J

TEMPTING the COWBOY

USA TODAY BESTSELLING AUTHOR
KENNEDY FOX

Copyright © 2022 Kennedy Fox
www.kennedyfoxbooks.com

Tempting the Cowboy
Circle B Ranch, #8

Cover designer: Outlined with Love Designs
Cover image: Wander Aguiar Photographer
Copy editor: Editing 4 Indies

All rights reserved. No parts of the book may be used or reproduced in any matter without written permission from the author, except for inclusion of brief quotations in a review. This book is a work of fiction. Names, characters, establishments, organizations, and incidents are either products of the author's imagination or are used fictitiously to give a sense of authenticity. Any resemblance to actual persons, living or dead, events, or locales is entirely coincidental.

Each book in the Bishop Brothers World can read as stand-alones but if you wish to read the others,
here's our suggested reading order.

BISHOP BROTHERS SERIES
Original Bishop Family
Taming Him
Needing Him
Chasing Him
Keeping Him

SPIN-OFF'S
Friends of the Bishops
Make Me Stay
Roping the Cowboy

CIRCLE B RANCH SERIES
Bishop Family Second Generation
Hitching the Cowboy
Catching the Cowboy
Wrangling the Cowboy
Bossing the Cowboy
Kissing the Cowboy
Winning the Cowboy
Claiming the Cowboy
Tempting the Cowboy
Seducing the Cowboy

Could be forever or we might break
That's just the kind of risk that we take
My head is yelling that I could get hurt
But I'm gonna jump right in
Baby, with my heart first

"Heartfirst"
-Kelsea Ballerini

PROLOGUE
KANE

"MERRY CHRISTMAS," I say to my dad when he calls.

"Don't be late today, okay? Your mom's already hangry and ready to start without y'all," he warns as I look up at the clock. We weren't supposed to meet for lunch until eleven, and I have twenty minutes to drive to my parents'. All of my family lives on the ranch, and it doesn't take long to get there. But I know when Mama ain't happy, nobody's happy.

"Okay, okay. I'm puttin' on my boots right now," I tell him.

"Are ya gonna be okay with everything?"

My face heats. "Like what?"

"Hadleigh and Knox," he confirms, but I knew what he was referring to. Hadleigh has been my best friend since childhood. I had a crush on her for years but recently realized it was nothing more than an infatuation. Everyone knew I had a thing for her. Well, everyone except her. For weeks, my identical twin brother and I fought for her attention. So instead of making her choose, I conceded. She deserves to be happy, and my brother could love her in ways I never could. We're better as friends, and I told her as much. Now she and Knox are a thing, and I'm very happy for them, even if my jealousy got the best of me in the beginning. But it's all water under the bridge now.

I smile. "Dad, I swear I'm completely over it."

"Really?" His tone slightly changes as if he doesn't believe me.

"Yes, absolutely. Scout's honor. We won't be havin' a repeat of Thanksgiving. I promise."

"Good. I don't want to have to reprimand my grown-ass son for actin' like a child in front of the family again," he confirms.

My brother and I got into a huge argument over Hadleigh in front of our large family at the Bed & Breakfast and embarrassed the hell out of my parents. Not to mention, I'd given Knox a black eye a week before that. I'd allowed my emotions to get the best of me because I wanted the absolute best for Hadleigh. At that point, I thought Knox was just using her, and she deserved better than to be another one of his one-night stands. I realize how much I overreacted and allowed my temper to control my actions, something that had never happened before.

"You'll find your person," he states, pulling me out of my thoughts. "Now hurry up and make your way over. I've got to remind your sister to leave now too. If you're late, your mother is giving you all a bag of coal."

"Damn, I'll be right there."

The call ends, and I go to the table where the finished leather journal lies. It's the first one I've ever made, and while I'm not one to toot my own horn, I'm proud of it. It's a symbol of how much I care about Hadleigh. I started this project before I knew how I truly felt about our friendship. It only felt right to continue working on it and give it to her as I'd always intended. Over the past six weeks, I experienced many ups and downs, and at times, I felt like I'd gone to hell and back but making this for her was my saving grace. With the learning curve, it took a lot of time and dedication. It calmed me when nothing else did, and I will forever be grateful for that, considering how wound up I was at times.

I pick it up, feeling the weight of it in my hand. The earthy smell of the worked and burned leather reminds me of horseback riding and saddles. I carved her name on the front by hand and embossed flowers around it. I untie the leather straps that hold it closed and flip through the blank cream-colored pages. After a minute of staring at the first page, I grab a pen and scribble a note for her to read later.

> *I'm so damn happy you're happy.*
> *Don't break my brother's heart.*
> *He couldn't handle losing you.*

A small smile touches my lips as I tie it closed, then tuck it in the bottom of the red-and-green gift bag I bought. I stuff candy cane–striped tissue paper inside and let out a sigh of relief. Giving it to Hadleigh after the last month feels right.

She may have been the woman I crushed on for fifteen years, but I know deep inside that she wasn't the one for me. Knowing that means I can search for the woman I'm going to start a family with and spend the rest of my life making happy, and I hope to God I find her sooner rather than later.

CHAPTER ONE

IVY

**PRESENT DAY
2 ½ YEARS LATER**

Although the pollen tends to coat the hood of my car, I love late spring, right before summer. I always find something special about the grass and flowers coming out of hibernation after a long, brisk winter. Just another reminder that the seasons are changing and days are passing. Pretty soon, outside will feel like an inferno, so I try to enjoy the warm mornings while it's still bearable.

After I grab my book and walk inside the goat soap warehouse where I work, my boss, Harper, greets me with a smile. She also gives me her signature good morning expression, but she looks exhausted while chugging coffee from her "Boss Mom" thermos.

"Rough night?" I ask, noticing the wild strands of hair that aren't quite in her ponytail.

"You have no idea. Hayden was up at four and wouldn't go back to sleep. Thankfully, Grandma asked to keep the kids this mornin'. There's some pre-summer thing they're having at church. Honestly, a literal godsend."

I snicker. "I was wonderin' where they were. But hey, at least Hailey-Mae is a little angel."

Hayden is almost three, and we celebrated Hailey-Mae's first birthday last month. Together, they're a handful, so Harper usually brings them to work with her. The shop has an area for the kids, and honestly, I love having them around. They always keep it interesting and make me laugh, especially Hayden with his mini-Bishop personality.

"My son will probably be a devil. He was already cranky when I dropped him off."

"Well, if he is, a handful of women over the age of seventy will take him off her hands because he's adorable."

"He is when he wants to be. I know he's not even in kindergarten yet, but I'm dreading his high school years because he's already giving me a run for my money."

"Hopefully, he'll grow out of it," I say, setting my book on the counter and rummaging through the pile of orders to fulfill today.

She gives me a pointed look. "I highly doubt it, considering how sexy Ethan is. I swear he's going to age like a fine wine. I tell him not to forget to wear that wedding ring because the old ladies at the diner give him the eye, knowing he's married to me and has kids!"

"Cougars want to have fun too, ya know?" I tease, knowing I shouldn't because it's too early to get her riled up.

Harper shakes her head and playfully scoffs.

"Do you blame them, though?" I smirk. "A fine cowboy with a big appetite." I can't even get the words out.

"Hell no! If he weren't mine, I'd be lookin' too, especially now since he's letting a little more scruff grow." She finally bursts into laughter. "Hot as hell."

"Keep that up, and you're gonna have a third baby." I snort, and she does too. "Orders in the morning, then soap mixing in the afternoon?" I ask, realizing just how much we have to get done tonight. Harper gives me a nod, and then we get to work like busy bees.

Our routine doesn't change too much each day, but it's extremely dependent on what's been launched and what sales we're doing. This week, we're focusing heavily on packaging before lunch so most packages can be postmarked on the shipment day. In the afternoons, we've been prepping for the announcement, then pre-order launch of the first wave of summer scents. Since it takes almost six weeks for our homemade soaps to cure, running this business successfully means being ahead of schedule and overstocked for launches.

"You know my sister's gonna go into labor at any moment," I sing-song. My sister, Hadleigh, is ten years older than me and has been best friends with Harper for as long as I can remember. A few months ago, Harper and I made a bet on which date we thought the baby would be born.

"We'll see," she says with a chuckle.

"The fact that Hadleigh is married to Knox Bishop and is now having a baby still shocks me."

"It still shocks me too, but we need to go over the terms of this bet just so we're both clear," she reminds me.

"Oh no, ma'am, we already shook on it. If I win, I get an entire paid weekend off...my choice!"

She gives me a mischievous grin. "And if you lose, you're gonna babysit for an entire weekend for free."

"Seems like I win either way." I shrug because I love kids so much that it's not really a losing situation.

"That's what you think," she playfully warns. "I'd almost feel bad for you if this wasn't your idea."

Considering I don't have any friends my age and only chat with Hadleigh and Harper, I'm fine with babysitting, especially now that I'm on my summer break from college.

Harper's increased my hours to full-time for the summer since she needs the extra help, and I want to save more money. Plus, I love being on the Bishops' ranch and hanging out with her.

The warehouse contains several long tables for packaging in the middle, a kitchen area for mixing ingredients, a curing area after the soaps are molded, and then shelves upon shelves of stock that's ready. It's a whole process, but a fun one.

Harper walks by the counter where I set my book and glances at it. "The cover is interestin'. What's it about?"

"I dunno, some girl who went missing or something. It was recommended in one of my book groups, and I wanted to try a thriller between my fantasy books. I'm going in completely blind!" I grab soaps and place them on top of the order sheets.

"That actually sounds creepy."

"I'll let you know how it is tomorrow. I'll probably finish it tonight." I shoot her a wink.

"Between reading and listening to books, how many do you finish in a year?"

"Close to three hundred. Maybe three fifty with audiobooks."

Her eyes widen. "I wish I had that much time!"

That has me snorting. "You mean, you wish you had no boyfriend or friends? Because that's what happens when you're a book nerd. Book boyfriends over real ones."

She chuckles. "Still, I should make more time for other hobbies."

I smile, trying to find my words so I don't stutter over them. Harper's patient and waits for me while I articulate my thoughts. "Well, it's understandable why you don't. You have a super successful business. A husband who loves you. Two beautiful kids. And you live on the ranch. I'd trade reading a thousand books per year for all that."

She gives me a somber look. "You're only nineteen and have plenty of time to have all those things too. You'll graduate with your business administration degree, and then you'll be unstoppable." Harper lifts a case of boxes that needs to be folded and taped for shipments.

"I'm glad you have faith in me."

"Always," she says.

Once I pop in, I scroll through my phone to find the fantasy book I started yesterday. It's been on my to-be-read list since January, and now it's May. Once I'm fully immersed in a different world, I start my tasks.

The two of us work together like a well-oiled machine, and she doesn't micromanage me. Sometimes, when the kids are here and she has to take care of them, she lets me work alone. I'm an introvert and thrive in this type of environment. At this rate, I'll retire here because I love it, and it pays well. This job is why I decided to get my associate's degree in business. I want to help Harper grow it to be even bigger than what it is now.

When I turn around, Harper waves her arms to get my attention.

I removed one of my earbuds. "Have you seen the Strawberry Shortcake soaps?"

"I think it's up top, above the Cotton Candy ones," I explain. I placed them there after their six-week cure time. After a while, all the bright colors start to look the same.

I restart my audiobook, then continue what I was doing. Another reason I love working with Harper is because she doesn't force me to talk. She's just like my older sister and brings out the best in me, and I'm comfortable around her. I'm the stereotypical quiet book nerd, and I proudly wear that badge of honor.

After another hour passes, my phone buzzes in my back pocket.

Hadleigh: Water just broke! Going to the hospital now.

Ivy: YAY!!! Should I meet you up there?

I yelp with excitement and run over to Harper.

"Hads is in labor!" My grin is so wide it almost hurts.

"Right now?" Harper pulls her phone from her pocket just as giddy as me and reads her text. "I didn't even feel it vibrate, but you're right."

"So what do we do? Do we go now?" I ask, overcome with emotions. I'm finally going to be an aunt, and I can't wait to spoil my nephew.

"Babies don't just fall out when your water breaks. Especially not a Bishop baby," she explains. "When she arrives at delivery, they'll see how dilated she is, and then I'll tell you if we need to rush or wait."

"Thank goodness you're a pro at this," I admit. "I don't know how any of this works."

"I'm not sure I'd consider myself a pro, just got a tiny bit of experience." She chuckles. "I'll text her and get the low down."

"Awesome!" I go back to packaging, but I don't restart my book because I'm too wound up. "Oh yeah, I won!"

Harper playfully rolls her eyes. "You did, fair and square. Any weekend you want, and it's yours."

"Heck yeah."

"But I know you're going to spend it reading in bed," she adds.

"Damn right." I shoot her a wink.

My phone buzzes again, and I check it.

Hadleigh: You might want to wait until after work because the waiting room will be crammed with family, and I know how you get around big crowds of loud people.

Ivy: LOL! I can do that! Thanks for sparing me.

Hadleigh: Don't want you to be too anxious before meeting Hendrix :) I'll make sure Knox keeps you updated. Love you.

Ivy: Love you too! Also hurry up and push that baby out.

Hadleigh: If ONLY it were that easy.

I read the texts to Harper, and she laughs. "Oh, I almost forgot about how many people will be there. She's probably right, honestly. It can be extremely overwhelming up there, fair warning."

"I'll probably wait until after my shift, then drive up so I don't have to rush around to wait."

Harper grins. "That's smart, but if she delivers early and you change your mind, just know I'm fine with ya leavin' early. Your sister can only have her firstborn once."

"Very true," I say, but I'm certain I'll visit after most have seen the baby. Until I was reminded, I forgot how crazy the entire family is when it comes to newborns, especially their grandma—Rose Bishop.

"I'm gonna finish checking inventory and see what needs to be restocked. I'll have to leave to pick up the kids once they're back," She explains while grabbing the additional shipping materials I need.

I give her a nod. "Perfect."

"You've got this." She moves to the computer and printer located on a stand-up desk, then grabs her clipboard with product numbers.

I turn my audiobook back on and get lost in the world of fairies that make women orgasm just by looking at them. Seriously, I'm surprised Harper hasn't asked me why I'm blushing. At least reading keeps life interesting, considering how boring it is in the small town of Eldorado.

Knox texts me random updates from my sister's phone throughout the day. When it's finally lunchtime, Harper waves her arms and points at the clock.

"Don't skip lunch again," she reminds me. "I've gotta go get the kids."

"Yes, Mom. Also, I can handle getting everything prepped this afternoon so we can start on the strawberry margarita soaps tomorrow."

She grins. "You sure?"

"Absolutely. I've done this a million times. Plus, it'll keep me busy all day which I need because I'm so excited to meet Hendrix."

"Okay, thank you so much. If you need any help, please let me know and be very, very—"

"Careful, I know." I chuckle. "I'm a pro at pouring milk into ice trays. I can handle it, promise."

"You're the best, Ivy."

"Thanks, boss." I finish packaging the last few items as she makes her way out the door. If I don't take a break right now, I'll skip lunch, so I stop and warm up my food. Sure, I could go to the B&B and get some of Maize's amazing cooking, but I don't want to eat alone. It would be too awkward, and I only like to go when Harper or my sister joins me. When the ranch hands try to talk to me, I turn into a stuttering mess, so it's easier to stay in my comfort zone at the warehouse.

As I eat my lasagna for one, I grab my thriller book and start reading. After I finish three chapters, I text Knox on my sister's phone.

Ivy: How's it going? Has the baby popped out yet?

Hadleigh/Knox: Not yet. But soon. He'll be here any minute.

Ivy: Better send me a pic after he's cleaned up!

Hadleigh/Knox: Will do!

I can't explain how damn excited I am. Hadleigh has always been a mother figure since our mom worked so much to provide for us. My dad left before I was old enough to remember him, so it's just been the three of us. Hadleigh pushes me to do better, and I can't explain how grateful I am that she's my older sister. She's helped me break out of my shell, and I can't imagine how I'd be without her. Now, she's going to be a mom and raise her own babies, something she's always wanted.

After eating, I wash my hands and look over the list of soaps we're launching for the summer season.

We use the cold process when making goat soap. That means twenty-four hours before we stir the ingredients together, we freeze about 750 ounces of fresh milk in cubes. It keeps the mixture from having a chemical reaction with the lye, which makes the bars look discolored and brown. When the process is done correctly, the soaps are ivory white, and it allows the brightness of the colorant to stand out. Harper's known for her hot pinks and blues, neon greens and yellows, and it all stems from the prep work we do the day before we're set to mix and mold.

I carefully lay the trays on the prep tables, then walk over to the goat farm where Ethan, Harper's husband, works. As soon as I enter, one of the ranch hands greets me with a smile. I don't have to ask for milk anymore. Instead, a few of them carry the gallons pumped this morning over for me.

"Thank you," I say, and they're out the door with a head nod. Once I'm alone again, I carefully pour the liquid into the rectangles. The key is not to overfill or waste a drop. I turn on my audiobook and do this for nearly an hour before my arm gets tired. While I rest my biceps, I look at my phone and notice some missed notifications. I quickly unlock it and am in awe by a picture of my beautiful nephew wailing.

I'm overcome with joy as I hurry and text them back.

Ivy: Congrats y'all. Can't wait to hold baby Hendrix in just a few hours. I love you two!

Hadleigh: Love you too, sis. I'll see you later.

With a pep in my step, I stack the trays on top of one another and make my way toward the commercial-sized stand-up freezer. As I'm walking over, I trip over absolutely nothing, and several trays spill down the front of my shirt and jeans.

I'm infuriated with myself for being so damn clumsy, but I also know I'll smell rotten by the time I get off work. I close my eyes, count to ten, and make a note of how many ounces I'm wearing so Harper's aware of my mistake. She won't care, but I hate it when I do stupid things because I want her to take me seriously.

Although I'm full of dread, I send her a text to get it over with.

Ivy: I spilled six trays of milk...on myself.

Harper: Aw, it's okay. Do you need to go home and change?

Ivy: No, I deserve it for being clumsy.

Harper: You're harder on yourself than I am on you.

Ivy: I know, but I can't help it. This was stupid.

Harper: What's my number one rule?

Ivy: No crying over spilt milk.

Harper: That's right. It happens!

Ivy: Thank you! Good news is I'll have everything prepped so we can kick ass tomorrow and make a thousand bars.

Harper: Looking forward to it!

For the rest of the afternoon, I take more breaks so I can focus on what I'm doing. By the time I finish, it's nearly five, and because I smell gross, I'll need a shower. I double-check the freezer, clean my prep station, then turn to leave.

During the drive home, my excitement begins to take over. I'll finally get to meet my nephew, something I've been waiting all my life for because I've dreamed of being an aunt. I knew it'd happen before I became a mom because of Hadleigh's age compared to mine.

When I walk inside my house, I find a note from Mom telling me she's leaving for the hospital. I quickly shower, throw my hair into a ponytail, and head that way in fresh clothes. Considering it's an hour's drive, I have plenty of time to finish the current book I was listening to at work.

As soon as I turn onto the country road that leads to San Angelo, my nerves get the best of me. It's impossible to push it away because I know Kane will be there. Having conversations with people is already hard enough, but it's almost impossible for me to chat with the man I've had a crush on since I was a kid. I'd see him around because he and my sister were such good friends, but he always treated me as Hadleigh's kid sister.

I've run into him a few times on the ranch, and he's been nothing but polite, even if I struggle to get out a simple hello. It also doesn't help that I'm an introvert who thinks he's the most gorgeous specimen I've ever laid my eyes on. Now that my sister married his identical twin brother and we'll be sharing a nephew, I'm sure we'll run into each other more, or at least, I hope.

Knowing I'm not paying attention to my book, I turn it off and continue in silence, practicing what I'm going to say if I get the chance to chat with him alone. Since I started college last year, I've been trying to work on my self-confidence and focus on my social skills, so I won't pass up the opportunity to talk to him if it arises.

When I finally enter the waiting room, it's packed with Bishops, but my mama is still chatting with Jackson and Kiera—the twins' parents.

"Hey. I was getting worried about you. Was just getting ready to call and check where you were."

"I know, sorry. I made a mess at the shop and had to shower," I quietly explain, not wanting to draw any attention.

"You should go back there now," Mom says, guiding me toward the double doors. She waves over a nurse who scans me in and walks me to Hadleigh's room. I give her a smile, then gently knock before pushing open the door.

When I enter, Kaitlyn—Knox and Kane's sister who's in her late twenties—opens the door with a grin. My eyes immediately meet Kane's, and it feels like every bit of air escapes the room. I swallow hard and glance around the room.

"Hi." I silently celebrate not stammering when several sets of eyes are on me. "Sorry, I'm late."

"You're just on time," Hadleigh says sweetly. I move forward and sit in the chair right next to Kane. Our gazes lock, and it feels as if this moment is frozen in time. Eventually, I lean over to get the perfect view of my adorable little nephew. My arm brushes against his, and I feel butterflies flutter throughout my body. I swallow hard.

"You wanna hold him?" Kane asks, and I can't help but study

his perfect, beautiful lips. Realizing I'm staring, I slide my gaze up to his crystal-blue eyes.

"Yes, please," I nervously say as he stands inches in front of me and carefully gives me Hendrix. I can smell the light hint of his cologne and soap, and it's so intoxicating that I sit.

My heart pounds heavy in my chest as we study Hendrix. Knox is talking to Kane, but his attention is zeroed in on Hendrix and me. I can't help but notice how soft his expression is when our eyes meet.

"He's so perfect," I whisper, playing with my nephew's tiny fingers.

I look up at Kane and smile. Something electric lingers between us, something I want to explore. I understand how the heroines of my romance books feel. I'm almost at a loss for words as the butterflies in my stomach flutter.

"Did you hear me?" Knox repeats.

Kane clears his throat. "Sorry, what?"

"We should probably let some others in," he says, and I selfishly don't want this to end, not right now. I'd do anything to hold Hendrix for another ten minutes with Kane this close.

"They can wait their turn," Kane tells him, and I wonder if he's thinking the same as me. I meet Hadleigh's eyes, nearly begging her not to kick us out, but I can tell she's exhausted.

"That's right!" Kaitlyn says, moving closer so she can admire Hendrix.

"There will be plenty of time, y'all. I promise. You can come over and visit whenever you want. No invite needed," she explains.

Knox speaks up. "Excuse me, invites are needed. We might be busy." He waggles his brows with a smirk as Kane shakes his head. Hadleigh and Knox chat away, but I don't pay them any attention.

"Looks like we'll be sharing lots of nieces and nephews," Kane tells me with a smile.

I meet his gaze, trying to form my words. "I guess so."

A small smile touches my lips as I glance back down at Hendrix bundled tightly and sleeping so peacefully. I take in every second I can as Kane chats with his brother and Hadleigh. I was given the ten minutes with Hendrix that I wished for, but I know it's time to go because others are waiting outside.

Kaitlyn looks at the clock and groans, then we both quietly chuckle.

"I don't want to go either," I explain.

"I say we tell everyone else to fuck off and lock the door. We're his aunts!"

As I'm snickering, there's a light tap on the door, and their cousin Maize and her husband Gavin enter. Apparently, he's a retired bull rider. Kane glances my way as he leaves, and my heart races. After I hand Hendrix to Maize, I say goodbye to Kaitlyn, then walk over to my sister, who looks gorgeous as hell after giving birth.

"I love you so much," I say and awkwardly hug Hadleigh. "I'm so happy for you."

"Thank you, sis. Hope you're ready to babysit."

I grin wide. "Anytime. My schedule is wide open."

As Maize and Gavin chat about how adorable Hendrix is, I turn to Knox. "Congrats!" I tell him.

"Thanks, Ivy. So glad you came by."

"Me too," I admit. "Both of you need some sleep."

"Now who's acting like Mom?" Hadleigh throws my way with a wink.

I give her a quick wave, then walk into the hallway. I'm pleasantly surprised that Kane is patiently waiting, and when he falls in line next to me, my stomach fills with butterflies. He's never made an effort before, but I'd be lying if I said I didn't like it.

"Wow, I can't believe we have a nephew."

"I know, it's insane," I say honestly, glancing his way as he pushes open the door for me.

"Babysitting is gonna be a blast. I'm sure he's gonna be a breeze to watch and a lot of fun as he gets older. I might be biased, but Hendrix is adorable."

He smirks. "I agree wholeheartedly. He looks just like Knox and I did."

This makes me laugh, but I notice the resemblance. Before I get the courage to start my next sentence, I suck in a deep breath and lick my lips. "So…" I say, hoping my words don't get stuck in my throat. "I know this might come off a little awkward but—"

Before I can spit out what I want to say, a raven-haired woman with big boobs and bright blue eyes walks up and interrupts us.

"Sweetheart," Kane mutters, almost surprised. "I didn't think you were going to make it."

She glances at me, like she's sizing me up, then presses her lips against his. "I didn't think so either, but I was able to get off work early. I didn't want to miss this."

It's awkward standing here, listening to their conversation, but I can't just walk away either.

"You should go in and see them really quick. They're in room 585. I'll meet you there in a bit," he tells her. She agrees, kisses him again, then walks away.

My heart thuds in my chest, and my cheeks heat when their lips touch again. I stare off into the distance, wishing I could disappear. When she's completely out of sight, Kane turns to me.

"Sorry, what were you saying?"

"Oh, it was nothing." I smile and try to keep my tone light and fluffy, but it feels impossible. "Well, I should probably get going. It was really good seeing you."

"Yeah, you too."

Awkward silence returns, and it seems to draw on for eternity. Neither of us moves.

"Let me walk you to your car. You can tell me about school," he suggests, but I feel like he's just being nice for the sake of it.

"No, no, it's fine. I'm parked right up front. You should probably go meet up with your girlfriend. I don't wanna keep you," I truthfully say.

"You're not," he states. "I'll be happy to—"

"Take care of yourself, okay? Have a good night." I don't want his pity or for him to feel like he has to be kind to me for the sake of it.

"You too," he tells me, almost sounding defeated.

I give him a nod and make my way to the elevator, needing fresh air. I almost made one of the stupidest mistakes of my life and asked Kane to hang out when he had a girlfriend. Thankfully she walked up and stopped me from embarrassing myself. Though, it sucks because I'd finally found the courage to ask the man I've had a crush on since I was twelve to hang out or grab some coffee sometime, and now I can't.

CHAPTER TWO

KANE

"Shit." I roll over, trying to turn off my blaring alarm. My phone drops to the floor with a loud thump while the annoying siren screams. I lean over my bed, blindly reaching for it, and miraculously find it. I check the time, and it's almost five in the morning. Waking up early is the norm around here, but it doesn't make it any more palpable.

I get up to piss, then brush my teeth. After I'm dressed, I grab my baseball hat, then leave. One good thing about living alone, I can be as loud as I want whenever I want. Since Knox and Hadleigh's baby boy is finally here, I'm on double duty so my brother can have some bonding time with his son. I'm more than happy to cover for him because I know he'll do the same for me when my firstborn comes.

Once I'm in my truck driving down the long drive toward the barn, I realize I didn't make any coffee. I contemplate running by the B&B on the way over but decide to wait until after the horses are fed. When I pull up to the barn, Payton's carrying two buckets of feed in both hands. I walk up to him.

"I've fed stalls on the right already, workin' on the left."

"I've got the rest," I tell him, going to the storage room and measuring the feed for the rest of the boarded animals.

A few years ago, my brother pitched the idea of running a breeding facility on the ranch. After it was approved by the family, I was asked if I'd join him and help manage the operation. I couldn't say no. After we acquired more stud horses and expanded our boarding stalls, we had Payton transferred here to help full-time. Before that, we all worked in different areas on the ranch and often did the same bitch work. He's a hard worker and friends with my sister, Kaitlyn. While we keep him as much as we can, we'll send him to the goat farm when our cousin Ethan is shorthanded. He mostly keeps to himself but also does his fair share of shit-talking.

Spring through summer is the fertile season for the females, so we're always very busy. We board mares for a month to ensure they get pregnant. Considering we have twelve different studs, we're taking care of twenty-four horses at a time for six months of the year. It's a lot of damn work, but it's worth it for our one-hundred percent pregnancy rate.

Payton passes me to refill his empty buckets and then finishes. As the horses eat, we hop in the truck and make our way to the B&B to quickly eat breakfast. Since we're the only two working all week, we don't have any time to waste.

"I didn't expect you to be working so early," I admit as I drive us there.

"I know. Thought I'd get a head start so we'd have plenty of time to have seconds. Woke up starvin'."

I chuckle, and we go inside. "I know the feelin'."

My mouth waters as I take in the scents of frying bacon and butter biscuits that fill the room. Dishes clank, and chatter fills the dining room. It's just a typical work day at the B&B. A handful of other ranch hands are already taking advantage of the first round of food to come out of the kitchen for the morning. As soon as I grab a plate, my cousin Maize comes from around the corner, shaking her head.

"Y'all are gonna make me work extra hard today, aren't ya?"

I chuckle. "You know you'd be bored out of your mind if it weren't for us. How much food can twenty guests who are stayin' here really eat?"

She pokes me in the shoulder. "Exactly my point. I wouldn't have to work nearly as hard, and then maybe I could really focus on my catering business. Ya know?"

"We love ya for it, though, cuz. Nobody makes a buttered biscuit quite like you."

She cracks a smile. "Okay, now you're just tryin' to butter me up. Smart. You can have extra."

I pile up sausage, bacon, biscuits, blueberry pancakes, and a hefty scoop of western scrambled eggs, then join Payton at an empty table.

"What's on the schedule today, boss?"

"I think a quarter horse is showing up today, so we'll have to sign contracts, unload, and get the stall setup connected to Blitz's pasture." The registered Arabian stallion is the son of a champion racehorse. The breeding fees for him bring in a small fortune, not to mention what we make for housing the mare.

"That's it?"

"I believe Juniper Blossom, the fire engine red quarter horse we've had since the beginning of May, is being picked up around eight. So we'll have to deal with customers for a few hours, contracts, loading, and then make sure the stall is clean for tomorrow. Then rinse and repeat. Oh, we need to probably check the cameras we have installed to see how many times the horses mated yesterday so we can keep track."

Payton swallows down a bite of eggs. "Sounds good. Is Knox coming in today?"

"He said he might stop by in the afternoon, but I'm not sure yet. I told him to stay home and enjoy his time off, but you know how well he listens."

He nods and chuckles. "Yeah, as well as a screaming toddler."

"You're right 'bout that." I put butter and strawberry jam inside my warm biscuit, then eat half in one big bite. Payton gets up and grabs another plate of food, then returns. Guess he wasn't kidding about being hungry.

"Seems like we've got a busy day," he continues.

"Yeah, pretty sure it'll be like this for the rest of the week, and next month, oh, and the next."

Payton shrugs. "That's life on the ranch, ain't it? Beats the alternative."

When we're almost finished clearing our plates, my cousins Riley and Ethan enter. They're being loud as hell too.

Uncle John comes from his office and glares at them. "Y'all need to quiet down. We still have guests sleepin' upstairs and don't need y'all wakin' them up being rowdy."

He manages the B&B and has since he was our age. Without him, I'm not sure this place would be as successful as it is. My cousin Maize is his daughter.

"Yes, sir," they say in unison, but as soon as he walks off, Diesel bursts into the B&B, yelling at them to wait up. I shake my head and put my dishes in the tub.

"What's so damn funny?" I finally ask as I reposition my hat.

"We pranked someone, and they're pissed," Diesel states.

"It better not have been Kaitlyn."

They laugh harder, and Diesel's nearly gasping for air.

"You're messin' with dynamite. She'll explode on y'all without apology."

"There's a problem with that. Kaitlyn doesn't know it was us," Riley says like he's smarter than my sister. Spoiler alert —he's not.

I shake my head and look at Ethan because I thought he was smarter than those two idiots. "I can't believe you let Tweedle Dee and Tweedle Dum rope you into these shenanigans. What did y'all do?"

Ethan zips his mouth, locks it, then throws away the pretend key. "They threatened me, so I can't say shit."

"Fine. Maybe I'll text and ask her what happened today, then accidentally tell her who's responsible."

"Okay, okay," Diesel says. "We put her truck on blocks."

"You did what?" Payton asks from behind me.

Riley snickers. "She cursed me out, then threatened to slit my tires for parkin' behind her the other day when I came for lunch. Apparently, I was makin' her late to a training session. She cursed me out real good, so this is payback."

"I feel sorry for y'all when she finds out," Payton warns. "Real sorry for ya."

"As long as you two keep your damn mouths shut, she won't know."

I laugh. "I ain't gettin' involved in any of this. When she burns your houses down, just remember this day."

Payton and I go back to the truck, and we're both shaking our heads.

"You're gonna tell her, aren't ya?" I ask him because I know they're good friends.

"Nah. But if she asks for help getting them back, I'm fuckin' game."

"They started a shitstorm."

"She'll destroy them like a tornado," he confirms as we arrive at the facility.

I go into the office as Payton goes to get Juniper Blossom ready. We've got a few hours, but I make sure all the release forms and disclosures are signed along with the total for the final payment. Once I do all that, I find Payton.

"Got'er together?"

"Yep, just waitin' for her owner."

"Great."

Before I make it to my office, my cell buzzes in my pocket. When I pull it out, I see a notification from my sister.

Kaitlyn: You responsible for this shit?

She sends a picture with her truck suspended on concrete blocks. The tires are stacked in a pile beside it. I wonder how early those fools got up to do this and still have time for breakfast before their shift.

Kane: Hell no. I would never.

Kaitlyn: You know who did?

Now, this is a question I don't want to answer. They'll know either Payton or I told Kaitlyn, and they'll retaliate against us. I don't have time for their games, at least not until Knox gets back.
"I told her," Payton says with a chuckle. "They're done."

Kaitlyn: Never mind. Riley and Diesel, even Ethan are dead meat! They just started WW3!

Kane: Don't do anything dangerous.

Kaitlyn: They. Fucked. Up. That's all I'm saying.

"Ya think I should give Diesel and Riley a warning?" I ask.
"Nah, they made their bed, now they're gonna get buried in it. Riley shoulda just ignored her temper. He brought it to this level."
"Yeah, you're right. But I'm staying out of this."
Payton and I walk around the property to do a perimeter check on the fence lines of the segregated pastures. It's something we do each Monday just to make sure we don't have any escapees. Since we're responsible for other people's horses, it's important they stay safe and are well taken care of. While we

have insurance to cover any sort of disaster that could happen, we must avoid it at all costs. We have a reputation to uphold.

Before the clock strikes eight, I see a large diesel truck pulling a gooseneck horse trailer kicking up dust.

"Mr. Henderson's here," Payton leans into the office and tells me.

"Thanks," I say and go outside to meet them in their vehicle.

"Howdy," Mr. Henderson says, and we exchange handshakes. This time his wife stayed home. "You think my mare took?"

"Yes, sir. Considering how things have gone, I'd almost guarantee it."

"That's good news. Hopefully Juniper ain't the exception."

"They've been cozy," Payton explains.

Mr. Henderson grins wide. "Good."

He follows me into the office, signs the forms, pays the final bill, and then Payton loads her up.

"Don't forget to send us some pictures once the foal is born," I remind him as we pass the wall full of all the babies our studs are responsible for.

"I won't." He gives us each a final handshake and then is on his way.

It took about an hour to take care of everything, and while Payton cleaned the stall, I check my phone.

Knox: How's everything going so far?

Kane: Great. Got it all under control.

Knox: Might stop by after Hendrix goes down for his nap.

Kane: You don't gotta.

Knox: I know, but I'm already missing it. Plus, Hadleigh has told me several times I'm hovering.

Kane: Have you been?

Knox: Truthfully? Yeah. I'm not used to just sitting around so I'm going stir-crazy. Oh, before I forget. You know who took Kaitlyn's tires off her truck?

I chuckle.

Kane: Riley, Diesel, Ethan, and I think they got a few ranch hands to help.

Knox: Idiots. They're utterly fucked.

Kane: That's what I said. Anyway, I need to catch up on emails and return a few calls. I'll talk to ya later.

Knox: Yep. See ya.

It's important that we stick to our scheduling because we've pre-booked our years. We require non-refundable deposits and have a waitlist for cancellations within twenty-four hours. I'm solely responsible for the back-end work while Knox takes care of the front end. We work well together, and I'm grateful my brother trusted me enough to be his partner in crime in real life and in business.

I finish adding things to our weekly task list and updating the whiteboard on the wall so Payton knows which horses are coming in and going out. It's a revolving door, and we're slammed from March to early September. When mating season ends in the fall and winter, we put the studs on mounting mares and collect sperm, freeze it, and sell it online. It's not quite as reliable as the real deal, but we've made a pretty penny and have an eighty-percent pregnancy rate. So while we're not as busy during those seasons, we still have stuff to do. Shipping and freezing horse sperm isn't something I'd ever expected myself to be doing, but it's honest work.

After I've responded to fifty emails, printed out new website orders, and checked in a new mare, it's nearly time for lunch. We usually take an hour from twelve to one, so we have plenty of time to eat and get back for the afternoon rush. The B&B is busy as hell, but Payton and I eat quickly then we head back. As soon as we park, Knox drives up and meets us.

"Hey, Daddy," Payton says with a chuckle.

"Don't say it like that, ya sick fuck," Knox tells him.

"Just couldn't stay away, could ya?" Payton likes to give Knox a hard time. That hasn't changed from when we were all doing bitch work together. As Knox and Payton go back and forth, I feel my phone vibrate in my pocket. I pull it out to see a text from my girlfriend, Raelyn.

Raelyn: I was just thinking about you, baby. How's work been today?

A small smile touches my lips.

Kane: It's going okay. Busy as always.

Raelyn: That's my stud master.

This causes me to chuckle. Knox looks at me.

"Who're you chattin' with? Your girlfriend?"

"Something like that," I tell him.

We became exclusive only a couple of months ago but went on our first date six months ago. Raelyn and I met at Hadleigh and Knox's wedding last year, but our schedules rarely synced up to get to know each other. Finally, after some consistent dates, we made it official. While we can only spend time together a few times per month because of our conflicting schedules, we have a good time when we do.

She sends a text. I open it to see a picture of her standing in her bathroom wearing only a bra and panties.

Raelyn: Wish you were here.

I smirk.

Kane: Damn girl, I do too.

Another picture comes over, and this time, she's completely naked. I swallow hard.

Raelyn: Sure you can't step away for a few hours? Promise it's all it'd take.

Kane: Sorry, I can't. We're already shorthanded, but trust me, I really wish I could.

Raelyn: Maybe next time.

Kane: I'll take a rain check.

I lock my phone and shove it in my pocket before adjusting myself. Raelyn's a beautiful woman and very independent, but she's also very flirty with every man she meets. It's something that bothers the fuck out of me, but I'm trying hard to get over it. We've agreed to be exclusive. While our relationship dynamic is different, and I don't know if she's really the one for me, we're both willing to see where things go.

CHAPTER THREE

IVY

As I open my laptop and log in to my college's online portal, I suck in a deep breath. Final exams were last week, and our grades will be released today. I think I did great on all of my tests except for calculus. Thankfully, I don't ever see myself using the concepts in real life. I'm not trying to be a rocket scientist. I just want to make goat soaps.

After I log in, I wait for my grades to load and nearly burst into tears when I see a row of A's. The first thing I do is text my sister.

Ivy: I MADE A 4.0!

Hadleigh: Oh my goodness! Congrats! We're totally going to have to celebrate.

Ivy: Thank you! I'm shocked. Math kicked my ass.

Hadleigh: You're smart! I had no doubts.

Ivy: At least one of us was confident. How're things going today? Do you need anything?

I watch her text bubble pop up and disappear a few times, then finally, the message arrives.

Hadleigh: Only if you were planning to come visit...

Ivy: How did you know I was going to ask to see my gorgeous little nephew today?

I laugh at how well my sister knows me.

Hadleigh: Just a hunch. You can say no, but I would love it if you could pretty please pick me up some food from the B&B. Maize texted me today's menu. She made chicken fried chicken, and it's one of my favorites. Knox had to go to the office, and they're busy, so I don't want to bother him.

Ivy: I'll be happy to stop by there on the way. Do you want dessert too?

Hadleigh: Who passes up triple chocolate cake?

Ivy: You're right. Probably a dumb question. :)

Hadleigh: Thank you. You're the best sister in the world! Hendrix can't wait to see his favorite auntie.

Ivy: I'm gonna give him all the chubby cheek kisses when I get there.

Hadleigh: See you soon. I'm so proud of you!

Ivy: Thanks so much!

I check the time and then pull my curly hair into a high ponytail. Of course I'm wearing a bookish T-shirt and some jean shorts, but 'I'm not like other girls' is my style. Hopefully, the stop at the B&B will be quick, and no one will want to chat. Though, I'm already mentally preparing myself to have to socialize.

When I walk out of my room, I pass my mom, who's knitting on the couch. "Oh, new project?"

"I'm working on a blanket for Hendrix for Christmas," she explains.

"Starting early." I give her a grin and compliment the gray and blue yarn she chose.

"With how busy things are at work, it might take me the whole seven months to finish it." Mom chuckles. "Headin' out?"

"Yep, I'm gonna take Hadleigh some lunch and see Hendrix," I explain, slipping on my sandals.

"Send my love."

"I will," I tell her, then go to my car. As soon as I get inside, I connect my audiobook app so I can listen to my book on the way there. While I love fantasy romance, I'm listening to an erotic werewolf romance right now, and it's so damn hot. I wouldn't be surprised if my car caught on fire.

When I pull into the B&B, the parking lot is full. Visiting during the lunch rush probably wasn't the best idea. I walk up the steps and say a little prayer that there's no line. I don't visit the B&B often, and I never stay and eat unless Harper or Hadleigh are with me.

As I enter, I hear chatter in the dining area and know it's packed. I stop at the end of the line and wait. When I turn and look over my shoulder, I see the man I've had a crush on since I was twelve years old. The electricity streaming between us is like an inferno ready to swallow me whole. The intense eye contact causes my temperature to rise, but I can't stop staring. He walks toward me with a sexy as sin smirk and falls in line behind me.

"Hey, Ivy," he says, and right now he has my full attention. Kane is much taller than me, and I can just imagine what it's like to be wrapped in his muscular arms. Listening to that sexy audiobook on my way over probably wasn't the best idea.

"Hi," I finally say, heat meeting my cheeks as I try not to care. But damn, he's mesmerizing as he confidently stares at me. When he licks his lips, I nearly melt into a puddle on the floor. The line moves forward, and before I pick up a to-go box, Kane speaks up. "You stayin' to eat?"

"I was gonna grab something for Hadleigh, then head over."

"You're missin' out on one of the best meals on the ranch. Stay and eat with me."

Unable to resist the opportunity to spend time with him after our hospital chat was cut short, I agree. "You talked me into it."

"Didn't take much convincing. I like that," he admits, and we fill our plates full, then each take a glass of sweet tea.

Kane walks to a table by the large window, and I follow him. My heart flutters when I realize there's only enough room for two. Feeling self-conscious, I look around, but no one is paying any attention to us. He sets down his tray, then pulls out the chair for me. No man has ever done that before.

"Thank you."

He shoots me a wink and then sits in front of me.

As soon as I take my first bite of steak, I let out a moan.

Kane's eyebrow pops up with amusement. "Maize's perfected Grandma's recipe, but she hardly ever makes this anymore, so it's a special occasion."

"That's a shame," I say. "It's the best thing I've had in my mouth in months."

His cute smirk that I love so much is on full display, and I realize the slip of my tongue.

"Well, that came out wrong." My nerves are getting the best

of me. I've never really had the opportunity to have a private conversation with him like this without interruption, and I want to say and ask so much.

"You're going to see Hendrix after this?" He easily keeps the conversation moving.

Since it's not polite to speak while chewing, I cover my mouth with my hand. "Yes. I've been impatiently waiting for Hadleigh to catch up on sleep so I can bombard her without feeling guilty."

He chuckles. "I've been doing the same."

"You should come with me," I say, and I'm kinda shocked the invite tumbled out so quickly.

"I wish I could. We've been super busy in the office, and I gotta get back right after lunch."

As if he can see the disappointment in my expression, he hurries and adds, "We should plan it sometime soon when I can break away."

"Deal," I say. I appreciate how he waits for me to speak and actually listens when I do. I think this might be the most I've talked to anyone in months. Well, other than my sister and Harper. "So you said you were busy. What is it that you do again? Watch horses bang all day?"

Kane lets out a roar of laughter, and the ranch hands sitting at the long table across the way turn and look at us. After he catches his breath, they go back to their conversation and pay us no mind at all.

"Not exactly, but that's hilarious. Next time someone asks me, I'm just gonna tell them that."

"Hey! It's plausible, considering it's a stud farm."

He shoots me a playful expression. "It's a bit more complicated than that, but at the most basic level, we're horse pimps."

His response catches me off guard and causes me to snort. "That's interesting."

"We basically breed horses and deal with owners, online

sperm sales, and a lot of paperwork. But it's fun. Beats being a ranch hand floater who does the bitch work every day. What about you? Whatcha up to these days?"

I swallow hard and take a sip of tea. I'm not used to talking about myself very much. "I..." I stammer. "I finished my second semester of college and made all A's."

He has no idea how much I appreciate him waiting for me to finish my sentence, or maybe he didn't even notice. It's hard to tell because his eyes don't leave mine.

"Wow, congrats. That's incredible, Ivy. So you're a genius?"

"Not exactly, but thank you. I was just as surprised. But now I'm on summer break, and Harper's letting me work as much as I want. So I'll be hanging out at the warehouse for the next few months."

He looks at me over the rim of his glass as he takes a drink, then sets it down. "I'm actually looking forward to seein' you more."

Blush hits my cheeks, and I try to contain my smile but find it impossible. "Yeah, maybe we can have lunch again one day?"

"I'd like that." Kane meets my gaze, and I swear he wants to say something more but doesn't. "So other than working this summer, do ya have any other plans? Any crazy vacations? Road trips?"

I giggle because it's funny he thinks I have a social life. "Just hanging out with fictional men."

He pops a brow. "Fictional? You still read a lot? I remember Hadleigh talking about how many books you used to read back in the day."

Him remembering that I'm a huge bookworm warms my heart. "Oh yeah. I think it's only gotten worse now that I'm reading adult books."

"Adult? As in por—"

"Fantasy. It's my favorite, but I'm not opposed to trying other genres. In the past year, I've dipped my toes into some erotic fantasy." I'm tempted to tell him about the plot of the sexy werewolf book I'm listening to, but I keep my nerdiness to myself.

"Sounds...kinky." His words come out rough, and it causes my skin to prickle.

"It's very, very scandalous." I love being under Kane's microscope.

His gaze sweeps from my eyes down to my lips, and for a moment, time feels as if it stops. "So Ivy Callaway. Hobbies include reading and working. Goes to college. Anything else I need to know?"

Oh God, there's so much I'd like to tell him right now, especially when the underlying current streaming between us is ready to pull me under. When I look into Kane's baby blues, my heart rate increases. Heat streams through me, and I wonder if he feels it too.

I clear my throat. "I'm a hopeless romantic."

"At the core, I think we all kinda are."

With a nod, I smile, realizing how true that is. "I think everyone wants to find love and be in love." I'm tempted to ask him questions about his girlfriend because I'm curious, but I also don't want to make it awkward. The reality is I don't have the courage to mention her, especially not after how she treated me like I was invisible at the hospital.

Kane tilts his head. "I've never heard such truthful words spoken."

There are only a few more bites of food on each of our plates, and then we'll go our separate ways. I've had a good time chatting with him, even if it was completely unexpected.

Once we've finished eating, I speak up. "Thanks for inviting me to stay."

He winks. "It's been fun. We really should do it again sometime."

"I'd like that," I admit. We stand and Kane takes my plate to the dish tub, and I go back through the line to grab Hadleigh's food. He comes over before leaving, and he hesitates.

"Tell Hads I said hey," he finally says.

"I will."

A smile plays on his lips. "Don't be a stranger."

"You'll see me around," I confirm, and he patiently waits for me. The fact that he gave me any attention today is enough to keep me coming back for more. I might be Hadleigh's little sister, but it's more than obvious that something is brewing between us, and I want to find out what that is.

I drop two gigantic slices of triple chocolate cake in the box because it looks too good to pass up.

"You need any help carryin' all that?" Kane asks, but I decline his offer.

I stack the Styrofoam boxes on top of each other and keep a firm grip as he leads the way through the B&B. When we're close to my car, he opens the door for me.

"Thank you," I breathlessly say when I smell his mixture of cologne and sweat.

"Any time. Have a good day, Ivy. Enjoy your fictional men," he teases.

"Oh, I will. Enjoy watching horses have sex." I slide into my seat, carefully setting the food on the passenger side. He chuckles, then closes my door. Before walking away, he gives me a quick glance, then heads to his truck. My eyes are glued to his ass and how he confidently strides across the parking lot. I'm sure I look like a love-sick puppy right now.

I crank the engine, then back out. My heart pounds, and I know my cheeks are flushed. On the way to Hadleigh's, I try to calm down so I don't look suspicious. My sister can usually see straight through me.

As soon as I walk up to her house, the door swings open.

"Damn. You look cute today," she says.

"Really?"

"Yes, ma'am. Might wanna start carrying a stick around to beat those ranch hands off ya."

I set the food down on the breakfast bar, and Hadleigh grabs a fork.

"I need one too, please. I got some extra cake."

"You're eating cake for lunch? You havin' a bad day or something?" she taunts.

I snicker and shake my head. "No, I already ate, but I couldn't pass up that icing."

She laughs, handing me the utensil, then I open the box and dig in.

"Ugh, this is amazing," she says around a mouthful of mashed potatoes.

"Yeah, this cake is orgasmic," I blurt out. Just as she cuts into her chicken, I hear Hendrix's little cries in his bassinet.

"I've got him." I stand, then go pick him up.

"Thank you."

I hold him against my chest and whisper sweet things while I rock us back and forth in the chair. Within minutes, he's back asleep.

"Wait, are you a baby whisperer?" she asks quietly.

I snort with a shrug. "Maybe it's one of my superpowers. Do you think he's hungry?"

"Not yet. I fed him about an hour ago."

"Did you notice his onesie?" Hadleigh asks.

I carefully reposition him so I can see it.

My aunt Ivy is my number one fan. "Oh my God, this is adorable! Wait, did you make this?"

"I was practicing with my new vinyl cutter. Gotta keep my mind busy before I go crazy."

I can't stop smiling. "It's perfect. And true. Hell, you might be a pro by the time you go back to work."

"If I go back…" Her words linger.

"Are you thinkin' about quittin'?"

She shrugs with a somber look. "I'm already on part-time hours. It's just gonna be difficult being an hour away from Hendrix each day. I guess I really didn't think this through."

"You'll figure it out, Hads. You always do. Just enjoy your time off the best you can."

"Now you sound like Mom." Hadleigh sighs. "So what are your plans this summer?"

"To read, work, and lose my virginity."

Hadleigh nearly chokes on a green bean.

"I was kiddin' about the last one," I quickly add.

"You almost gave me a heart attack." She swallows hard.

"I can't keep my V-card forever. It's bound to happen at some point. I swear, right now, I'm the nun of Eldorado."

"Nuns don't have sex toys," Hadleigh reminds me.

"No, but…"

"I don't wanna know what you're about to say. You read so much, and I can never predict what's gonna come out of your mouth."

Hendrix's head slightly bounces as I giggle, and he fusses. It makes me feel guilty that I've woken him again. "I was just gonna say…but they still have their fingers."

She bursts into laughter. "You're gonna make me blush."

I clear my throat. "Excuse me. I'm pretty sure you know what you're doing, considering I'm holding your love child. This kid wasn't delivered by a stork."

A mischievous grin slides across my sister's lips. "You're right about that."

"But yeah, I'll be working a lot. Harper gave me a rundown on everything we need to do, and there just isn't enough time in the day. She's talked about hiring someone part-time, but I told her I'd stay as late as I need to help her catch up. I think we can handle it. It's just going to take extra hours at the shop."

"Oh good. If you stay late and get too tired to drive home, my couch is always available."

"Thanks, sis."

"I hope after everything settles down and I've figured out my new normal and what I'm going to do about my job, I can start helping y'all again."

"That'd be awesome. I'm actually excited about working more because my paychecks will be amazing with all the extra hours."

"That's a plus!"

Hendrix eventually settles down and falls back to sleep. Hadleigh finishes eating her lunch, then takes a bite of cake. "Okay, you're right about this."

"I wasn't exaggerating. Oh yeah, Kane told me to tell you hi."

"Really? What was he up to?"

"Nothin'. Just eatin' lunch at the B&B." I don't tell her that we ate together. It's something I want to keep to myself for a little while, though I'm sure she'll find out because there are no secrets on this ranch.

"Was Raelyn with him?"

I meet her gaze. "No, he was alone."

"Gotcha. Sometimes on her days off, she'll meet him for lunch."

"Oh, okay." I don't want to discuss that witch right now.

My sister thankfully continues. "He owes me a visit. Lately, he's been so busy with the shop and his girlfriend that time slips by. But then again, I also understand we're growing up, and things are different."

"Yeah, totally. He did mention he was letting you catch up on rest. We'd all be over here every day bugging you, but no one wants to overstep. That's my biggest worry."

"Aw, you're not. Ever. You're always invited over because I enjoy hanging out with you."

"I'm gonna hold ya to that."

"I hope you do. Eventually, you're gonna be too busy for me too."

"Now who sounds like Mom?" I snicker.

"Guilty," she tells me. "Guilty as charged."

After an hour passes, Hadleigh lets me feed Hendrix while we watch a few episodes of *Impractical Jokers*. When I check the time, it's nearly three in the afternoon. Eventually, we say our goodbyes. I thank her for allowing me to come over, and then I head home.

As I pass the B&B, I check to see if Kane's truck is there, but when it's not, I keep going. This summer, my real goal is to help him realize what's always been waiting right in front of him—me.

CHAPTER FOUR

KANE

I can't believe it's already peak summertime. However, considering how goddamn hot it is outside, I can. It feels like this year is passing by so quickly. Another sign that I'm getting older.

Of course, it's Monday, and our day has been jam-packed. I've already had three mares picked up this morning, and this afternoon, we'll receive three more. Knox has returned to full-time hours, though he occasionally leaves to help Hadleigh if she needs anything.

Once things settle down and I can breathe again, Payton and I head to the B&B for lunch. I look for Ivy, hoping to run into her again, but unfortunately, she's nowhere in sight.

For the past few nights, she's shown up in my dreams. I guess they'd actually be considered fantasies. Since we talked a few weeks ago, I haven't been able to stop thinking about her. She's consumed my thoughts, and I find myself wanting to get to know her better. It makes me feel guilty because I have a girlfriend, but it's not like that. I'd never cheat on Raelyn, not in a million years, and especially not because of a platonic infatuation.

But it's proof that I always tend to want what I can't have.

Hadleigh would cut off my balls if she knew half the things I've thought about her little sister. While Ivy isn't a kid anymore and is old enough to make her own decisions, my best friend is overprotective when it comes to her.

"You searchin' for someone?" Payton asks, noticing my eyes scanning the room.

"Nah, just seein' who's all here."

His expression tells me he's not buying it, but he doesn't press any further.

I had such a good time chatting with Ivy and learning about the things she likes, and I selfishly want to do it again. While we were eating, I wanted to ask her what she was going to say at the hospital, but my nerves got the best of me. Although it's been bothering me for nearly a month, I chickened out at the last minute.

The way she looks directly into my eyes when I speak drives me absolutely fucking wild. She's quiet, but I've learned those are the ones you have to watch out for.

Ivy's been a bookworm for as long as I can remember, and I think it's awesome she still is. A million questions flip through my mind, and I'm intrigued to learn more.

"Did you hear me?" Payton asks as he takes a bite of his macaroni and cheese.

I shake my head. "Sorry, what'd you say?"

Payton slowly shakes his head at me. "I need a day off next week so I can go to my dentist appointment."

"Should be fine. If you need a tooth extracted or anything, ya know we've got some pliers that'll do the trick."

"Hard fuckin' pass. I'd never be desperate enough to let any of you near my mouth with or without tools. I ain't stupid," Payton tells me.

"Good answer," Riley mutters from behind us as he sets his plate down on the table. Of course, his sidekick, Diesel, follows him.

"How's work goin'?" Riley asks, shoving half a roll in his mouth.

"Busy as hell. But I'm not complaining. I like what I'm doin' at least," I tell him.

"Being a ranch hand bitch were the good ole days, though," Diesel interjects. "We used to get into so much trouble. Honestly, I'm surprised we're still alive."

I laugh, thinking about all the shit we used to get into when we weren't being watched like hawks by our uncles. "Yeah, that's true. But I don't have any complaints."

Ethan walks up to our table, and before he sits, I notice he's covered from head to toe in dirt.

"Don't even ask," he says sternly before anyone can speak.

I lean forward. "You know we're going to hound you until you tell us."

"Yeah, well, I ain't in the mood to talk about it."

I don't push him any further, but it doesn't stop Diesel from asking every few minutes.

"Shut the fuck up," Ethan snaps, picking up his cornbread and throwing it at Diesel's head. It bounces off and lands on the floor with a thud. Seconds later, my uncle John comes from around the corner wearing a scowl.

"Do it again, and I'm kickin' you all out," he warns, looking directly at me.

"I didn't do anything," I explain. "I'm just sitting here tryin' to peacefully eat my lunch."

"Then I guess that means you're guilty by association." His eyes scan across the table, daring us to push him, but we're so quiet a needle could drop, and we'd hear it. When my uncle turns his back to return to his office, I see a smirk playing on his lips in the reflection of one of the pictures on the wall.

"You're chickenshit," Diesel tells Ethan.

"Better than bein' a dipshit."

"Okay, okay," Payton interrupts. "Can we at least try to get along today?"

All I can do is chuckle. "Why are you always the mediator?"

"Because y'all are a bunch of damn fools with too much testosterone."

This makes Ethan's face split into a smile, and we finish eating without arguing. Even Diesel gives him a break.

"You're gonna tell us, though, right?" Diesel says as we pick up our dirty dishes and put them away.

"Fuck no," he mutters. Payton and I tell everyone goodbye, then we hop in the truck and head back to the stud farm.

On the way back, Payton cracks up laughing.

"What?" I ask.

"You know what happened to Ethan?"

I shake my head.

"Kaitlyn put boobie traps around his shop, and he has no idea who did it. Apparently, he had a meeting with every single one of his employees today and wanted someone to confess. None of them did."

"Damn. Unfortunately for him, I know she's not done."

"Not in the slightest. They should've never put her truck on blocks," he says.

"You're right because she will spend the rest of the summer fucking them up."

We have a good laugh because my sister is just getting started.

The rest of the afternoon goes by so fast, I can barely believe it when Payton's filling buckets with grain for the evening feeding. Once this is done, we can both leave, so I help out to make it go faster. As I'm walking to the stalls at the end, my phone vibrates in my pocket.

Raelyn: Can you call me when you get home?

I check the time and respond.

Kane: Sure, should be within the hour.

Raelyn: Perfect!

After we finish our task, I tell Payton bye, then lock the office. One good thing about summer is it gets dark later, so there's no need to work against the clock. I get in my truck, roll down the windows to take in the warm air, and head home.

When I walk inside my house, I kick off my boots, then call Raelyn as I promised.

"Hey," she says. Light music plays in the background.

"Hey, Rae. You still comin' over Friday?" I ask with a smile, looking forward to spending some time with her since she's off.

"Actually…" she lingers.

I swallow, anticipating some bad news.

"I wanted to chat with you about that. Some college friends invited me to hang out with them in Houston this weekend."

"Oh. What are y'all plannin' on doing there?"

"We're supposed to go clubbing. Relive our heydays," she explains.

"Alright," I deadpan.

"Is there something wrong with that?"

I suck in a deep breath, not wanting to argue with her, but I'm frustrated as hell. "We made plans to see each other this weekend since you had off. It's not a big deal, though, so do whatever will make you happy." We compared our schedules a month ago, and she's known since then.

"I'm sorry, I honestly don't remember that."

That fucking hurts.

She continues, "My friends messaged me a few days ago, and I already committed to driving out there Friday mornin', then we're gonna do a pub crawl that night. I'm sorry, baby. I wouldn't have agreed to it if I'd remembered our plans."

"It's fine."

"Thanks for understanding. I'll make it up to you. I promise."

Her response is the exact opposite of what I want to hear, so I wait for her to say something else. If she doesn't want to hang out with me and would rather be with her friends, that's fine. I won't beg her, but I'm actually hurt that she forgot. I'm not a priority in her life, and she doesn't seem to notice or even see an issue. I can't be bribed like a kid who didn't get an ice cream cone as promised. The thought of it annoys me.

"Oh, there's something else I wanted to talk to you about, but we can discuss it later. You sound tired."

"Can you just tell me now? I don't wanna obsess about what it is for the rest of the night. If you can mention it, you can spill it." I don't like being held on a line like bait.

"Well..." She lets out a drawn-out sigh. "I didn't want to have this conversation right now."

"It's probably for the best if you go ahead and get it over with," I say with annoyance. "You at least owe me that much since you're canceling on me this weekend."

Thirty seconds pass without either of us saying a word, but it feels like an hour.

Eventually, she clears her throat. "What do you think about us having an open relationship?"

My heart pounds so hard in my chest, I can hear it beating in my ears.

"What does that exactly entail?" I ask, wanting her to make it crystal clear what she means.

"An open relationship, you know, like we're still together, but we can also see other people at the same time. Since we don't get to be together very much, keeping our options open makes sense."

I open my mouth, then close it, completely blindsided by this.

She doesn't have time for me now as it is, so I know she wouldn't if she had a handful of other dudes at her beck and call.

Memories of Hadleigh fill my mind, and I remember how jealous I was thinking about her with another man. She dated my brother and me at the same time while she took time to figure out what she wanted, and although at that time I agreed to it, I learned that I'm not cut out to share my girlfriends with anyone. Even though I knew deep down that Hadleigh wasn't the woman for me, I can't go through that agony again.

It brought out the absolute worst in me.

"No, sorry. If we're datin', then that means we're exclusive. If that ain't the case, then we're just fuckbuddies. I've told you before that I'm not lookin' for that kinda relationship, and I'm still not."

"I know you did, but it could be really fun for both of us, Kane. We'd still be together, but there'd be no cheating if either of us wanted to see someone else on the side," she explains as if I don't know how this shit works. I thought what I said made it obvious that I'm not willing to share. Guess not.

"Not happenin', Raelyn. I'm not interested in fucking around, and I don't want the person I'm dating to have that option either," I say sternly, growing more irritated with each passing minute.

"I understand." She sounds defeated, like she truly thought I'd be into this idea.

No woman will force me to cross my boundaries like that, especially her. The fact that she even asked doesn't settle well with me. It makes me question our relationship even more. We don't live in the same town, she's always working, and when she isn't, she's hanging out with someone other than me. For all I know, she's already seeing other guys.

"I was only offering the option because I don't want to hold you back in any way. I'm the one who's too busy to hang out, and I feel guilty that I can't give you more time and attention. But if you're fine with how things are right now and seeing me sporadically, then I am too."

"Okay." That is all I can say.

"Are you going to be up for a while?"

"Nah, I think I'm gonna take a shower, then go to bed. I've had a long day." It's not lost on me how quickly she changed the subject.

"Oh okay. I'll text you tomorrow. Good night."

"Night."

After the call ends, I lean my head back on the cushion and stare at the ceiling. This is the first time we've disagreed on something, and I don't like the way it makes me feel.

While I want to trust Raelyn, part of me knows she'll do whatever she wants regardless of whether I agree. There's no way I'd ever find out if she did cheat, and the fact she mentioned this right after telling me she's going clubbing in a big city leaves me even more concerned.

At this point, I don't know what to do and need time to think.

Maybe it's a good thing she won't be here this weekend.

The last time I saw her was at the hospital when Hendrix was born. I haven't found it to be an issue that we don't get together that often, but maybe it is. We text and chat often and have had phone sex a few times over the past few weeks.

My thoughts are all over the place. I don't want to hold her back if she wants to be with other people. If all the signs point to this not working out between us, why am I so dead set on staying with her? That's the question I need to figure out the answer to. I'll give her a chance to prove herself, even if my heart is wary.

Since my chat with Raelyn earlier this week, things have been distant between us. We've texted back and forth a few times, but she hasn't offered to call me, and I don't have anything to say. We're in a weird limbo right now, but it could just be me. I'm trying to shake off this feeling. I've reminded myself that one disagreement doesn't mean it's over, at least not yet.

But if I ever find out she's cheated, I will break up with her without a second thought. She knows exactly where I stand.

After my shift, I go home and take a shower. I couldn't stand the way I smelled and needed to wash the sweat off my body. When I step out and dry off, I slip on some joggers, then go to the kitchen where my leather working supplies are laid out. I do some research online about hand binding paper because I'd eventually like to start making my own journals too. Before I get too lost in a rabbit hole, I check the time and call it a night. It's nearly nine, and I'm actually pretty exhausted after the day I've had.

Just as I'm turning off the dining room lights, I hear a light knock on the door. Confused, I move forward and look through the peephole to see Ivy standing there. Loose strands of hair have fallen out of her ponytail, and she nervously tucks the corner of her bottom lip inside her mouth as she waits for me to answer. A lump forms in my throat as I admire her under the glow of my porch light. Before she knocks again, I undo the deadbolt and turn the knob.

"Thank God you're home," she says breathlessly.

"Prayers answered." I laugh, surprised but also very happy to see her. "Everything okay?"

Her eyes wander up my pants and trail their way to my mouth. She unapologetically drinks me in, and I actually like the heat in her gaze. It has me smirking as I cross my arms over my chest, waiting for her to speak.

"My car won't start," she explains.

"Did you walk here in the dark from the warehouse?" I ask, stepping outside and looking around to see if she's alone.

"Yes, but it's fine. It's not that far, and I had the flashlight on my phone if anyone was driving down the road. Honestly, I walked without it, though. Vega was too gorgeous."

"Oh, so you know your night sky?"

"I know a few of the summer and winter constellations and of course, which star is Polaris, so I'll always know north."

I tilt my head at her and grin. "That's awesome. Come on in. Sorry. Guess I lost my manners."

"Thought you'd never ask," she says, walking past me smelling like sugar and spice. I can only imagine what scent soap is on her skin, but it reminds me of fall.

"Do you want me to look at it now?" I ask, reaching for my keys. "I really don't mind."

"No, that's okay. You look showered and like you're gettin' ready for bed. We might need some jumper cables, but I'm not sure if it's the battery or something else. Right now, I kinda don't care about it that much." She yawns, and I can tell she's just as tired as I am. She and Harper have been working really hard lately to fulfill all the orders. Ethan gave me all the details at lunch yesterday.

"You can crash on my couch if you want, or I'll be happy to take you home," I offer.

"Your couch actually sounds great. I'm exhausted, and I have to work early in the morning. Probably just call roadside service to come down and help me with it in the mornin'," Ivy explains. "That's what I pay them for each month."

"Whatever you'd like." I grab a few extra blankets and a pillow for her.

She meets my eyes as I hand them to her. "Do you happen to have a T-shirt or something I can borrow to sleep in?"

"Absolutely." Right now, I'm so damn tempted to kiss her pouty lips because she's like a magnet, pulling me closer to her every chance she gets. I force myself to take a step back and create some space between us.

"Thanks, Kane. I'm so happy you were up."

I grin, then walk away, knowing her eyes are on me as I go to my bedroom.

My quickened pulse gives away my excitement. I can't believe she's here, standing in my living room. Ivy acted like her prayers were answered, but damn, I feel like mine were.

No woman has ever made me feel this way, and I'm not sure how to react. I want and need to know everything about Ivy Callaway—her likes, dislikes, fantasies, and dirty secrets.

I meet her in the living room, exactly where I left her. I give her a shirt I won at the rodeo a few years back when I barrel raced one of Kaitlyn's horses. It was the runner-up prize, even if I'm still convinced it was rigged.

Without saying anything, she peels the orange tank top off her body. My eyes graze over her beautiful breasts nearly falling out of her hot pink bra. I turn my head, needing to be the perfect gentleman as she slips on my shirt.

I hear her shoes plop to the floor and her shimmying out of her shorts. Once the movement stops, I turn and meet her eyes.

"Do you need anything else?" I help her spread the quilt out over the couch as she positions the pillow at one end. Ivy crawls under the blankets and looks up at me with hooded eyes.

"Nah, I think I'm good," she says with airiness in her tone. "Your couch is comfy and smells like you."

I swallow hard and smile as the intense urge to be around her nearly consumes me. The conversations we have and the things she says always hit me on a personal level, even if it's everyday things. While I want to be around her, I know we're both exhausted.

"Good night, Ivy. Sweet dreams."

"Night, Kane."

I turn off the kitchen light and walk to my bedroom, tormented by the fact that the woman haunting my dreams is here in the flesh. If she were any other woman and I were any other man, I'd have kissed her right in my living room. I'd have given her compliments and told her how damn pretty she is, but instead, I said nothing at all.

The fact that she commented on how I smell has my dick twitching with anticipation. I lie down and close my eyes as images of Ivy's beautiful breasts fill my mind. Reaching under the covers, I roughly grab my cock and stroke myself to thoughts of her. The orgasm builds so damn quickly that it rips through me like a category five hurricane. Guttural grunts slip out as I come harder than I have in my life, and the woman to blame is my best friend's little sister.

CHAPTER FIVE

IVY

When I roll over, sunshine splashes across my face. Opening my eyes, I look around, and at first, I don't remember where I am. Then the familiar smell of Kane hits me, and a small smile plays on my lips. It wasn't a dream, and I'm really here.

Pushing myself up, I lift my hands above my head and stretch. I stand and grab my phone, realizing it's just past seven, which means Kane is already at work. A tinge of disappointment hits me until I notice a note on the coffee table along with my car keys. I immediately grin when I pick it up.

Ivy,

Good morning. I left early this morning while you were still asleep and changed the battery in your car. It's parked outside, so you won't have to walk all the way back to the warehouse. If you need anything else, I left my number at the bottom. Next time you're in a jam, I'll be happy to help. No need to be alone in the dark. I'll come rescue you. Anyway, I hope you have a good day. Don't work too hard today.

-Kane

PS—Feel free to keep my shirt. It looks better on you anyway :)

I blink hard as my excitement bubbles. I'm almost tempted to pinch myself to make sure this is really happening. The fact he's letting me keep his shirt has me walking on cloud nine. I lift it to my nose and inhale his scent again, grinning like a teenager in love. In a way, I guess I am. I set the letter down and immediately program his number into my phone, overjoyed that he willingly gave it to me. My shyness would've never allowed me to ask him for it, so thankfully, I don't have to. There are a million different things I want to text him, but I'm trying not to scare him away by sounding too eager.

Ivy: Thanks for everything. I really appreciate it.

His text bubble immediately pops up.

Kane: Anytime.

Ivy: I owe you!

Kane: Nah. But it'd be nice to have lunch with you again.

My cheeks immediately heat.

Ivy: I'd like that. Oh, also, do you mind if I use your shower?

Kane: Feel free. Make yourself at home.

Damn, I wish I could.

Ivy: You're too kind.

Kane: :)

There's an extra toothbrush in my car, so I walk out and grab it, then I head inside. Thankfully, Kane's house is not off a main road on the property, so I'm not concerned about anyone seeing me here. I'm sure if my sister caught wind of my car being at her best friend's house, who's ten years older than me, she'd ask a million questions, even if it's harmless.

I go into the bathroom and look around for any signs of Raelyn. But there's no sign of her existence in his entire house. Trust me, I looked. There are no pictures, makeup, or hair care products—*nothing*. It makes me wonder what kind of relationship they have if none of her things are here.

His cologne sits on the counter next to his razor. I'm tempted to pick it up and inhale it, but don't. Instead, I take off my clothes, then hop in the shower. As I stand under the hot stream, I think about everything that's led me here.

Sure, I could've called Hadleigh last night, and she'd have willingly picked me up. But it was around nine, and I knew she'd be in bed, so I felt too guilty to ask. For once, I didn't want my sister to rescue me. When my car wouldn't start, I went through all the options. I selfishly allowed my heart to decide and started walking toward Kane's. He actually lives closer to the warehouse than anyone else, so it conveniently worked out.

Once I was close, I realized it was a stupid idea because he had a girlfriend. Raelyn could've been staying over, and that would've been extremely awkward. I contemplated turning around, but when I saw the glow of his porch light, I was committed.

It took me a few minutes to work up the nerve to knock. I'd talked myself out of it a handful of times, then just went for it. When he didn't open the door immediately, I somewhat started to panic, but then he did. As he stood in front of me like a Greek god—shirtless with chiseled muscles—I drank him in without apology. At that moment, I knew I'd made the right damn decision. The sexual tension between us was so sharp it sliced through the air, and I wanted nothing more than to taste his lips.

After I wash my hair and body, I step out and wrap myself in one of his large towels. Then I walk to the living room to check the time on my phone and grab my clothes. While I wish I had something else to wear, I'm sure no one will notice. Honestly, I couldn't tell you what Harper was wearing yesterday, and I'm sure she didn't pay any attention to me.

Once I'm changed, I look at the T-shirt Kane gave me and smirk, smelling it one last time before leaving. Right now, the thoughts of him overpower me, even if he has a girlfriend, and I wish he didn't.

Kane's a nice guy just doing nice guy things, but I could've sworn I saw him study my curves for a brief second last night. The underlying current streaming between us threatens to pull me under, and soon, I'll drown under his spell.

When I arrive at work, Harper is already there. I walk inside, and she gives me a look but smiles.

"Inventory today, right?" I ask as she sips her coffee.

"Yep, I'm gonna mix the next scent for the launch." She already has the ingredients laid out and has started the process. "Once we have a final count, we can start pouring our evergreen scents for a restock."

"Perfect." I grab my AirPods and turn on an audiobook. After ten minutes, I stop listening and put on a drama YouTube video about influencers because I can't shake those images of a half-naked Kane out of my head.

I climb up and down the ladder, counting all of our current stock. It takes me nearly three hours to go through everything we have available, but I have a solid list of what has to be made when I'm done. Harper likes to keep her signature scents in stock so we never run out, but lately, we've been slammed more than usual. While it's great for business, it becomes overwhelming to juggle everything, especially when soap has a six-week cure time.

After I go over what we need with Harper, she grabs everything to mix the formulas. Before we get started, I look at the time.

"It's nearly noon. You should probably grab lunch. I've got this."

"Shit. I didn't even notice." Harper smiles. "This is why I keep you around, lunch reminders. When I worked alone, I skipped so many meals."

"Go ahead. I can finish this up while you run home and eat."

She sets down the goat milk and sucks in a deep breath. "I won't be long."

"Take your time," I explain, and she grabs her keys and leaves.

Just as I'm measuring out the milk to pour into the trays, my phone vibrates in my pocket. I pull it out, thinking it's Harper reminding me of something, but I'm pleasantly surprised when I read who it's from.

Kane: How about that lunch date? I'm headin' to the B&B in ten minutes.

I don't know whether to smile because I was invited or frown because I'm busy.

Ivy: I'm really sorry, but I can't. We're super swamped, but maybe we can some other time?

He has no idea how much it pained me to write that reply. Even now, I'm contemplating how I could make it happen, but considering what needs to be done, there's just not enough time in the day. I haven't even had a chance to read the book I bought last week, which never happens.

Kane: Sure, that's no problem at all.

Ivy: I'm really sorry!

Kane: It's fine. I'll just have to keep askin' ya.

Ivy: Please do.

I wish I knew what he was thinking right now. The fact that he's making an effort has my insides squirming, and I can't stop smiling. Knowing I don't have time to play around, I start pouring fresh milk. After I've gotten every filled tray in the freezer, I pull out the ones we did yesterday so I can mix the ingredients together.

We have at least ten different soaps to restock right now, and I can't waste any more time. I carefully measure the lye and pour it in the pot, then drop the frozen cubes of goat milk inside. After it's stirred together and begins to thicken, I carefully pour the liquid into the mold. If I wait too long before I put the final product in the fridge to cool down, the milk will scald due to the chemical reaction. It would be devastating to waste this entire batch.

Patiently, I sprinkle raw oats on top, and when it's complete, I'm proud of how pretty it looks. After I put it in the oversized refrigerator, I turn around and am shocked to see Kane standing in the warehouse with to-go containers in his hands.

"Oh my goodness. What are you doin' here?" I ask, unable to hide how happy I am to see him.

"I couldn't let you go without a hot meal, considering how hard you've been working. Ethan told me how much y'all needed to do today when I showed up at the B&B, so I brought you some chicken spaghetti and garlic toast. Oh, and some apple cobbler too because we all need a little sugar rush."

"I could seriously kiss you right now," I tell him, and I watch his Adam's apple bob as he swallows before he smirks.

He sets it down at one of the tables and hands me a fork. It's not until I dig in and take a bite of dessert first that I realize how hungry I am.

"Startin' with dessert, huh?"

I shrug with a smile. "I'm just in that kind of a mood," I admit as I eat a piece of cobbler.

Kane takes a step closer, and I look up into his baby-blue eyes. With his thumb, he swipes the corner of my mouth. Then he pops it between his lips, licking off the filling. I swallow hard, watching him, wishing he'd make a move, though knowing it'd be terrible considering he's taken.

"Mmm…sweet," he says, temptation coating his tone.

For a brief second, I contemplate standing on my tiptoes and gently sliding my lips across his, and if I had an ounce of courage, I'd do it. Before I can say anything, the door of the warehouse swings open.

I look past Kane, who's standing awfully close, and meet Harper's eyes.

"Hey," she says. Walking closer, she glances back and forth between us, then heads to the kitchen area to set down her purse. I'm so thankful she doesn't say anything and acts as if she's not fazed by him being here, though he doesn't come in here often.

"Well," he says. The roughness in his tone isn't lost on me as something swirls between us. Warmth rushes through my body when I meet his eyes again, and I feel as if we're doing something we shouldn't. "I gotta get going."

"Thank you again," I say breathlessly, drunk by his proximity.

He shoots me a wink, then heads toward the door. "See ya, Harper."

"Bye," she says with her back turned. I dig into my food and wait for her to question me. When she talks about work instead, I'm more than relieved. I quickly eat, and then Harper and I tag team the work for the rest of the afternoon. My mind is all over the place, and I try to focus on the task at hand.

The only man I've ever crushed on is giving me the attention I've wanted for years, but he's taken. Sometimes life really isn't fair, but I try not to dwell on that. Honestly, I'll take what I can get from Kane, even if that means just being friends. But I can't deny the way he's always made me feel. He's my dream man, kind and sexy as sin.

I busy myself with work, and by the time I look up at the clock, it's nearly seven. Harper and I are exhausted after pulling long hours all week, and I can't wait to shower and go to bed.

"Let's clean up and call it a night," she says after we finish pouring our final batch of soap. "We can start back up in the morning."

"Sounds good," I agree with a yawn.

For the next thirty minutes, we pick up our mess and stage our area with supplies so we can get started first thing tomorrow. After she locks up, we walk out together.

"Have a good night," I tell her with a wave.

"You too!" she says as we go our separate ways.

When I get home, Mom's sitting on the couch knitting again. Her entire face lights up when she sees me.

"I wasn't sure if you'd be home tonight," she says.

This causes me to laugh because it's her way of asking me where I was. We're close, and I don't usually keep things from her, but I also don't tell her where I am all the time either.

"I stayed on the ranch because my car battery died."

"At Hadleigh's?"

I clear my throat. "At Kane's."

She gives me a pointed look, the same look I expected Harper to give me today.

"Don't even. It's not like that. It was late when I left the shop, and he's basically the only Bishop who lived close enough for me to get help. And... I slept on his couch."

Mom's brow lifts as if she's not buying it.

"It's really not like that, I swear. He has a girlfriend who he seems to like very much."

"Whatever you say, honey. Men can have girlfriends and still be with other people. Your dad was a perfect example of that." Just by her tone, I know she's not convinced by my explanation.

"I'd never be a side piece, Mom. I've got more respect for myself than that."

"I'm glad to hear that, sweetie. You deserve to be someone's queen."

I'd let Kane put me on a pedestal and worship my body from head to toe, but I keep those details to myself.

CHAPTER SIX

KANE

Today we were slammed, and I dealt with people nonstop. I think I walked fifty thousand steps between dealing with horses and assholes along with asshole horses. Mondays are typically busy, especially during breeding season, but today was a different monster with three roaring heads. It was stressful because everything seemed to go wrong, and we got off schedule. All day we played catch-up, but it meant I was at the barn until nearly eight. I'm not just physically and emotionally exhausted but also mentally. Right now, I just need a vacation, but there's really no sleep for the wicked, at least not until the end of fall breeding.

After showering, I grab a beer from the fridge and plop down on the couch. I warm up a shitty microwave meal and flip through countless channels of nonsense. By the time I got off work, the B&B had stopped serving dinner, which was disappointing, so I'm resorting to this.

When I finally land on a documentary about the Wild Wild West that looks half-decent, my phone buzzes. I see Raelyn's picture and name flash across the screen and answer with a smile. We still haven't talked too much to one another since our little argument, but we're trying to work through it the best we can.

"Hey, babe," she says in her normal tone.

"Hi. How was Houston?" I ask since it's Monday, and we haven't talked since she returned.

There's a long pause after my question, and I check my phone to ensure I didn't lose connection. The service on the ranch can sometimes be spotty.

"It was…great, actually. I had a lot of fun, but it also gave me an opportunity to really think about things."

"Things? Like what?" I play coy, but deep down, I know where this is headed, especially since things have been tense and awkward.

"About us, Kane."

"And?"

"Well, I thought about our relationship and how things have been going lately. Our schedules don't line up all the time, and you've already told me that you wouldn't be okay with an open relationship."

"You're right about that. I'm not gonna share my woman with anyone," I remind her. I'm not on board with what she wants. Nothing will make me change my mind.

"I understand and respect that, and it's why I think it might be best if we take a break for a little while."

I stare at the TV, and it's cowboys shooting and riding through mountains.

"You know, to make sure we're right for one another," she adds.

I want to ask her what that means exactly, but I'm aware of why.

Raelyn wants a break so she can see other people.

"Okay, if that's what you want," I tell her, not wanting to argue because there's no point. She'll do what she wants, and I can't do anything about that. But I won't be with someone who sleeps with other people. I'm not looking for a fling or random pussy. I want a solid relationship with someone who wants to be with me just as much.

Deep inside, I think this is about something else, and I want to ask if she hooked up with anyone while she was away. But I guess it doesn't really matter in the grand scheme of things. I'm not sure I'd want to hear the answer anyway.

"Before I settle down with someone, I need to make sure I'm making the right choice. Ya know?" she confirms.

"Yeah, sure. I get that."

"Thanks for understanding, Kane. We'll chat soon."

She hangs up before giving me the opportunity to respond. I set down my phone and lean my head back on the couch. Honestly, I didn't expect to get broken up on one of the worst days I've had in a long time. Being single wasn't on my bingo card this morning, but I'm not that upset.

We've only been seeing each other for a couple of months, and she was a nice girl, even if she didn't check all the boxes. I remind myself it's for the best, and everything will work out exactly the way it's supposed to.

Needing a distraction, I slip on my boots and decide to go over to my brother's to see Hendrix. That kid always brings a smile to my face. He's almost a month old now, and he's a little bigger each time I see him. Hadleigh has told me to stop by and see the baby when I want without an invitation, and tonight I'm going to take her up on that offer.

As I pull up to their house, I'm pleasantly surprised to see Ivy's car outside. My heart gallops, knowing we'll get to hang out again.

"Good one, universe." I laugh, then I reposition my baseball cap and head toward the door. Moments later, it swings open, and Ivy's wearing a sweet ruby-red-lipped smile.

"Hey," I say, meeting her eyes and noticing the way her breath hitches when our gazes lock.

"Hi. My sister told me to let you in," she explains, stepping to the side. She smells like honeysuckle flowers when I pass her, and I wish I could bottle it up.

"Ooh, look both your aunt and uncle are here," Hadleigh says to Hendrix as she breastfeeds him. It's crazy to see Hadleigh as a mother. Once he's done eating, Ivy happily takes and burps him. She's so careful with Hendrix, and I'm mesmerized watching her with him.

"So did you hear what Kaitlyn did to the boys?" Hadleigh asks, wearing a smirk.

"No," I tell her.

Knox chuckles. "She had all of their vehicles towed away, and this morning, they woke up and thought they were stolen. Not just that, she took all the keys to their side by sides too."

"How'd you find out?" I ask because we were so busy today I didn't know my ass from my head. We didn't even get a chance to go to the B&B for breakfast or lunch. Instead, we ate frozen pizzas.

"Dad told me when I went to bring him last month's financial statements."

I laugh because she's been kicking their asses all summer. Hopefully, they're done, and each got their revenge. "That's the thing about Kaitlyn. She's sly. She waits, then strikes when you least expect it. Don't ever want to get on her bad side. I think her temper is worse than ours combined."

Ivy snickers. "She's always been really nice to me."

"She's nice if you're nice. But as soon as she's crossed, watch out."

Hadleigh is grinning wide. "Good. I'm glad she's giving them a run for their money. They're always pickin' on someone. You'd think they'd have grown out of that."

"Are you kiddin'? They'll never grow up," Knox states. "I thought havin' kids woulda helped them clean up their act. Nope."

"It's never a dull moment on the ranch," I add. "At least it keeps it interesting."

Hendrix spits up on Ivy. It drips down the rag and onto her shirt.

"Eww," she says, making a face. "It's running, oh man."

Hadleigh takes Hendrix from Ivy.

"I'll get you something to wear home. Sorry about that," Hadleigh explains, looking at the mess on her sister's shirt. "He's a little piggy sometimes. Just like his daddy."

Knox lifts a brow. "I only like to devour one thing and one thing only."

I shake my head, but that's nothing new around these two. After Hadleigh has Hendrix cleaned up and a new shirt for Ivy, she hands him over to me. Hendrix stares at me, and I wonder what's in his head right now.

"I'm not your dad," I explain softly. "I'm the cooler one out of the two."

"You wish," Knox says from across the room, and it has me cracking into a smile.

"Grandma reminded me about the Fourth of July party when I brought Hendrix by to visit today," Hadleigh says from the other side of the couch.

"Each year, it just keeps getting bigger and bigger. Should probably just make it a town celebration at this point." I glance over at Ivy. "You're gonna come, aren't ya?"

"I was thinkin' about it," she says.

"You better," Hadleigh tells her. "Can't miss it."

"Yeah, and Dad ordered a volleyball net. So there will be way more activities for the young adults. His words, not mine," Knox tells us.

"I'll try to make it," she explains. "Depends on how busy we are at the warehouse."

"Not me about to text Harper and tell her you're going to the party," Hadleigh says, reaching for her phone. Ivy blushes when I meet her eyes.

Hendrix lets out a big yawn, and I smile wide.

"My nephew is the cutest," she whispers, moving to sit right next to me. I'm mesmerized by her in ways I can't fully explain, and the way she smells has me thinking terrible thoughts.

"Do you want to hold him some more?"

She nods, and I can't deny her. Carefully, I hand him off, and her breath quickens when our arms brush together. My body instantly reacts to hers too, and I know it's not just a coincidence this time.

"Thank you." She gently cuddles Hendrix. The way her eyes twinkle when she kisses him on the cheek is adorable. One day she'll be an amazing mother, just like her sister. Ivy's the epitome of kindness and grace.

Knox yawns, and I know he's tired as hell because we ran our asses off today. I stand and stretch. "Well, I should probably get goin' so you two can get some rest."

"Yeah, me too." Ivy catches the hint, and hands Hendrix to Hadleigh.

I give Hadleigh a side hug and my brother a pat on the back while I wait for Ivy to say her goodbyes.

"We'll have to do this again sometime," I tell them with a grin, meeting Ivy's smoldering gaze. I love the dark eyeliner she's wearing tonight with those deep red lips. If I didn't know better, I'd say she's trying to catch my attention.

"Yeah, I'd like that," she adds, blinking up at me with a smirk.

"Good night, y'all," I walk toward the door with Ivy trailing behind me. I open it and allow her to go first, then follow her outside.

"You really should come to that party," I say, slowing my pace, not wanting this moment to end so quickly. The moonlight splashes across the ground, lighting the path to our vehicles.

"I think I will." She grins, and I swear she's going to say something else. "It was really nice seeing you again."

"You too," I admit, tempted to grab her hand and pull her into me. There are too many unspoken words streaming between us, and it's something I want to explore. "Don't be a stranger, 'kay?"

She laughs. "I'll try. Bye, Kane."

"Bye."

She gives me a sexy little wave before she gets into her car. I sit in my truck, watching her back out of the driveway, but the whole time, she's looking at me. Something about Ivy Callaway has me intrigued, and I kinda wanna fuck around and find out what's burning between us.

CHAPTER SEVEN

IVY

After launching the lemonade-scented soaps, business has exploded. It was so popular that we sold out within the first twenty minutes. Luckily, Harper and I predicted this outcome, so we made a second batch that will finish curing next week. We've hinted that there'll be another drop very soon.

Our customers are losing their minds over it and should because nothing like it has been done before—layered goat soap that changes colors. Harper always gives me a bar of whatever scents we make, and I used the pink lemonade one last week. It was cool to watch it go from yellow to pink as I used it. My skin felt silky smooth after I showered. When I finish my bar, I'm going to be sad because the scent is perfect for summer.

As we're packaging, Harper comes over to the long table next to my shipping station.

"So I've been doin' some thinkin'," she says.

"Are you going to fire me?" I don't know why my mind goes straight there every single time.

"What? No! Absolutely not." Harper laughs because she's used to this reaction.

"Okay, am I in trouble?"

She throws her head back and laughs. "Girl, no. I've been thinking about the business and how we've accomplished so much in the past year. A lot of that is because of you, Ivy. You make great suggestions, and you want to improve the efficiency of the processes. Because of that, I think I'd like to eventually make you my business partner. You've been with me for three years, and so much has changed since then. We have all this room for expansion, and we're bringing in enough to hire more people so we can get more accomplished. But I can't do it alone."

I'm in a state of shock and wait for her to say she's joking, but those words never come. "Wait, you're serious."

"Dead serious. Obviously, I want you to finish school first and have your business degree because I think it will be helpful, but I want you to know where my mind is right now."

"I don't know what to say. I'm honored, but I really don't know what it means to be your business partner."

"You'd be more involved with the behind-the-scenes things, like decision-making, campaign and scent launches, marketing the product, and helping expand. I'd hope to eventually be able to take more of a back-seat approach to the business and let you fully manage the place. I mean, you are a decade younger and all, so you have more working years in you than me. Especially after those kids are graduated and gone."

My face hurts from smiling. "I'd love that."

"It also comes with a nice raise and a percentage of the profits every quarter. So the more we sell, the more we make."

"Holy shit, Harper."

"You've earned it, and I trust you. We'll do some test runs for a few events later, but in the meantime, focus on school. Just know the opportunity is yours when you're finished. Gives you plenty of time to prove that you're the right person."

"I won't let you down. I promise."

She nods. "I know you won't. Now, since that talk is out of the way, give me an update on where we're at on our tasks."

Pulling my clipboard from the table, I hand it to her. "We had five hundred orders. I've got a quarter of them done." I point over at the pile ready to be picked up. "The rest of the labels are printed, and I've set out the quantities for each order on top of the shipping label. Once I finish taping some boxes, I should be able to hit the halfway mark today."

"Amazing. I've finished what I need to do so I can help out. How about I take care of taping, and you finish grabbing inventory?"

I give her a nod, and we get busy working like carpenter bees. My mind is reeling, and my face hurts from smiling so much. I can't believe Harper wants me to become a partner. Partner?

It's a huge deal because I can visualize how big this operation could potentially grow. This is the beginning of something that could be a household name. I try to calm down so Harper doesn't change her mind.

Of course, it's been hard working while going to school full-time, but I only have two more semesters left. I'll graduate in a year and will get to use the things I learned to help Harper. I know that with that title and raise, more responsibility will come. While my absolute answer is yes, it's still a lot to think about. My first job could be my forever job. Who else is really this lucky? Well, other than a Bishop.

We move around the shop for hours like we're running out of time, and if we want these to be postmarked today, we are. With about fifty orders left to fulfill, I climb up the ladder to grab the rest of the soaps off the top shelf when I hear screaming over my sound-canceling headphones.

I take an earbud out and look at Harper. "Everything okay?"

"Not sure." She sets down a handful of thank-you cards, and I place the bars of soap on the table, then we go to the door.

Fifty goats are roaming around the property.

"Oh no," Harper whispers. "They shouldn't be outside of the fence."

Seconds later, Kane, Ethan, and Payton round the barn as one jumps on top of my car.

"Get off there," I say as it prances over the hood, roof, then plops down.

Harper shakes her head at Ethan. "What the hell happened?"

"Someone left the gate open, and they all followed Cupcake out. I got a call on the radio from Payton. We were just heading back from the B&B."

Kane's chasing a few, waving his arms in the air, but the goats aren't paying him any attention. All they do is *baa* at him as they sprint past.

"How are we going to catch them all?" Payton huffs, repositioning his hat.

It's hot, and just standing here for these few minutes has me sweating.

"Maybe you two can help? We kinda need all hands on deck to round up what we can. Then we're gonna have to take a head count to make sure we don't have any wanderers," Ethan explains to Harper. She hesitates before answering, and I can tell she wants to say no. We have personal deadlines that she wanted to make. But with one look, Harper caves and gives me the go-ahead.

Sweat drips off Kane's forehead as he tries to keep several goats from moving past him.

I walk toward him. "We need some rope so we can lasso them. Isn't that what real cowboys do?"

"That's not a bad idea. If you don't watch out, these little bastards will use you as a springboard. It's worse than herding cats." He gives me a smirk, and butterflies flutter in my tummy.

"What can I do to help?"

He laughs. "Put me outta my misery?"

"I don't think so. We're gonna have to suffer together. Oh look. Where are they going?" I ask, pointing behind him. At least a handful of goats are walking down the road in a straight line and others are joining in.

"Shit," he whisper-hisses.

"Ethan," Kane yells and points. "You need a side by side to stop them."

"Y'all need a sheepdog to help guide them around and keep them in line," I tease.

Kane's face breaks into a huge smile. "You're right. That'd be a great idea. I'm gonna tell Ethan that."

I shrug nonchalantly. "Might be life-changing."

"You sure you weren't a ranch hand in another life?"

I snort because I know I would've never survived doing ranch chores.

Kane leads me to the barn. Grabbing a handful of lead ropes, he gives me half. "We'll catch them eventually."

"I'm going to apologize in advance for sucking at this. Not really experienced with physical activity or dealing with any sorta livestock," I admit. Everyone knows I grew up in town and busied myself in books.

Kane places his hand on my shoulder and laughs. "Experience won't help you with these little assholes, so it's not a big deal."

When he removes his hand, I feel the instant loss of his touch. Being this close to him is intoxicating in all the wrong ways. If I had to chase animals just to spend more time with him, sign me up every day of the week.

We walk down the road next to the fence line, and he starts catching them one at a time. Unfortunately, it's nothing like walking a dog, and I understand why Kane called them bastards.

One of them starts screaming and tugging against me. I nearly drop the rope, and Kane comes over and grabs it from me.

"This is a feisty one." He wraps the rope around his gloved hand and guides the little booger back to the barn. Then we do it all over again. We pass Harper and Payton, who each have one too.

"Did you expect to be chasing goats today?" he asks me.

I snicker. "No, but I'm actually having fun."

He smirks. "Only 'cause of the company."

"Yeah. But it's kind of like an adventure. I expected my day to go a certain way, and it's always a pleasant surprise when it changes, and I run into you."

"That's a good way to look at it," he admits. "I like that."

He meets my eyes with such intensity that I have to look away. As I stare at the number of goats in front of us, Ethan blocks them in with a side by side. Since they can't easily continue any farther, they turn around and head toward us.

Harper catches up to us, chuckling. For the next hour and a half, we chase and capture these animals that scream like old ladies. At one point, one screams so loud, I start laughing and can't stop. I got so tickled by the sound that I could barely catch my breath. Kane even started laughing because I was.

When we return to the barn, Ethan takes a head count and realizes one is missing.

"Dammit," he seethes. "I'm hot, sweaty, and now I have another to find."

"You're gonna have to be on your own for that one," Kane states. "Payton and I need to get back to the stud farm. Knox is already blowing my phone up."

He looks at me and smiles. "Thanks for the adventure today."

I grow giddy and give him a wink. Harper raises a brow at me as Kane gives me all his attention.

"Maybe we can do it again sometime." Kane smirks, and I swear I'm going to internally combust.

"I'd actually like that," I admit, happy for another opportunity with him. Unfortunately, he still has a girlfriend who he seems to like a lot.

I'd never do anything to sabotage his relationship, but I can't help but wonder if he'd give me the time of day. Sure, I'll always be Hadleigh's little sister, but the reality is I'm a single woman. If only he were available.

"If your goats get loose again, call some extra help. Ivy and I have a lot of stuff to take care of."

Ethan pulls her in and slides his lips across hers. "I'll make it up to you, baby," he whispers, but I can still hear him.

"Yeah, make it up to me by letting me sleep until at least nine on Saturday." Harper laughs and kisses him again.

"Deal," he tells her, and we walk back to the warehouse.

"Ugh," I say when the A/C hits my face. "I'm disgusting now."

"Me too. My underboobs are sweating." Harper looks at the clock. "How 'bout we call it a day and start back up first thing in the morning?"

"Yes, thank you. I need a cold shower and some deodorant."

Harper grins. "What were you and Kane chattin' about?"

"Goats."

She tilts her head. "And that's it?" She doesn't sound convinced.

"Yep, pretty much." But my mind wanders when I think about how he was looking at me.

"He's a nice guy," she adds.

"Yeah, he is. I met his girlfriend at the hospital," I add.

"Raelyn, right?"

"I dunno, she didn't introduce herself to me. Just kinda acted like I didn't exist."

"Yeah, I dunno what to think about her. But if he's happy, then everyone will accept her with open arms," Harper explains. "It's the Bishop way."

I swallow hard as a tinge of jealousy sweeps through me. "Yeah, I'm sure she's a sweetheart. I can't imagine Kane being with someone who isn't. But anyway, ya sure you don't want me to finish this up before I go?"

The products and packing slips along with the thank-you cards are all exactly where we left them on the table.

"Nah, it's fine. Another day won't make that much of a difference at this point."

"Thank you so much. I've got a date with a book tonight."

"Really? Another one?"

"Yeah, it's a little different than what I'm used to. It's an erotic lizard shifter romance."

Her eyes go wide.

"Did you know they have several penises?"

Her mouth falls open.

"Yeah, the sex is wild. Several—you-know-whats—in the same hole. Wild."

"One day I'm gonna have to get you to make me a list of must-read books."

I chuckle and grab my stuff. "You tell me when and I'll give you a list of a hundred. Anyway, see ya tomorrow."

"Yep! Have a good evenin'. Enjoy your quad penetration lizard sex."

I snort. "Oh, you know I will."

"You're gonna make some man really happy one day, Ivy. All this research you've been doin' over the years with those books."

"Let's just hope he can satisfy my needs," I say matter-of-factly.

She laughs, and so do I, but I'm not joking. I have many things I want to mark off my sex bucket list, but first I gotta get rid of my sacred V-card. I've been saving it for one man, but unfortunately, he's not even an option. At least not yet.

CHAPTER EIGHT

KANE

I WAKE up at the butt crack of dawn to help Knox and Payton feed the horses. Afterward, we head down to the B&B, grab a quick breakfast, then set up the tables for the Fourth of July party. The past three weeks have been hectic, and I can't wait to relax and enjoy myself before returning to the craziness.

"Ready for tonight?" Riley asks.

"Yeah, it's actually one of my favorite traditions," I admit. "It's something I loved as a kid and still enjoy as an adult. Even when my dad's being an asshole and throwing water balloons at us."

Diesel snickers. "I heard this year he got something even better."

"No," Knox says from behind me. "What is it?"

"I promised I wouldn't tell anyone," Diesel adds with a shit-eating smirk. He loves knowing something we don't.

"You're bullshittin'," Riley throws back.

"No, I'm not. I only know because it was accidentally delivered to my house, and well, I opened up the boxes to see what it was."

"You really aren't gonna tell us?" Payton shakes his head. "That's cruel."

"Jackson told me he'd kick my ass if I said a peep to anyone. And I believe him."

"You should," Knox confirms. "If nothing else, he's a man of his word."

"I know what he's planning as well," Gavin states, and I almost forgot he was here.

"What the hell!" Knox grows more agitated. "Someone needs to spill the beans so we can retaliate if it's even possible at this point."

"It's not. Nothing you could buy in a four-hundred-mile radius would help you," Gavin explains. "Y'all are all fucked."

"Dammit," I mumble. My dad usually isn't happy until every person under the age of thirty-five is soaked. "That's what I get for hoping this year would be different."

We continue making small talk, but Diesel's and Gavin's lips are sealed tighter than a slot machine in Vegas. It's annoying they won't tell, but I know Dad threatened them with his wrath.

All the younger Bishops have been tasked with setting up, so we take care of it after eating. Of course, we usually get together during the holidays, but this one is different. It's always the most laid-back event, in my opinion, and the weather is typically really nice, so there's plenty of room for the entire family to be together. Which honestly is an accomplishment within itself, considering most of my cousins are grown with spouses and babies. Red-and-blue-checkered tablecloths are clipped on every flat surface. We set out folding chairs and hay bales for extra seating. Grandma demanded a large tent be put up this year so we at least had some shade, and it takes us at least an hour to get it right. The party officially starts around lunch and ends with fireworks, and always includes plenty of food and activities.

"Wanna give me a hand with the volleyball net?" Knox asks, carrying the large bag over his shoulder.

"Sure." I follow him toward the poles Dad cemented in the ground a few weeks ago.

Knox carefully unfolds the net, and I grab the opposite end so we can stretch it out.

"So you bringin' Raelyn to the party today?" he asks.

I'm not shocked it came up in conversation, but I can't believe it took this long for news to spread, considering Hadleigh knows her.

"Actually no. She won't be coming."

He gives me a puzzled look. "Is she workin'?"

"Raelyn said she wanted to take a break after I said no to being in an open relationship with her."

Knox shakes his head. "Don't blame ya. I wouldn't want to share my woman with every man in town either."

"I dunno if it's like that, but she went to Houston and partied. Pretty sure she cheated, but I didn't care enough to ask."

"Sometimes, it's better to just let people like that go. In the end, way less drama."

"Almost positive she wasn't the marryin' type anyway. Being with someone like that is just wastin' my time."

"Sorry to hear that. You'll eventually find the one and settle down. Just have to put yourself out there more."

"That's for damn sure."

Except the first person who comes to mind is Ivy.

After everything's set up and in place, we go our separate ways and plan to meet up for lunch.

Once I'm home, I instantly fall asleep and take a three-hour nap. Hopefully, I'll be ready for whatever my dad has up his sleeve. Even as an old man, he's always up to something with his antics, which is tradition at this point. Only Grandma and pregnant women get a free pass from his wrath. Everyone else is fair game.

Before I leave, I change into shorts and a T-shirt. I learned the hard way that wearing jeans in the July heat is a bad idea.

When I arrive at the B&B and see the number of vehicles parked on the side of the road, I realize I should've left earlier. There's nothing I can do other than park and walk. Music and laughter echoes across the pasture. I try to take in the moment because I know I'll look back at this and cherish it one day. Grandma's getting older and so is everyone else, and I'm not stupid enough to think they'll live forever. They say you don't realize you're living in the good ole days until time passes, and I don't take things like this for granted.

As soon as I walk up, Dad comes running with the most gigantic Super Soaker water gun I've ever seen. He's wearing gallons of water on his back. With his finger on the trigger, he squirts me from head to toe, then makes sure to spray my crotch so it looks like I pissed myself.

"Are you fuckin' kidding me?" I seethe and run toward him.

He laughs like a maniac, shooting water into the air and still somehow hits me.

Maize, Kaitlyn, Knox, Riley, Rowan, Ethan, and Kenzie join in on the attack. That's when I notice they're wet too. Dad's laughing so hard he trips on unlevel ground, and before any of us notices, Grandma Bishop comes from around the B&B. She's holding the water hose nozzle right at Dad.

"Put 'em up," she demands like she's holding him at gunpoint. Dad cocks the Super Soaker and points it right at her.

"Jackson Joel Bishop, you won't live to regret pulling that trigger if you do."

The family bursts into "Ooohs" as Grandma and Dad have a full stand down. I cross my arms and watch what's about to unfold. Dad soaks Grandma's red toenails with water, and then she lays into him with the hose until he runs away. We laugh so hard that I can barely catch my breath. Looking like I pissed myself for the next hour was worth it. Grandma drops the nozzle like a mic and grins wide.

"Way to go!" I tell her, holding my hand up for a high five. She slams hers into mine.

"Sometimes, you gotta play dirty."

"Thanks, Grandma," Kaitlyn says. "He probably would've gotten us all if you hadn't stopped him."

She shakes her head. "I raised him better than that."

"You showed him who's boss," Knox says, wrapping his arm around her shoulder.

She nods. "That's right. Never forget it. Now, y'all make sure to eat plenty. There's enough to feed an army."

Uncle John and Uncle Alex are busy grilling hamburgers and hot dogs. The hearty scents float through the air and my stomach growls. I wait at the end of the line, where Hadleigh and Knox join me.

"Where's Hendrix?" I ask. Hadleigh points at my mom, who's holding him under the tent.

"She won't let me take him." Hadleigh chuckles. "I'm not complainin', though. He's gettin' heavy." She quickly changes the subject. "Where's Raelyn? Is she comin'?"

I glance at Knox. "You didn't tell her?"

"Ain't my business," he admits.

"Tell me what?" Hadleigh looks back and forth between us.

I lower my voice and fill her in on what I told Knox earlier.

Hadleigh's brow furrows. "I can't believe that. Wow. Honestly, though, her loss."

"That's what I said, in a roundabout way," Knox says, then adds, "Actually, I said, fuck her."

"I appreciate it, but I'm not that upset. Guess deep down I knew she wasn't the one for me."

"Everything happens for a reason," Hadleigh reminds me. As the conversation comes to a lull, the line starts moving. I grab a plate and some buns, then my uncles load me up with meat.

We find an empty table and chairs under the canopy and sit.

Just as I shove a hot dog with extra mustard in my mouth, Ivy walks toward us, and I nearly choke.

"You okay?" Knox asks.

"Yeah, just went down the wrong way." I sip my punch to try to coat my throat. Ivy looks as if she's gliding across the grass wearing a tank top, cut-off shorts, leather boots, and a cowboy hat to top it off. I'm at a loss for words by how damn gorgeous she is without even trying. Her hair up in pigtails is enough to nearly break me.

"Hads!" Ivy says, sliding down beside me.

"You made it." Hadleigh grins wide. "Go grab some food. There's plenty."

"Good idea," she says and gets up.

"So when did your sister grow up?" Knox asks. "Did that happen overnight?"

Hadleigh snickers. "Basically. Makes me even more worried about her. Eventually, some man is gonna break her heart, and I'll have to go all psycho big sister."

"You never know. She might meet the person she's supposed to spend the rest of her life with right off the bat," I tell her.

"Maybe. She's just too cute for her own good." Hadleigh takes a big bite of her burger.

When Ivy returns, she plops down next to me and takes off her purse that she had slung around her body. She smells amazing, almost good enough to eat.

Before I can start any sort of conversation, Harper comes over with a wide smile.

"Ivy!" She leans over and gives her a side hug. "Glad you decided to come after all."

She playfully narrows her eyes at her. "It's only because you and Hadleigh literally threatened me."

"Whatever will get your nose out of a book for a day," Harper quips, squeezing her shoulder. "Gotta give those eyes and ears a rest and live a little."

"But a fantasy world is so much better." She glances at me with a seductive expression, then focuses back on her food.

Did she just eye-fuck me? No. I must be delusional.

"Well, I'll let ya get back to eatin'. Don't forget to try the tres leches cake. It's to die for."

"Oh, I won't," Ivy says before Harper walks away. "So what's been goin' on so far?"

"Other than my dad startin' shit, not much," Knox explains, then tells her exactly what happened.

Ivy falls into a fit of laughter.

Knox pops a few chips in his mouth. "Every damn year, it's some sort of prank."

"Did your junk get sprayed too?" she asks me.

"Yes, but it's almost dry now, thankfully," I say, not wanting to stand because I don't want her to look at the chubby I'm currently trying to hide.

"That would've been funny to watch. I always miss the good stuff." She smirks.

"The best part was when Grandma stopped all the commotion," Hadleigh explains.

Right on cue, Dad walks by, and he's dripping wet. Ivy snickers, and I shake my head as Dad shoots winks and antagonizes anyone who will give him a sliver of attention. We've all learned to ignore him.

"The trick is not to make eye contact," I lean in and whisper to her.

"Got it," she confirms, focusing on her plate while she snickers.

After eating, I catch up with Ethan and Harper, who are sitting on a blanket and enjoying the sunshine. Hayden and Hailey-Mae are busy playing with their toys on the grass. While we talk, my gaze drifts over to Ivy. She's smiling at Hadleigh and Knox, but I notice her pull a small bottle of something from her purse and pour it into her red cup. I vow to keep my eye on her throughout the day and night because while she's safe here, some ranch hands'd happily take her home. That shit isn't happening on my watch.

Uncle Alex asks Ethan a question, and I take the opportunity to step away. Ivy's back at the punch bowl filling her plastic cup full.

I lean in and whisper in her ear. "I know what you've been doin'."

She immediately giggles, and I can tell she's already tipsy. "What have I been doin'? Please enlighten me."

The confidence in her tone is undeniable.

"The booze. I've been watchin' ya."

Intrigue covers her face. "Have you now? And do you like what you see?"

Heat rushes through me, and I can feel my pulse pick up in my neck. "Depends," I linger, not finishing my sentence.

"So whatcha gonna do about it? Tattle on me?"

I burst into a hearty laughter. "Maybe I'll call the cops and get you arrested."

"With handcuffs? Sounds erotic. Call them. I dare you," she taunts, lifting a brow.

I shake my head. "Nah. But if you don't slow down, you're gonna be sick as hell."

She opens the flap of her purse, and I see a bottle of Fireball. The fact that she's mixing it with fruit punch makes my stomach turn. "That stuff will sneak up on you if you're not careful."

"I guess we'll see, won't we? I mean, you admitted to watching me, so sit back and enjoy the show."

"Never experienced feisty Ivy before."

She lifts a brow. "Then you're missing out."

I can't help but study how she licks her lips.

"So where's that girlfriend of yours?" Ivy looks around. "Haven't come across her yet."

"Not sure." I'm tempted to tell her that I'm single as a Pringle, but I keep it to myself. It would be awkward to offer that information right now.

"Her loss," Ivy states, pouring another shot into her drink.

"Kane!" Kaitlyn yells from across the pasture. She's holding a volleyball in her hand. "Bring Ivy too!"

Payton stands off to the side as Kaitlyn waves us over.

"You two are the only ones under the age of fifty who aren't holding a baby at the moment. We can play in pairs. You in?" Kaitlyn asks.

I look at Payton, and all he does is shrug. He's only trying to appease her because Kaitlyn can be pushy at times.

"I'll play if Kane does!" Ivy glances at me. "But fair warning, I was into academics, not sports. Sorry you've got the worst partner, and we haven't even started."

A chuckle escapes me. "I'll be the judge of that."

"Who's serving first?" Payton asks.

"They can," Kaitlyn demands, then throws the ball toward us. Ivy misses, and I hand it to her.

"Told you," she whispers.

I lean in close. "The booze probably ain't helpin' any."

She places her finger against her lips and shushes me. When I turn around, Kaitlyn and Payton are in place. Ivy tries to do an overhand serve, and her hand slams against it. The ball whips forward and bounces against the top of my head. Somehow, it goes over the net where Kaitlyn spikes it.

"Damn. I'm sorry," Ivy tells me.

"At least it went over," I encourage.

"I hope this whole game ain't gonna be like this," Kaitlyn complains.

"Stop shit talkin'," I say when it's their turn. The ball goes back and forth a few times, mainly between Kaitlyn and me. She's way too competitive for her own good.

"Next time, we're playing chess," Ivy states as I help her up after she tripped. I give her a little too much oomph, and she slams against my chest.

"Sorry," I mutter.

"I have a feelin' you're enjoyin' this a little too much," she playfully mutters as she tugs on the bottom of my T-shirt.

"Not too much, just the perfect amount." I smile as Hadleigh brings us bottles of water.

I dunno what happens, but the next time Ivy serves, it's like her competitiveness decided to show up. She sends the ball over the net, and Payton misses it. Another serve missed. We go through this a few times, and before I know it, we're all sweaty, and the game is over.

"What the hell?" Kaitlyn comes over, giving us each a handshake. "I'd say good game, but damn Ivy, you smeared our noses in it."

She chuckles, then shrugs. "I dunno what came over me."

"Y'all make a good team," Payton states.

I playfully swing my arm around Ivy's shoulders as she grins at me.

"Best two out of three?" Kaitlyn eyes us, and I know exactly what she's doing. I grew up with her being a poor sport and learned to quit when I was ahead.

"No way, loser," I state, and she rolls her eyes with a huff as we walk away.

"Oh my goodness, that was so mean." Ivy furrows her brow. "We could've played again."

"No. That's the thing, she'd want to keep going until she beat us, and I wanted to relax. She's always been like this, so I like to rub her nose in it. And trust me, it ain't often, so I gotta take the opportunity when I can."

Ivy and I mosey over to the food area and grab drinks, then we plop down on a spare blanket in the grass that's not taken. My uncles are across the pasture in the distance setting up the display.

"You gonna watch the fireworks with me?"

She leans in a little closer. "Only if you want me to."

I swallow hard, unable to stop staring at her pouty lips. "I'd like that a lot."

"Twenty-minute countdown." I hear my mama yell. Her voice is the only thing that snaps me back to reality. For a moment, I was entirely under Ivy's spell. Then again, I'm not complaining either. She makes me feel things I haven't felt in a long-ass time.

When I turn around, I see so many of my cousins scattered around on the lawn, and it makes me happy. I make eye contact with my brother, and he lifts a brow before glancing at Ivy. Before he uses his twin superpowers and reads my mind, I look away. I can't have anyone thinking something is going on, but then again, maybe I don't give a shit.

Deep down, I wish there was.

Ivy opens her purse, takes the Fireball out, and empties the rest into her cup. As she chugs, I shake my head.

When Ivy finishes her drink, I meet her eyes. They're glassy, and she's wearing a goofy grin.

"Why are ya lookin' at me like that?" The flirty nature in her tone isn't lost on me.

"Just thinkin' how pretty you look tonight," I explain.

Her eyes look off into the distance, and I swear I see her blush. "Thank you," she whispers and scoots closer to me. It's electrifying when her arm brushes against mine, and it drives me fucking crazy.

The first boom happens in the distance, and seconds later, the shells explode up above, leaving trails of silver and blue glitter in the sky. Everyone lets out oohs and aahs. This happens time and time again until the grand finale. During the end of the show, Ivy leans her head on my shoulder. As she stares up, I glance over at her and see the reflection of fireworks in her eyes.

There's so much fire in her gaze that not even a kiss could

extinguish it. When the fireworks are over, disappointment strikes.

I stand, holding out my hand for Ivy. She takes it, and she stumbles into me when I pull her up.

"You good?"

"Of course."

Liar.

One of the younger ranch hands walks by. I think his name is Joey, and I catch him checking out Ivy's ass. She notices and looks back over her shoulder at him. It seemed like he was going to come chat with her, but then he noticed my locked jaw. I slightly shake my head, and he must be smart enough to keep going.

When Ivy looks up at me, I realize how drunk she is. Not wanting anyone in my family to notice, I place my hand on her back and steady her. "You're going home with me tonight," I demand.

"Ooh, I actually love the sound of that."

I smirk. "No, not like that. I can't let you drive. You've had too much Fireball, and now it snuck up on your ass. You need lots of water so you don't get dehydrated."

"You're worse than my mother. I'm *fiiiiine*," she sing-songs.

"You're not *fiiiiine*." We sneak away before anyone notices, and I lead her to my truck. After I unlock it, I open the door and let her in.

"Always the gentleman." She chews on her lip as I move to the driver's side.

"You don't have to take care of me. I'm grown," Ivy states on the way to my house.

I nod. "I know you are. Which means you're also old enough to know better."

"Oh please, you can't tell me you didn't sneak a few drinks before you turned twenty-one."

"I did, but not without consequences."

She lifts a brow. "Sounds scandalous."

I chuckle. "Oh, sweet Ivy, the stories I could tell you."

"You should." She doesn't take her eyes off me.

"Maybe some other time."

When we pull into my driveway, I help her out of the truck. When she wrapped her arm around my waist, I'd be lying if I didn't admit I liked the way her touch felt. As quickly as possible, I unlock the door and lead her to the living room.

"You good?" I ask, turning on the lamp.

"Yeah," she says breathlessly. Ivy's palms rest on my cheek, and seconds later, she's leaning in to kiss me. Quickly, I pull away, but not because I want to. No, I want to wage war with her tongue and devour her mouth, but she's not in the right state of mind. When I kiss her, I want her to be completely sober.

"Ivy," I whisper when she meets my gaze with disappointment. I want to give in. I fucking want to. "I can't."

Instead of being upset, she laughs. "Is it because you slept with my sister?"

The words tumble out of her mouth like a dust storm in West Texas, and it shocks me. Something that doesn't happen often.

"Absolutely not." I search her face. "How did you know about that?"

"Everyone heard about it, Kane. Rumors fly 'round here like songbirds. So it's true?"

Adrenaline courses through me, but I refuse to lie to her. "It happened, but it was a long time ago, and all that is in the past."

"Thanks for admitting it, even though I don't really care about it. I know you aren't in love with my sister."

"I'm not," I admit. "I don't think I ever was. It was just a thing that happened."

"And I respect that," she says, not shocked. While it should be weird to talk about this with her, it's not. There's nothing accusatory about her tone. She treats it like what it is—something that happened in the past.

Ivy wobbles on her feet, and I lead her to the couch. I grab the extra blankets and pillow like I did before, then give her another T-shirt to wear. She puts it to her nose and inhales, then lets out a sigh. "You just always smell so good."

"Not a compliment I'm used to gettin'," I admit.

"That's a pity." She grabs the bottom of her shirt, and I turn my head. My cock hardens as she throws her shirt, bra, and jean shorts in a pile. If I didn't know better, I'd say she's teasing me on purpose and testing every bit of willpower I have. While she gets settled, I make her a tall glass of ice water. I return and set it on the coffee table.

"Drink as much as that as you can so you don't feel like total shit tomorrow," I explain as she looks up at me from the couch.

"Thank you. I will. Good night, Kane."

"Night, Ivy." I hold her gaze for a few more seconds, then turn off the lights and go straight to the shower. It's not the first time she's made me hard as fuck, and I'm sure it won't be the last.

I stand under the stream, roughly stroking my cock to thoughts of her until I desperately come with the faint taste of her lips on mine. If she hadn't been drinking, I'd for damn sure have kissed her until the sun rose.

CHAPTER NINE

IVY

When I roll over, I immediately realize where I am. A glass of water sits on the table next to a bottle of over-the-counter pain meds. Kane predicted I'd have a raging hangover, and damn, he was right. Drinking was the stupidest idea I've had all year.

I see the clothes I wore to the Fourth of July party on the floor and notice I'm wearing another one of his shirts. Hopefully, he realizes I'll be keeping this one too. The other shirt hasn't been washed yet, but his scent has unfortunately dissipated. It's okay because the memories of him giving it to me live rent-free in my head.

Just as I grab two pills and gulp them down, Kane comes from the hallway wearing a pair of black joggers. They sit haphazardly on his hips, and I can't help but linger on his abs. Kane looks good enough to eat, and I'd love to lick him from head to toe.

"Mornin'. How're ya feelin'?"

"Go ahead. I'm waiting for a big fat I told ya so."

"Oh, I don't have to rub your face in it 'cause you already know I was right. Feel like shit, don'tcha?"

"Ugh yes," I admit, leaning my head against the couch cushions. When he opens the blinds in the living room, then meets my eyes, I begin to recall the stupid things I said to him last night. Embarrassment doesn't even describe how I feel. I'd love to crawl under the cushions and hide.

"What?" He chuckles, noticing me having an internal meltdown.

"I'm sorry about everything I did and said."

He crosses his arms over his chest and smirks. "Oh, so you *do* remember?"

"Everything," I whisper, burying my face in my hands. The fact that I asked him about Hadleigh after trying to kiss him is so ballsy, and something I'd never have the courage to do sober. Honestly, it makes no difference to me that he hooked up with my sister years ago. She's beautiful and fun, so I'd almost think something was wrong with *him* if he didn't. But to call him out on it? I guess tipsy me needed confirmation from the horse's mouth.

I shake my head. "I'm *never* drinking again."

Kane's chuckle almost lightens the mood, but then I replay my desperate attempt to kiss him. "It's fine. We've all been there."

"Yeah, but you have a girlfriend, and I acted inappropriately toward you. Kane, I swear I'd never do anything to ruin that for you, and I didn't mean to put you in such an awkward situation. I'm so sorry. I obviously wasn't thinking clearly."

"It's fine. I'm used to sloppy drunk girls trying to stick their tongues down my throat." He smirks, almost as if he's enjoying it.

I groan, wishing I could disappear. "And now I'm officially deceased."

I stand to grab my clothes, trying to escape my mortification. "I'm just gonna change back into my clothes and get going."

Before I can take a step, he gently places one strong hand on my shoulder. I'm standing directly in front of him and find it hard to look into his baby blues.

"Ivy," he whispers, placing his fingers under my chin and prompting me to meet his heated gaze. "I didn't kiss you because you were intoxicated. Trust me, if you hadn't been drinking, last night would've turned out completely different. I can guarantee you wouldn't have slept on that couch."

His admission has my breath hitching as he continues. "I don't take advantage of women who can't give sober consent, even the ones who...ya know, forcefully throw themselves at me." He chuckles. I search his face, wondering if I'm dreaming.

"Wait, you would have kissed me back?"

"Hell yes, I would've. But that moment has come and gone." For a brief second, I feel as if the world stops around us. What he said begins to settle into the crevasse of my heart, and I swallow down the knot that works in the back of my throat. I wish he'd just pull me into his arms, thread his fingers through my hair, and devour my mouth right here, right now.

"What about Raelyn?"

"We're not together anymore."

My mouth falls open, and my eyes go wide, a reaction I can't hide. "Oh, I'm sorry. I didn't know."

"It's fine."

"Do you want to talk about it?" I don't want to pry, but I also know sometimes it helps to have people listen.

"Three weeks ago, she told me she wanted an open relationship. I'm not cut out to share the woman I'm with, and I told her as much. So she said she wanted a break," he explains, and I see the flicker of his dominant and possessive side. I'd be lying if I said I didn't like it.

"Wow."

"I know. But things work out the way they should." Kane

gives me a wink and makes his way to the kitchen. I follow him, but when I pass by the dining room table, I can't help but scan over all the tools covering the flat space.

He opens the fridge and pulls out a jug of orange juice, then pours a glass for us both. I take two big gulps, hoping it fixes the dizziness taking over.

"You're into crafting?" I ask.

He laughs. "I wouldn't call it *crafting*, but I like to do leatherworking in my spare time. It's relaxing to carve out shapes and emboss covers for journals."

"I had no idea." I scan over the dark-colored leather that looks soft to the touch.

"It's a long process, but nothing more than a side hobby. It really helps me clear my mind when I feel like things are spiraling out of my control. Grounds me in a way," he admits.

"That's cool. Are you self-taught?"

"Pretty much. I met a man at the rodeo one year and was intrigued. When I got home, I started researchin' and bought the supplies to start. I made your sister one for Christmas one year."

My eyes go wide. "*You* made that? I thought she bought it online. Color me impressed."

He proudly smiles as I reach out and touch the cut edges of the intricate flower close to the left side of the cover. "It's gorgeous. I'd love to see your process. The detail of this is... Actually, I think I'm speechless. What other secrets have you been keeping?"

Kane lightly chuckles as he moves closer, then turns on the overhead light. "Sweet girl, if only you knew."

I bite my lip, intrigued as hell.

As he sits, he pats the chair beside him, an invite I won't refuse. I plop down, and I'm so close that our arms brush together each time he reaches forward. I don't move an inch because I want to be as close as humanly possible without it being awkward.

Sparks fly, and the excitement builds in the pit of my stomach as I think about his earlier admission.

He would've kissed me.

Now I feel even more stupid for needing any amount of liquid courage for that party. I just didn't want to be nervous around so many people, and at the time, it did help.

I try my best to focus on what he's doing.

"If you look at the leather under the light, you can see the design I still need to carve."

"Oh yeah, that will look incredible," I admit as he holds it at an angle.

"So to start, we'll use this tool. It's called a swivel knife, and I'll use it to gently trace what I've already drawn. You can't go too deep, or it will cut through the material and ruin it." He looks over at me and smiles, then goes back to it.

I can't take my eyes off him and how precise he's being as he carefully moves the sharp edge around the stem and leaves of the flower. The soft sounds of his breathing as he works, combined with the intensity of his gaze, have heat rushing through my body. The muscles in his triceps flex, and I love watching him work so precisely with his hands. Honestly, Raelyn is an idiot for letting him go, but her loss is another woman's gain. Hopefully mine.

While I study him, I wonder who else knows about their breakup or if he's keeping it to himself. It actually makes sense why she wasn't there yesterday and explains why he's been so flirty with me. I knew I didn't imagine it, even if my self-esteem told me I was.

Kane continues carving, and it's impossible for me to forget about how enamored I am with his man as the faint hints of his soap and cologne drift through the air. Being with him like this is intoxicating, and I don't want this day to end even though I feel like crap.

He picks up another tool and a small hammer, then taps it into the leather a few times.

"Wow, it creates a shadow effect."

"Yes," he nearly whispers. "Gives the image depth and makes it almost three-dimensional. Do you want to try?"

I blush. "I'll probably mess it up."

"You can practice on scrap first," he offers.

"Sure." Kane positions the square piece of leather in front of me, then tells me to draw whatever I want, so I do the easiest thing—my name. He hands me the swivel knife and walks me through the steps.

"You'll hold it like this." He places his large hand on top of mine. "But be careful because it's very sharp. Take your time to steady your wrist."

I slowly draw out the I, then the V, and Y. The canvas I'm working with is even slicker than I thought, and the tool cuts through it like butter. It makes me respect how perfect his lines are because it's not as easy as he makes it look. Thankfully, my name is short and without curves.

"Perfect."

He guides me through the next steps, and I appreciate his patience. "You're a good teacher," I offer.

"You're a good student," he encourages, and it makes me smile.

After an hour of leather working together, my stomach growls. It's loud enough for Kane to hear so he speaks up.

"Wanna grab some food at the B&B?"

"Together?"

He nods. "Well, yeah."

I tuck my bottom lip into my mouth and turn my body until I'm facing him in the chair. He searches my face.

"It's probably not a good idea. I'm not working today, and I'd prefer not to be questioned because someone will ask why we're together."

"It's no one's business, Ivy. I'll tell them as much," he confirms.

"I know, but you're aware of how rumors spread around here. I'd just rather not be bombarded by it or have to explain what happened last night to my sister. Trust me, I'm already embarrassed enough after how I nearly humped your leg."

His head falls back with laughter. Kane rests his palm against my cheek when he catches his breath as his thumb lightly brushes across my skin. "Just know I'm not embarrassed to be seen with you, Ivy. I wouldn't care what they said, but I'll respect your wishes. Having a big family can be overwhelming at times, especially when everyone is in your business. So whatever you want, I'm game."

He has no idea what I want right now, but it includes him naked in his bedroom with me under him. The dirty thoughts are almost too much for me to handle.

"Thank you. I appreciate it."

He gently tucks a loose strand of hair behind my ear as my heart urges me to go in for another kiss, but I wouldn't be able to stand the embarrassment if I were denied again. Still, even after everything he's said, it's hard for me to believe he'd ever really give me a chance. I'm ten years younger and his bestie's little sister. I have nothing to lose compared to him.

"What if I grabbed us some food to go? We can eat here, and then you can leave if you'd like, or you can hang out for a little while."

My eyes go wide when I remember I parked at the B&B, which will only encourage questions. "My car…"

"It's right outside. I picked it up this morning after I fed the horses so no one would be curious and to make it easier for you today."

"Are you always this thoughtful?"

He laughs and stands. "You leaving the keys in it just made it easy. So on a scale from one to ten, how hungry are you?"

"Eleven. My head feels weird, and I think food will help with that."

"Got it. And dessert?"

"Always," I say.

"I'm gonna change clothes, then head out. Shouldn't take me very long."

"Perfect," I tell him, going back to the living room. "Oh, do you think it will be okay if I use your shower? I think I need to wash yesterday off my body and out of my mind."

I watch his Adam's apple bob in his throat.

"Sure. I'll get you some clean clothes when I change. Be right back," he tells me, and I watch him stalk down the hallway toward his bedroom. I give a little fist pump and grin because for the first time in my life, Kane Bishop is giving me the attention I've always desired.

When he returns, he's holding a small pile. "They'll probably be huge on you, but it's the best I could do."

His hand brushes mine as I take them. "I'm sure it will be better than putting on yesterday's clothes. I should probably just bring an overnight bag from now on, considering your couch has quickly become my second bed."

Kane meets my eyes, and I immediately feel stupid until he speaks. "Probably not a bad idea. It's always good to be prepared."

His eyebrow pops up, and I know he feels the underlying current between us. It's undeniable when he looks at me with that intense Bishop gaze. It's what wet dreams are made from.

When he grabs his keys from the counter, I get a good look at what he's wearing. Running shorts, a T-shirt, and some athletic shoes. His biceps are huge, and when he slaps on his Astros baseball cap, I nearly melt.

Goddammit, now *he's* testing *my* willpower.

"I'll be back." He catches me gawking.

"I'll be waiting here."

He shoots me a wink, and a few seconds later, he's out the door. When I hear his truck crank, I let out a loud squeal. Kane is finally single, and I'm gonna make him mine.

CHAPTER TEN

KANE

Knowing Ivy is in my house, wearing my clothes, and no one can know gives me an adrenaline rush like no other. While the attraction is mutual, a part of me feels guilty.

She's my best friend's much *younger* sister.

Although what happened between Hadleigh and me is water under the bridge, I can't imagine she'd be okay with me dating Ivy. Hadleigh's always been fiercely protective of her sister, and just because we're besties doesn't mean I'd get special treatment.

Ivy's sweet and innocent, so I should keep my distance, but a dark part of me wants to corrupt her in all the right ways. I try to push the thoughts away before they consume me.

As soon as I walk into the B&B, I contemplate turning around when I spot Hadleigh putting food on a plate. Grandma's happily holding Hendrix and sees me before I can escape.

"Kane, sweetie. How are you?" Grandma motions for me to come closer. I lean down so she can kiss my cheek.

"Hey, Grams. Doin' fine. How's my nephew?" I take a peek and see he's fast asleep in her arms. The drool on his chin makes me chuckle.

"Kane, hey!" Hadleigh comes up and smiles. "Wanna sit with us? I heard most of the ranch hands are hungover today."

I fidget and stumble over my words, unable to make eye contact. "Yeah, that's why I took a half day. Just gonna grab some food to go so I can watch TV and eat."

"No, you should stay. Spend some quality time," Grams insists.

Hadleigh encourages with a nod.

"Maybe another time. I need to shower and do some laundry for the week. I'm also supposed to meet Payton later for—"

"Meet me later for what?" Payton inconveniently strolls over.

Fucking hell.

Does no one eat at home anymore?

Like I should talk.

I scratch my two-day-old scruff along my jawline. "Some paperwork stuff."

He shoots me a confused look, and I beg him with my eyes to go along with whatever the fuck I say. "I don't remember you tellin' me anything."

"*Maybe you didn't hear me then,*" I grit out, lowering my tone so he gets the goddamn message.

He shrugs. "I guess. Text me when you wanna meet up then."

"I will." Then he goes to the buffet, and I grab a container to fill.

Without looking too suspicious, I try to fit as much as I can into one box.

"Jesus, Kane. You feedin' an army or what?" Maize goads, peeking around me as I add a second scoop of potatoes, then set it down before it gets too heavy.

"Can't help myself when it's your food," I taunt, then pat my stomach. "I'm a growing boy."

She snorts, shaking her head. "Y'all are the reason I need to double everything."

"And we appreciate it so much." I flash her a grin.

"Put any more shit in there, and you won't be able to close the lid," she warns, then walks off with an eye roll.

Once I've filled it to the brim, I grab another box and add in desserts I think Ivy will like. A variety of pies, bars, and cakes.

"You're gonna puke your guts out eatin' all that." Hadleigh gawks as the Styrofoam threatens to burst.

"Nah."

"Kane Bishop, I know you can eat a lot, but I don't think I've ever seen you eat *that* much." She stares me down.

My heart races at her suspicious tone. She knows me well enough to realize when I'm lying.

"It's hangover food, whaddya expect? Don't worry. There'll be *no* food wasted. Grandma taught me better than that." I smirk because it's actually the truth.

"If you say so," she drawls, putting Hendrix in the car seat so Grandma can eat.

"I'll see ya guys later." I kneel to give Hendrix's little fist a bump. "You too, little man. Be good for your mama."

Once I give Hadleigh and Grandma hugs, I drive home.

"That smells delicious," Ivy says as soon as I walk in.

"Hadleigh was there with Hendrix and Grandma," I explain, setting out two plates. "Maize too. They all gave me shit for how much food I was getting."

"Oh no. What'd you say?"

When I repeat how it went down, Ivy laughs. "Well, I hope you don't expect me to eat half of *all* that."

"Don't worry, I'll devour whatever you don't." I flash her a wink, and she blushes.

We take our plates to the couch, and I grab two glasses of sweetened tea, then sit next to her.

"So have you read any new books lately?" I ask as I dive into the beef tips.

"Yeah, I've been bingeing a *Beauty and the Beast* retelling fantasy romance series. I'll read in bed and get sucked in, and then before I know it, it's after midnight." She chuckles, angling her body toward mine as she eats.

"I can't remember the last time I read for fun. You'll have to give me some recommendations. Maybe a reading fantasy for dummies manual."

She beams. "I'm gonna give you a thousand recs, so I hope you're ready."

"Well, prepare for it to take me a year to finish one book. I can't afford to stay up late when I gotta be up at five the next day. And I definitely can't read as fast as you," I admit. "Miss I can read a book in a day Callaway."

"It comes with practice." She shrugs. "But there are always audiobooks."

"That's true. What got you into reading so much?"

Swallowing hard, she lowers her gaze as she plays with her food, and the silence lingers.

"You don't have to tell me, Ivy." Guilt creeps in as she brings her eyes to mine.

"It's just kinda embarrassing," she admits. "I've had a speech impediment since the first grade and got teased in elementary and middle school. It made me not want to talk very much because I'd get super frustrated when the words would get stuck in my throat. Eventually, my therapist suggested reading out loud to help me rewire my brain. She said the more I practiced, the easier it'd get, and I'd eventually grow out of it."

"Did you?" I ask, somewhat shocked because I've never noticed it.

"For the most part, yes. It got significantly better in high school, but at that point, I was still shy and reserved. Most of my asshole classmates were the ones who picked on me, so I didn't want to be their friends anyway. However, if I'm anxious or nervous about being in a situation, the stuttering and stammering are more noticeable. Over the years, I've learned how to trick my brain and merge words or use different variations so I don't get stuck. The thesaurus and I became good friends in high school." She nervously giggles.

"I never knew that," I say, surprised Hadleigh never mentioned it, but she probably didn't want to share without Ivy's permission.

"That's because you're easy to talk to," she says sweetly. "I get social anxiety around strangers, and it's the worst when I'm nervous. It's why I tend to stay quiet and keep to myself. I hid in my books for so long that now I can't help comparing the fictional world to reality. And let's just say, I'd rather live in a magical alternate universe some days."

Smiling, I nod. "I can understand that. I can't wrap my head around the concept of high fantasy."

"It takes some getting used to, and you really have to focus so you don't miss anything. Maybe I could read to you sometime?"

"I'd love that."

"Maybe I'll find a reverse harem romance for you before I bring over the thick fantasy ones." She snickers.

"What the hell is that?"

"One woman with multiple men."

"She's with them all at the *same time*?" My brows pop up.

"Yeah, sometimes. It can be just her with one of the guys or a few at once if more wanna join in. Sometimes, they watch and take turns, but also the guys might get with the other guys too. So basically, it's one girl with multiple boyfriends, who can also be with each other."

I must have a look of horror on my face because she bursts out laughing.

"And none of them get jealous?" I ask.

"Not with the other men in the harem. They're one big happy family!" She beams, and it takes everything in me not to think of the time Knox and I shared Hadleigh. It was definitely a one-time thing that we're all very much over. I will never share a woman again.

"Yeah, that's *definitely* fictional," I muse, removing my ball cap and brushing a hand through my hair.

"I could also read you one that's not focused on romance. Some fantasy books aren't as dirty as others, but it's usually at least a subplot."

"Whatever you want to read, I'll listen to. Who's your favorite author?" I ask, and her loud gasp nearly has me dropping my fork. "*What?*"

"You *can't* ask that!"

I furrow my brow. "Why?"

"That's like askin' a parent to pick their favorite child! Or askin' you to pick your favorite food."

I chuckle, amusement floating through me. "Biscuits and gravy. Cornbread and beef stew. Fried chicken and homemade mac and cheese."

She points a finger at me. "See? You can't choose just one. But if you could only eat one of those for the rest of your life, which would it be?"

"Fuck, you're right. That's too hard."

Her wide smile makes my heart pound. I love being the reason for it.

"Okay, so how about your top three authors?"

"That's still impossible."

"You're being taken to a stranded island for a whole year. But you can only take five books. What are they?" I ask.

Her eyes bug out, and I chuckle at her expression. "Oh my God, I'm sweatin'. I feel like I'm at a job interview."

I bark out a laugh as she fans herself.

"But fine, if you're gonna ask the hard questions, I'll do my best to answer my top three authors."

Though I won't know any of them, I'll do my best to remember them. I want to know everything and anything about her.

"K.F. Breene, Brandon Sanderson, and..." She chews on her

bottom lip as she contemplates her final answer. I study her mouth, wishing I could close the gap between us and feel her lips against mine. But I'll wait until the timing is just right. "Ugh, this is hard." She blows out a breath as if it pains her to choose. "Karen Marie Moning, K.A. Tucker, Kresley Cole and…Scarlett St. Clair," she spouts out so quickly it sounds like a different language.

"That's cheating," I playfully scold.

She throws up her arms with a shrug. "I can't do it. I love them all. That doesn't even include my list of favorite smutty romance authors."

I chuckle. "You'll have to read me one of your favorites someday. I'd probably enjoy it more if I was listening to you."

"As long as you don't roll your eyes at the spicy scenes. Hadleigh always teased me for being a virgin who read too much lady porn and knew more about sex than most adults." She blurts out, then slaps her forehead. "I did *not* mean to say that."

I choke back a laugh to ease her embarrassment. I'm assuming she didn't want me to know that *little detail*.

"Can we pretend I didn't just humiliate myself, please?" She covers her face with both hands, and I reach over, pulling them down.

"I like that you're comfortable enough to say whatever's on your mind," I state honestly.

"Now you have to tell me somethin' embarrassing," she urges. "So I don't feel stupid."

"Umm…" I contemplate what to share. I've made an ass out of myself dozens of times. "Alright…I screamed like a bitch gettin' a piercing."

Her eyes widen as her lips form a perfect O. "Where? Not your ears, nose, or brow." She looks over my body.

"No, it's, uh…*lower*."

"Your nipples? I'd scream too." She giggles.

"Not exactly," I drawl.

She lowers her gaze to my groin. "You pierced your dick?"

"Yep. Went out for my birthday a few months ago, woke up with a double frenum piercing."

Her jaw drops again. "Let me just google that, one sec..." Ivy sets her fork down, then grabs her cell. She types and glances at me over the screen. "Holy shit. You did *this*?"

She shoves the phone in my face, and I see dozens of dick pics. "Two bars under the tip like that? *Why?*"

I shrug. "Knox dared me to get a Jacob's Ladder or Prince Albert. I wasn't about to do that, so I went this route. Apparently, he has the same one."

"Oh God, don't put that image in my head. He's my brother-in-law!"

I let out a hearty laugh. "He promised it was the most sanitary, so I drank a six-pack and went through with his stupid dare. Slept with an ice pack for two nights."

"Don't mind me, just looking up what a Jacob's Ladder is...*holy shit*!" She tilts her eyes as she stares at the screen. "Why would anyone do that?"

"Some really get pleasure out of it." I shrug.

"I can't imagine having sex with someone who has this many piercings. Do ya think it'd hurt going inside?"

I shift on the couch, needing to adjust myself so she doesn't see the chub she's giving me. Hearing her talk about dick piercings and sex so freely gives my cock inappropriate ideas.

Shrugging, I stay silent because I quickly need a subject change. I shove more food into my mouth, hoping we're done chatting about this topic.

"Do you remember when we ran into each other at the hospital?" I mention once we're finished eating.

"Yeah, why?"

I contemplate not asking her, but it's been driving me crazy. "You were about to say something to me when Raelyn interrupted. When I asked you to finish, you blew it off. I've been wondering what you were gonna say ever since."

"Oh...well, I kinda froze when I realized you had a girlfriend. She made me nervous, and I struggled to get the words out, so I took it as a sign to drop it. Saying never mind was just easier."

"Please tell me."

She draws a slow breath before responding. "I was gonna ask if you wanted to hang out or grab a coffee sometime. Since we now shared a nephew, I thought it'd be good to get to know each other better. But when I realized you weren't single, I worried it'd seem like I was askin' you out on a date."

"Is that what you wanted it to be?" I secretly hope her answer is yes.

"Maybe eventually, once we talked and hung out a few times. But I hadn't realized you were seeing someone and didn't want to make it awkward."

"I would've loved to have taken you on a date, Ivy. Obviously, not while I was with someone else, but I'm single now."

Her cheeks heat. "Me too, though, I've been single for like nineteen years."

"I find that really hard to believe."

"I've been on some dates but never with anyone serious or long-term. Boys my age are immature and annoying. So I stopped wasting my time on them and buried my face in fictional *men* instead."

"Probably for the best," I admit. "High school boys are dumb and only think about one thing."

"Is that so? What's that?" she muses.

The corner of my lips tilts up at her mischievous grin. "Getting into your pants and about a dozen other girls' before graduation."

"I bet you and Knox were the same way."

"Oh yeah, Knox was horrible."

"Don't even pretend you were so innocent. I might've been

young and naïve back then, but I remember Hadleigh talkin' about you two all the time. Even up to a few years ago, she'd gush all about the Bishop boys' antics."

"My previous statement still stands. High school boys are dumb as hell."

She chuckles. "I wanted to hang out with you guys so much. When I was like thirteen, Hadleigh came to pack the rest of her stuff after college graduation, and I heard her talkin' on the phone about all the trouble y'all got into after her grad party. I was so jealous and wanted to be a part of your group so bad."

"It's a good thing Hadleigh didn't let ya tag along then. We would've corrupted you big time," I admit.

She scowls. "I could've held my own."

"I'm sure. Then Knox and I would've had two women on our asses."

Laughter spills from her mouth, and I can't stop staring at her perfect lips that tried to kiss me last night.

"Yeah, I fear what would've happened if my sister hadn't been around to straighten y'all out. I've heard y'all been arrested, gotten into fist fights, snuck into abandoned buildings, stole alcohol from the bar...I learned all kinds of things from eavesdropping on Hadleigh's phone calls."

I shake my head with a laugh. Hadleigh put us in our places more times than I can count. "No truer words have ever been spoken. Believe it or not, most of that shit was either Knox's idea or he dared me."

"*Trust me*, I believe it."

"You ready for dessert?" I ask once our dinner is somewhat settled. "I wasn't sure what you liked, so I got some of everything."

"Sure."

I put up our empty plates, then grab the box and clean forks from the kitchen. When I return, I sit even closer than I was before.

"Okay, so the options are..."

"Surprise me!" She closes her eyes.

I stare at her open mouth for a moment as my cock hardens.

Before it grows awkward, I take a scoopful and slide it between her lips.

"Mmm...cherry pie."

She bites on her lip, and I swallow hard.

"Yep," I finally respond. "Want another?"

"Yes, please!"

I try to surprise her and scoop something completely different in texture into her mouth.

"Hmm...something with pudding."

"Mm-hmm. Want one more bite?" I ask.

"Yeah, I think so, just to be sure."

I give her a mouthful this time.

"Jesus," she says. "I wasn't ready for all that."

I chuckle. "Do you know what it is?"

"It's gotta be Tiramisu."

"You're right. The best I've ever had too."

After opening her eyes, Ivy wipes some powdered cocoa and pudding off her cheek.

"So delicious," she says after popping her finger into her mouth.

Fuck. I'm going to hell for the thoughts invading my mind.

"Here, you missed some." I brush along her bottom lip, contemplating if I should give her a taste or steal it.

She doesn't give me time to decide because her hot tongue licks the tip of my finger. My eyes don't leave hers as she smiles. "God, that's *so* good."

I swallow hard, trying to keep every ounce of willpower I have left.

Ivy takes the fork from me and turns the box toward her. "Okay, my turn to feed you. Eyes closed, no peeking," she sing-songs.

I do as she says, nervously waiting.

"Okay, open up," she demands. As soon as the flavors hit my palate, I immediately taste cream cheese frosting.

"Carrot cake," I answer.

"Is it good?" she asks.

I open my eyes with a nod. "The absolute best."

"Hmm, I've never had it." She cuts a forkful for herself, but I quickly take it before she can eat it.

"Let me do the honors," I offer. "You need an equal amount of frosting and cake to get the full effect."

She smirks. "Okay, I'm trustin' you."

Ivy opens wide, and I slide the perfect amount into her mouth. She bites down and moans. *Fucking moans.*

"You were right," she finally admits, capturing the leftover cream from her lips. "That's delicious."

Our eyes lock, and only our ragged breathing can be heard. Ivy's too goddamn tempting, and I shouldn't be this close to her.

"Ivy, I—" I begin, then stop, unsure of where I was even going with that.

"I'm not makin' a fool outta myself for a second time, so if you wanna kiss me, you're gonna have to make the first move," she confidently states.

For being a quiet bookworm, she sure can be blunt too.

"I want to. I'm just decidin' if it's a good idea or not," I say honestly.

"Why? Because I'm Hadleigh's sister?"

"That, and I'm much older than you."

"Only ten years, Kane. Not like you're about to sign up for AARP anytime soon."

I crack a smile, shaking my head at her sassy tone. "Well, I *will* be thirty next year."

"And then I'll be twenty. And then twenty-one the year after that and twenty-two the—"

I cup her face and crash my mouth to hers. She goes stiff for the briefest second before her body melts into my chest and her lips move with mine. Her tongue dips inside, and the taste of her has me groaning.

My hands move to her waist as she straddles my legs. Then she wraps her hands around my neck and presses down on my erection.

"Ivy..." I breathe out her name, lowering my mouth down her jaw and neck. "You're drivin' me crazy with those little whimpers."

"I can't help it. I've dreamed about kissing you since I was twelve years old."

"What?" I push back, meeting her eyes.

"I've had a crush on you for like, *years*. I figured it'd go away because it was just a typical teenage fascination, but as I got older, it never faded. But even then, I knew you liked my sister, so I figured it'd only ever be one-sided."

Damn. Literally *everyone* knew but Hadleigh, apparently.

"I thought I did, but in reality, we were always better off as just friends." Too bad I didn't figure that out sooner.

"So the fact that you crushed on my sister while I crushed on you doesn't bother you? I kinda imagined you'd only ever see me as a little kid."

"I did up until a year ago, at your graduation party," I admit. Hadleigh invited me, and I realized then that Ivy wasn't a nerdy preteen anymore. She was a beautiful woman. It was hard to tear my eyes away from her, but I did so Hadleigh wouldn't catch me gawking. I had never seen Ivy as anything more than her little sister, so this revelation shocked me. At the hospital, I wondered if she felt the same undeniable connection I had.

She widens her thighs, grinding harder against me. "Glad to hear that because it'd be devastating to my self-esteem if I'd just humiliated myself a third time."

I brush strands of hair off her face and tuck them behind her ear. "Why do I get the feeling you're lookin' for trouble?"

She laughs, lightly scratching the pad of her fingers along my scruffy jawline. "The only trouble I'm lookin' to get into is the *fun* kind. You in?" With a popped brow, she challenges me. To what, I'm not exactly sure, but I'm willing to agree to almost anything if it keeps that adorable smile on her face.

"As long as it's with you, then you gotta deal."

I pull her in for another kiss and cross my fingers I'm not about to get burned by love again.

CHAPTER ELEVEN

IVY

ONE WEEK LATER

I ROLL over in my bed and face the harsh reality that the other side is empty. Last night, Kane snuck into my room like I'm not an adult who can have boys over. Mom would love the fact I'm dating and not spending an entire summer working. I didn't get the chance to discuss it with her because Kane texted me at nine o'clock last night telling me he was outside. Mom was already asleep, so we tiptoed through the house, then locked ourselves in my room. We spent hours making out and talking, but sadly, he had to leave early for work this morning.

Kane kissed me goodbye and promised to see me later. Though I was half asleep, I begged him to stay. He chuckled and said he couldn't because Knox would tear him a new one for being late. I missed him as soon as his warmth was gone.

I feel bad that he got three hours of sleep, but spending time with him is all I want to do. Every second of the day, I crave him, and I'm already itching to see him again. It's been a week since he first kissed me, but it feels like a lifetime ago. This past week, I've spent a couple of hours with him every night before he had to go to bed. I even started reading one of my favorite books to him while he engraved the leather journal he was working on. I appreciate his comments about the storyline and how he chuckles at the heroine's humor. While I've re-read this series several times, it still makes me laugh.

I explained how it's a *Beauty and the Beast* fantasy retelling but rated R. There's no sex in the first book—though there's tons of tension and *other* stuff—but book two brings the heat. He's in for a real spicy treat once we get there.

Though I'm self-conscious about my stuttering and stammering over certain letters, he never makes it known he notices. It's not as obvious when we're just freely talking, but sometimes, my brain goes faster than my mouth, and it takes a few seconds before anything comes out. I appreciate how he doesn't make me feel insecure. He's filled in the words for me a few times, which I appreciate because I get so flustered when I get stuck.

Regardless of his confusion over the story, he follows along and engages. Though we spend every spare minute together, I still can't get enough. And I hope I never do.

When I check my phone, it says 8:15, which means I need to get my ass up and ready for work. I don't have a set schedule, but I try to arrive before nine. Harper's up early with the kids and needs time to feed and change them before we buckle down for the day.

I miraculously manage to get to the warehouse two minutes before nine. Harper isn't here yet, so I unlock the doors and flick on the lights. On one of the workstations is a single stem rose with a handwritten note attached.

I saw this rose, and it reminded me of you—beautiful, vibrant, and delicate.
I hope you have a great day. Can't wait to see you later.

-K

PS—I'm not a shape-shifting dragon beast with a scaly tail or anything, but I hope you accept this rose anyway ;)

My heart flutters out of control as a stupid grin covers my face. His reference to my favorite book that we've been reading has me melting into a puddle.

Quickly, I take it to my car so no one questions anything. Then I pull out my phone to send him a message.

> **Ivy: You're the sweetest man on the planet, you know that?**

> **Kane: I've been told that a time or two. My grandma and mom are both very fond of me.**

I snort-laugh.

> **Ivy: Seriously, thank you. And the note. It was a beautiful surprise.**

> **Kane: Just like you ;)**

> **Ivy: It drives me crazy that I can't see you for eight more hours.**

> **Kane: I could meet you at my house around 1...I'll take my lunch break then.**

> **Ivy: I'll be there, Cowboy. I need to thank you properly.**

Kane: And now I'm gonna be hard just thinking about that all morning.

I giggle, my face flushing hot just imagining his cock. We haven't moved past making out, but I'm ready to move forward with Kane. As crazy and spontaneous as it sounds, I want to give him all of me.

Ivy: See ya soon :)

I walk back inside and start setting up our stations. Harper shows up ten minutes later with a big smile on her face. While we're busy packaging orders, she tells me about one of our rival goat soap companies who tried to take her down a couple of years ago. Apparently, karma got the last laugh because they just announced a going out of business sale. The owner supposedly joined a multi-level marketing company and is now using scammy tactics to recruit her previous clients.

"Do you think their customers will start buying from us?" I ask excitedly, though we stay plenty busy as it is.

"I think most of them already have. They quickly realized she was just copying my every move, and they actually liked the original recipes better," she says, trying to hold back a smile, but I giggle anyway.

"No one wants a knockoff. We work too hard. This usually happens when people aren't creative and can't come up with their own ideas."

All she does is nod. Her trying to be modest is the cutest thing ever.

At 12:50, I ask Harper if I can take my lunch break. She never tells me no, but I didn't anticipate her asking me to drop something off at the B&B first.

"Yeah, sure. No problem." I take the envelope. "Just hand it to John?"

"Yes, please." Then she lowers her voice as if someone can hear her. "Ethan asked me to do it yesterday, and I completely forgot. When he asked me about it this morning, I just nodded."

I smirk in amusement. "Don't worry, boss. I gotchu."

She tells me she's going to run home and feed the kids. Hayden's been playing all morning while Hailey-Mae crawled around in their circular baby gate. It has mats on the ground covered in toys, but Harper likes them to eat at home because it's easier.

Grabbing my phone, I head to my car and set down the envelope. Then I see a message from Kane.

Kane: I'm home. Come right in when you get here.

Unable to contain my excitement, I grin wide.

Ivy: On my way!

I try not to drive too fast since the gravel kicks up, but I'm excited to see him. I'm a woman on a mission, and nothing will slow me down.

As soon as I pull up to his house, I park on the side behind the tree. The east end of the ranch gets hardly any traffic, so I've been able to successfully hide my car.

As soon as I open the door, Kane swoops me in his arms and shoves me against the wood. His lips are on mine like rapid wildfire as I cling to him.

"God, I've *missed* you," he murmurs as his hands slide down my body and grip my ass.

"You just saw me," I retort with a smile.

"That already feels like forever ago," he admits, pushing his erection into my lower stomach.

I release a moan as his mouth lowers down my jaw and neck. My palm grazes his cock from outside his jeans, and he growls.

"I wanna taste you," I tell him bravely. I've never given head before, but I have read about it enough times to know the basics.

"Ivy..." He captures my chin between his finger and thumb, rubbing the pad softly against my skin. "You don't have—"

"Will you teach me?" I look up at him, hoping he won't deny us what we both want. "Show me what you like."

"You don't have to do that to keep me interested," he tells me.

"I want to touch you because *I* like it. Or at least, I think I will." I flash him a shy smile.

"Fuck." He pulls off his ball cap and scrubs a hand through his hair. "Does that make me the corrupter or the *corruptee*?"

I snort at his choice of words, then push off the wall and lead him to the couch. "Maybe a little bit of both."

Once he sits, I kneel between his legs and take in how sexy he looks. Wild hair, T-shirt tight against his abs and biceps, his dick begging to come out and play.

I'm really about to do this.

My body is hot all over, and I haven't even touched him yet.

Kane leans in and cups my face, pressing his lips to mine. "Take my cock out, sweet girl. I want your mouth on me."

Hell yes.

As soon as he leans back, I unbutton his jeans and lower the zipper. He lifts his hips slightly to help me pull them down, along with his boxers. The veins in his shaft look like they're about to burst as his erection springs free.

Oh my God...and the piercings.

"Will it hurt if I touch them?" I ask.

"Not at all." His voice is hoarse as if he can barely breathe.

Wrapping my fingers around the base, I stroke a few times and groan at how silky smooth it feels. Then I stick out my tongue and lick from his balls up to the bars of his double piercing.

"It's sensitive," he warns, gritting his teeth like he's barely holding himself together. "Especially when you do...*that*."

I smirk up at him as I lick him again. Seeing his body's response to my touch gives me a high I've never felt before. Kane's expression is a mix of pleasure and pain.

He rests his hand on my cheek, rubbing soft circles with the pad of his thumb. "You want me to come in this pretty mouth of yours?"

"Yes," I answer without a second thought.

"Put me inside. Your hot tongue and saliva will tear me apart," he admits.

I open wider, gripping his shaft and slowly covering the tip with my lips. Sliding down deeper, I stroke the base as I fit as much of him as I can.

"Shit, Ivy," he hisses, bucking his hips. "Suck me. Hollow your cheeks and bob up and down on my cock, baby."

His words have me squeezing my knees together as I feel how wet he's making me. God, Kane's dirty talk is like something I've only read in books.

I work him hard and fast, licking his crown and piercings. Each time my tongue slides under his tip, he twitches and groans with satisfaction. He said it was sensitive, but I think it's the woman's equivalent to a clit because his breathing grows shallow the longer I suck.

"You're doin' so good. Just like that...I'm gonna come soon."

I release him with a loud pop and gaze up at him. "Do you want to fuck my mouth?"

He blinks down at me, swallowing hard. "What?"

Holding back my embarrassment, I shrug. "I hear guys like that. You control my head while you thrust into me."

His dick twitches at my words, and I smirk in response.

"Ivy, I don't wanna hurt you." His voice is sincere and patient, but that's not what I want or need right now.

"I'm not as *delicate* as you think," I taunt, throwing his words from his note back at him.

He grins. "That wasn't meant to be an insult."

"I know." I smile in return. "But I want to experience everything with you. All my firsts. I trust you and know you won't hurt me."

Kane cups my face and captures my mouth. He pours heat and desperation into me as our tongues tangle together.

"Relax your jaw. Don't tighten, or you'll gag, and breathe out of your nose. If you need me to stop, tap my thigh twice."

"Got it."

"No, say the words so I know you understand."

"Relax jaw, tap twice if I'm gonna suffocate on your cock."

"So goddamn sassy," he murmurs with a smirk.

I rise higher onto my knees as he grips my hair at the back of my head, fisting it tight. When I open my mouth wide, he stalls briefly.

"Spit on it," he orders. "Then make it nice and wet with your tongue."

Hearing his breath hitch has me so hot and bothered, I'd do anything he wants.

He tightens his hand in my hair, guiding me down on him. I

grip his thighs as he shoves himself to the back of my throat. My eyes water as I choke and fight for air.

"Breathe through your nose, baby," he reminds me.

As soon as I do, my body relaxes, and I loosen my jaw. With each thrust, my head bobs, and I slide my tongue down his shaft.

"Fuck, you feel amazin'. You're gonna make me explode so hard."

I love knowing I'm the reason for his pleasure. It's so satisfying to hear his moans and feel his cock tighten between my lips. He continues to fuck my mouth as my pussy throbs with need. With one final motion, he releases with a loud groan. Hot liquid coats my tongue as I lick up every drop.

"Don't swallow," he demands as he tilts my head back. "Open up."

His wild eyes focus on me as I stick out my tongue.

"I love seeing my come in your mouth," he rasps, then leans in and tangles his tongue with mine. "See what you do to me? Drive me fuckin' crazy. I wish I could return the favor, fuck..."

He rests his forehead on mine as I swallow the rest of him down. "But I have to get back before the next mare arrives. Mrs. Townsend is coming at one thirty, and Knox and Payton left for the B&B after me, which means they're gonna be expectin' me there."

"It's okay," I reassure him. That wasn't my intention anyway. I wanted to do this for him *and* me.

He devours my lips again. "We taste so good together, don't we? Your sweet mouth is all I'm gonna be thinkin' about for the rest of the day."

I return to work just as Harper arrives. My stomach growls, but I try to ignore it and hope she doesn't hear it.

"You've been awfully smiley lately," she says as we get in the groove of packaging.

"Have I?" I play dumb and shrug.

"Yes, happier than usual, actually. Almost as if you're *datin'* someone."

I look over, and she's grinning wide.

"I'd say you're the one who looks extra smiley," I mock.

She playfully smacks my arm. "Oh, c'mon! I know you're seeing someone. You check your text messages more often, you're giddy, and I'm pretty sure I saw a hickey on your neck last week."

My eyes widen as I instinctively cover my neck with my hand.

She laughs as she points at me. "*I knew it*! So spill the beans, woman."

There's no getting out of this with Harper. She's persistent, and if I don't give her *something*, she'll keep on me until I do.

"Fine...I am kinda *sorta* seeing someone."

"And who is this kinda sorta someone? I want *alllll* the tea!"

"A guy I met at school last semester." I blurt out the first thought that comes to me. It's the most believable since no one around here knows who my classmates are.

"And does this guy have a name? What's his major? What class did you meet him in? Oh my God, he's not a professor, is he?"

I burst out laughing because my sister has warned me against that very thing.

"God, no!" I rush out but leave out that I prefer older men. "Winston is a business major like me. We met in one of our management classes, and one day, he asked for my number. We talked casually for a while, then he finally asked me out. I'd been too busy with work and finals, so I told him we could plan something this summer. And we finally did a couple of weeks ago."

I'm impressed by how quickly the lies fall from my mouth. I also hate that I'm lying to my boss and friend, but it has to be this way. Until we're ready to label what we are publicly, I can't act suspicious *and* pretend I'm not dating anyone.

"Winston, huh?" She pauses. "Sounds like a name for a Golden Retriever."

I try to hold back my laughter because it's what I call my vibrator. "Well, he is sweet and cuddly. Not to mention, he gives great orgasms."

She giggles. "I'm really excited for you, Ivy. Happiness is your style."

I chuckle. "Thanks."

Moments later, she stops what she's doing and glances over at me. "I knew somethin' was up. You wore the same clothes two days in a row."

I snort because I assumed she didn't notice. "I slept over at his house and didn't wanna be late for work."

"Get it, girl. Next time, just text me, then go home and change. Don't worry about it, especially if you're getting laid," she says so casually. Then just like that, Harper changes the subject, and we get back to it.

After an hour of packaging, we take a break to check the soaps curing on a shelf in the back. Tomorrow, we're launching a new scent—Watermelon Breeze. It's a red bar with cute little black seeds sprinkled on the top with a green bottom.

"My mom was telling me that she sold all the soaps we brought to the shop last week," Harper explains. Her mom owns a boutique in town, and we make custom soaps just for locals.

"That's amazin'. Oh, I saw the Back to School Fest sign-up sheet was posted online," I say, not wanting to forget.

"Oh yeah, I'll have to sign us up. Good job lookin' out. Thanks for the reminder!"

I'm trying to pay more attention to events and things of that nature for Harper to prove that I'm worthy of being her business partner. A few years ago, she asked Hadleigh, but that was before Hendrix, when she was fully dedicated to her nursing job. I'm still in shock that she offered it to me—after I graduate, of course.

Harper finishes printing the custom labels, and we spend the rest of the afternoon wrapping individual bars.

It's something I'm looking forward to once I graduate.

"I think we're done for the day!" she says once it's three thirty. "Gonna take the kids home, put Hailey-Mae down for her second nap, and catch up on laundry."

"Jesus. I don't know how you do it. You're superwoman."

She sighs with a grin. "I don't always feel that way. Especially during Hayden's witching hours of nonstop screaming and poop-diaper explosions in the middle of the grocery store."

I chuckle. "You make motherhood look easy, though."

She picks up Hailey-Mae and sets her in a stroller. "Meanwhile, you're out gettin' laid, reading about book boyfriends, and getting to pee in silence."

"Sounds like we're both thriving," I taunt as she grabs Hayden next.

As soon as Harper sets Hayden down on the ground, he takes off. "Hey, no runnin'!"

He runs around the warehouse giggling, then looks behind him to make sure she's not chasing him. "Don't make me call your daddy!"

Hayden freezes at her threat, smiling wide, then comes back.

"That's what I thought. Now hold the stroller and stay next to me. Don't need you gettin' run over by a tractor."

Harper shoves the diaper bag underneath. "I'm going to enjoy that extra glass of wine tonight."

"You deserve it, Mama."

I lean down and hold my hand up for a high five from Hayden. "Be good for your mommy, okay? I'll see you tomorrow. We can play tag during my break."

"Yay!" he squeals. Though the kids are there for most of the day, they stay busy in their play area. There's a kitchen set, tons of dolls and character figurines, dress-up clothes, and more. Oftentimes, I'll play with them during my lunch.

"See ya tomorrow!" I call out as I walk to my car, checking my phone.

I light up as soon as I see Kane's name on my screen.

Kane: My cock is still hard thinking about the way you sucked me off. Fuck, it's throbbing.

Ivy: I can still taste your come in my mouth.

Kane: Goddamn, don't tell me that. Now I need to go jerk off in the shower.

Ivy: I just got off work. Maybe I can help you out with that?

Kane: I really fucking wish you could. I'm stuck here waiting for another mare. The guy is an hour late, but Knox won't let us leave until she's boarded.

Ivy: Hmm...too bad. I guess I'll have to whip out Winston tonight.

Kane: As long as you think about me when you're getting yourself off.

Ivy: Don't worry, I always do.

Kane: Send me a picture after. I wanna see.

Ivy: See what exactly?

Kane: Your juices on the vibrator. Tease me with your come that I'm dying to taste.

God, this man is going to make me explode right here in my car.

Ivy: I'll even send you a pic of my soaking wet panties when I get home.

Kane: Jesus Christ.

I giggle, knowing how turned on he must be.

Ivy: Talk soon, Cowboy ;)

CHAPTER TWELVE

KANE

We've been busting our asses all day in this July heat, and the end of the workday is the first phone break I've had since breakfast.

I type a text response to Ivy. I'm still thinking about that wet panties picture she texted me three days ago.

"What's up with you?" Knox nudges me.

"Whaddya mean?" I ask, then look up at him. He's giving me one of his goofy shit-eating grins.

"Well, who is she?" He leans over, trying to read my screen, but I quickly lock it before he can. "I expected you to be all mopey and depressed after you and Raelyn broke up, but since you aren't, I know you're seein' someone new. So what's her name?"

"None of your damn business."

"Called it!" he shouts, pointing at Payton. "You owe me fifty bucks."

"What're you bettin' on?"

"That you were gettin' laid. You've been way too fuckin' chipper for my liking, so I just knew somethin' was up with ya."

His smug expression makes me want to punch his pretty-boy

face, but I refrain. I don't need our father or grandma getting pissed at me for throwing my fist in his face again.

"Proof or I ain't payin' shit." Payton huffs, crossing his arms over his bulky chest.

"I didn't admit to nothin'," I explain.

"Gimme your phone, and I'll have all the proof I need," Knox taunts with his palm out.

"You really wanna see me sexting with your *wife*?"

As soon as the words come out, Knox charges me. I'm quick on my feet, though, and outrun him. I purposely riled him up so he'd stop asking questions about my goddamn personal life.

"Not fuckin' funny," he mutters, giving up and shaking his head.

Payton's doubled over, laughing. "Dude, I'd pay a hundred just to see that expression on Knox's face again."

"The only reason I'm not beating your ass right now is because we have family dinner tonight," Knox hisses. Mom invited everyone over, and she wouldn't be happy if we were fighting.

"Oh calm down. I stopped jerkin' off to your wife two years ago."

Technically, Hadleigh was *my* best friend before Knox came in, and they fell in love. I'd wanted her for years, but we realized we were better as friends. That doesn't mean I don't enjoy giving my brother shit about it every chance I get. Especially since I know he's overprotective and acts like a caveman anytime I mention Hadleigh.

"You're a sick fuck," Payton says with a laugh.

I shrug because the plan to get Knox off my ass worked. He doesn't need to know his sister-in-law sends me pics of her soaked panties, and I got off to them. Honestly, Ivy's sexting game is on fire and gives me something to look forward to every day. That alone would've sealed the deal if I wasn't already crazy about her.

We've met at my house every day since we started fooling around. Spending all of my free time with her has been the highlight of my summer.

"See ya later," I call out to Knox as I walk to my truck. He responds with his middle finger, and I chuckle as I start the engine.

Mom and Dad expect us in an hour, which means I need to shower and quickly get ready. She only gave us a two-day notice that all three of her children were to show up, no excuses. Now that Knox's married with a baby and Kaitlyn's swamped with horse training, it's hard for the three of us to get together.

Ivy: Hadleigh invited me to come to the family dinner tonight. You gonna be able to keep your hands off me?

I read her message as soon as I'm out of the shower and smile.

Kane: Fuck, that's gonna be hard.

Ivy: I bet it is...

Kane: Behave. Unless you want everyone to see what you do to me.

Ivy: I wouldn't mind you showing me later.

Kane: Be a good girl, and I will when you come over tonight.

Ivy: Hmm...very tempting.

Kane: See you soon, trouble.

Once I'm dressed, I head to my truck. I can barely contain my excitement as I drive to my parents'. I know I need to keep my cool but seeing Ivy always makes me stupidly happy.

Mom hugs me as soon as I enter the kitchen.

"Smells great," I tell her, inhaling the hearty aromas.

"Can you help your sister set the table, please?" She points at the fancy china on the counter. "Remember, forks are on the right."

I chuckle. "I know, Ma. You taught me that when I was five."

"Just remindin' ya." She smirks, then takes the pot holders and grabs something out of the oven.

"No date tonight?" I tease Kaitlyn.

"You're one to talk," she throws back, setting the cups above the plates. "Before Raelyn, you spent Friday nights with Payton on stable duty."

"*You* spent Friday nights with Payton on stable duty," I mimic.

She rolls her eyes. "Dating is pointless."

"And why's that?" I ask.

"Because men ain't shit," she replies just as Mom walks in.

"Language," Mom scolds. "And don't say that. There are plenty of nice gentlemen out there for you to settle down with and make me grandchildren."

"Yeah, plenty of *gentlemen* to fill your womb," I mock in a feminine voice.

"*Kane Jackson!*" Mom hisses just as Dad struts in and smacks me upside the head.

"That's not appropriate dinner talk," he says as Kaitlyn laughs.

"Technically, we're not eatin' yet," I argue.

Moments later, Knox and Hadleigh enter with Ivy. I fight the urge to glance at her, but then she stands across the table from me, and I know it's going to be impossible to keep my eyes off her.

"Hi, Kane," she greets me in a sweet drawl.

"Hey, how's it goin'?" I ask in my best friendly voice. We take our seats and wait for the food to be put on the table.

"Pretty good. How 'bout you?"

"No complaints," I say, hoping no one else can feel the electricity streaming between us. We're both trying hard as fuck not to be obvious, but I'm worried we will be.

My eyes linger down her chest as her breasts swell against the fabric of her shirt. Her breathing increases, and I know she's caught me gawking. After she licks her lips, Ivy pulls them into a sultry smile.

Once we're all seated, and Mom says grace, we dig in. Dad and Knox make small talk while Kaitlyn and Hadleigh gossip about only God knows what. That leaves Ivy and my mother to chat.

"Are you lookin' forward to school starting up again next month?" Mom asks her.

Ivy is indifferent as if she's not really certain. "Kinda. I like being able to work every day, though, and being on the ranch. My school schedule keeps me busy usually."

That was the reason I hardly saw her last year. She helped Harper on the weekends, and those were usually my half days, so we barely crossed paths.

Hadleigh immediately chimes in like a gossip queen. "Speaking of school, a little birdie told me you're seeing some guy you met in class?" Hadleigh's question has my eyes bugging wide.

What the fuck is she talking about?

I don't want to look too enraged, so instead, I pretend I'm disinterested and pick at my food.

"Yeah, kinda," Ivy responds quietly.

My heart pounds as I eavesdrop on their conversation. We haven't had the *exclusive* talk yet, but I was under the assumption we were. Outside of work and spending time with me, there's no way she has time to see someone else. *Or does she?*

"Ivy! I can't believe you didn't tell me. You never dated in high school or talked about boys, so I was shocked when I heard. I'm just happy for you!"

Knox snort-laughs at Hadleigh's rambling, but I'm still stuck on the fact that she could possibly be seeing someone else.

"So what's his name?" my mom asks. "You should've invited him to join us tonight."

I don't want to hear this. No, wait. I definitely do. That way, I can confirm it's him before I knock him out.

Ivy clears her throat as I grab my beer, feigning boredom. "*Winston.*"

I choke on the sip I took, and Dad smacks my back with a laugh.

"You okay?"

"Uh-huh." I nod. "Just went down the wrong way."

I avoid eye contact with Ivy but can't help the smug smile on my face knowing she gave them the name of her vibrator.

"So when can we meet him?" Hadleigh asks.

"Umm...I don't know. It's kinda new. We're just seeing how things go right now. Don't want to rush or scare him off with my big sister's ruthless interrogations."

I finally sneak a peek as Ivy flashes a grin in my direction.

"It's my job to make sure he's good enough for you. Has good values and morals and won't corrupt ya."

"Oh, so like Knox?" Ivy counters, and everyone at the table roars with laughter except Knox and Hadleigh.

"Considering it brought me a grandchild, I don't really care to hear the specifics," Mom says, standing to take Hendrix from Hadleigh's arms so she can finish eating.

The rest of the dinner conversation focuses on the stud operation and Kaitlyn's horses. One of the Appaloosas she trained won a state competition last week, and now she's getting flooded with bookings. Though, she can barely keep up as it is.

"Why don't you ask Payton to help you?" I interrupt. "He's used to keeping up with the stables and boarding horses."

"Hey, no pawning off my guy," Knox interrupts. "Payton's mine. She can find someone else. In fact, why don't *you* go be her bitch?"

Kaitlyn rolls her eyes as I kick Knox's boots underneath the table.

"Payton would come help me in a heartbeat if I asked him, so don't *tempt* me," Kaitlyn threatens.

"You better not. I have him trained just the way I like." Knox gloats.

I snort. "Y'all talkin' about him like he's a dog."

"He might as well be with the way he follows Kaitlyn around." Knox chuckles, earning a fresh-baked roll to the face.

"Hey, no throwing food at the table," Dad scolds Kaitlyn.

"Yeah, only outside," I tease.

"Y'all are teaching Hendrix bad manners," Mom says, rocking him back and forth. "Don't you worry. I vowed not to let you turn out like my boys did."

"Hey!" Knox and I groan at the same time.

"You will be a pure angel child. No being a terror and definitely no pranking your mama at the grocery store," Mom explains.

Hadleigh chuckles. "If I hadn't known the twins my whole life, you'd be scaring me right now. But they've prepared me for the worst."

After dinner, Mama serves warm apple pie with vanilla ice cream. I try my hardest not to stare at Ivy, but it's nearly impossible with how gorgeous she is. Her dark-reddish hair is pulled back into a messy bun. Curly strands frame her face, and every time she smiles, her cute dimples appear.

Fuck, I get a chubby just thinking about her luscious lips being around my cock again.

Once we're in the living room, we take turns holding

Hendrix. Poor guy is the only baby in our family and has probably never been set down in his entire two-month life. I watch as Ivy holds him, smiling down and squeezing his little chubby cheeks. Our eyes catch, and I flash her a quick smile.

"Wanna hold him?" she asks from across the room.

"Sure, I'll come sit by you."

"Oh, that's perfect. I need an updated pic of the godparents." Hadleigh stands and pulls out her phone. I'm tempted to put my arm around Ivy when I'm close, but I don't want Hadleigh's fist in my face for being too close.

Ivy hands me the baby, and we smile for our mini photo shoot.

"Oh my God, that's *so* cute," Hadleigh gushes as Mom tells her to text her a copy.

"I will. I'll send it to you two as well," she tells us.

"Surprised you haven't announced baby number two yet," Ivy teases.

"Don't worry, we're tryin'." Hadleigh flashes her a wink.

"*Every night*," Knox adds.

"Alright, that's my cue to go if y'all are gonna start talkin' about baby-makin'." I hand Hendrix to Knox, who's wearing a shit-eating grin.

"It's not my fault I can't keep her off me."

I roll my eyes as Hadleigh smacks his shoulder.

"You're on hump duty tomorrow," Knox directs as I give Mom a hug.

Lovely.

"Excuse me?" Mom pulls back to scowl at Knox.

"Hump duty," he repeats. "Someone has to make sure the horses are mating."

"You actually just sit and watch until they do?" Mom asks.

"Only because he makes me," I clarify. "A few mares are leaving in a couple of days, so he wants to be certain they took."

"You're basically a voyeur," Hadleigh teases.

"Have another ranch hand do it," I tell Knox, ignoring the way Hadleigh and Ivy are giggling.

"Yeah, I don't trust those lazy pieces of sh—" He stops himself before Mom gives him hell. "It's all yours, bro. Don't be late."

"Yeah, yeah."

CHAPTER THIRTEEN

IVY

I steal glances at Kane as he says goodbye to everyone. Holding back a smirk, knowing I'll be going to his house later, I say, "Nice seein' ya again."

"You too. Have a good one," he tells me casually.

Tonight was a lot of fun, minus Hadleigh bringing up my *boyfriend*. I should've known Harper would tell my sister, but now I feel worse for lying.

I chat for another ten minutes before my phone vibrates. Cautiously, I look at the screen and hold back a smile.

Kane: Are you still planning to come over tonight, or do you have plans with Winston?

I choke on a laugh, trying my best to act indifferent, but Hadleigh notices. She arches a brow as if she wants to ask questions.

Ivy: Those are my usual Friday night plans, but I'd be willing to change them for you.

Kane: If you're looking to mix things up, I think I can provide much better entertainment. But then again, I'd hate to throw off your routine...

Ivy: I guess it depends if it'll be worth my time based on what you're offering.

Kane: I mean...I've had no complaints, but I could provide you with a free preview before you commit to having me as your Friday night plans.

My cheeks heat, and I can't help the way my thighs squeeze together. Shit, I need to leave before someone here notices.

Ivy: Ohh, like a sneak peek? Tell me more.

When I look at my screen again, the last thing I expect is a picture.

He's shirtless on his bed with his erection poking hard through gray sweatpants. As his fingers grip it, the veins in his hands pop, and I'm momentarily paralyzed.

Sweet Jesus. Kane Bishop will have me combusting in front of his entire family. I gulp, trying to contain my composure.

Ivy: That was cruel!

He sends back a purple devil emoji.

Kane: Come join me. I'm waiting for you.

Fuck, that does me in.

I stand and announce that I have to go. "Gotta get back to those book boyfriends," I mock, hoping Hadleigh buys it.

She pulls me in for a hug. "Let me know when I can meet Winston, okay? I promise I'll play nice."

I give her a wary look. "I'll think about it."

She lowers her voice. "Please be *careful*." Her silent implications are heard loud and clear.

Use protection.

Don't let him break your heart.

"I am," I confirm. Or at least I hope I am.

Once I've said goodbye to everyone and thanked Mrs. Bishop for dinner, I rush to my car while replying to Kane.

Ivy: On my way, Cowboy.

Kane: Better hurry.

I make it to his house in record time, which is a small miracle. The last time I drove here at night, I nearly hit a chicken. Little fucker had the audacity to cluck at me like I got in *his* way.

As soon as I park in my secret spot, I race up the porch, and before I can knock, the door whips open. Kane yanks me inside, then closes it behind me.

"Jesus," I breathe out as he pulls me against his rock-hard body. He's the epitome of a real-life book boyfriend with muscles for days and tattoos over his chest and arm.

"What took you so long?" he urges, hovering his lips over mine. "I've missed you."

I chuckle. "Your family is chatty."

He smirks. "That they are. I'm glad you escaped, though. I've been thinkin' of all the things I wanted to do to you."

Wrapping my arms around his neck, I bring our mouths closer. "Oh yeah? And what're you gonna do now that I'm here?"

He hoists me up until my legs wrap around his waist. "I'm about to show you."

Then he walks us toward his bedroom and lowers me to the bed.

"Pretty clever telling them you're dating someone named *Winston*. I nearly choked to death." He towers over me with a devilish smirk.

"Blame Harper. She caught me off guard, and I had to lie on the spot. And of course, she told my sister."

"Well, thank God I recognized the name because I was pretty pissed for about three seconds."

I wiggle underneath him, wanting more of him. "Is that right? Were you *jealous*?"

"Fuckin' right I was." He dips his head into the crook of my neck, licking just below my ear. "I would've marked my claim on you in front of everyone if I had to."

"Hmm...I kinda like the sound of that. What would that entail?"

Kane cups my breast as he sucks the flesh above my collarbone. "A little bit of this..."

My entire body shivers as goose bumps cover each area he touches.

"And a little bit of that..." He pulls down my shirt until he exposes my nipple, then blows warm air over it.

My back arches as I release a throaty moan, feeling absolutely unhinged at the way he's teasing me.

"And most importantly...*this*." His mouth widens as he captures my breast, then sucks hard. "I'd mark you everywhere," he tells me, gliding his tongue around my soft flesh.

"That feels incredible," I murmur, pushing against his lips.

"Has anyone ever touched you here before?" He swirls a finger around my pebbled nipple.

"No...only you," I breathe out. "You're the first."

He smiles as he massages the swell of my breast. As he lowers his hand to my stomach, Kane feathers light kisses below the hem of my shirt.

"How about right here?" He rubs over the fabric above my pussy. Just with that little amount of pressure, my body buzzes with desperation. I wish he'd rip off my clothes already.

"No..." I breathe hard, waiting in anticipation for the moment he removes them.

"Fuck, Ivy..." he hisses, kissing above the seam of my shorts. "I shouldn't want to corrupt you as badly as I do."

"Trust me, I want you to," I boldly admit. He's the only one I've ever wanted to touch me.

"Knowing I'll be the first man to give you an orgasm makes me hard as fuck. I'm going to blow your goddamn mind and pleasure you the way you deserve," he says confidently. My heart hammers even harder as his words repeat in my mind.

"Just this is driving me wild. I'm not sure I'll be able to handle anything more," I tell him, though I don't want him to stop.

"Don't worry, I'll break ya in nice and slow," he drawls, and I chuckle at his arrogance. Wish I was half as confident as him.

He kneels between my legs. "Watch me."

I lean up on my elbows as he undoes the button and lowers the zipper. His eyes land on my thin black panties, and nerves hit me as the realization sets in that I'll be exposed. I've only done oral on him, but I'm ready for his mouth and hands to be all over me.

Once my shorts are off, I try to relax as he stares intently at my body.

"You're so beautiful, Ivy." He leans down and presses his lips to mine. I curl my arms around him, not wanting to lose contact.

As his body presses against mine, I'm reminded that Kane can't go anywhere near my pussy.

"*Shit*..." My head falls back on the bed, and I cover my face with my hands to hide my embarrassment.

"What's wrong?" he asks, peeling back a finger, then two. "I won't do anything you—"

"It's not that," I try to explain as my arms fall back. "I forgot I just started my period tonight."

While at the Bishops' dinner, I used the bathroom and had to steal one of Kaitlyn's tampons since mine were in my bag.

"That's what you're worried about?" he asks with amusement, then laughs at my confused expression. "Do you trust me?"

I furrow my brow. "Well yes, but—"

"Then don't worry. I promised you entertainment, and I'm not letting *anything* get in my way."

"What does that even mean?" I ask nervously.

He flashes me a wink, then lowers between my legs again. Covering myself, I feel self-conscious and don't want him to get too close.

"You keep your hands off, or I'll be forced to bind them. Got it?"

"Are you sure you want to be...*down there* right now?"

"I live and work on a ranch. You think I'm scared of a little blood? Plus, there isn't any part of you I don't like or want to touch. And if you think Mother Nature is gonna get in my way of giving you an orgasm, you've underestimated how much I want you."

Before I can utter another word, Kane rubs the pad of his thumb over my panties. Instinctively, my hips arch for more of his touch as he teases my clit. He continues circling and adding pressure, but I can't stop thinking about how close he is to my tampon.

"Kane..." I murmur on a moan.

"Relax, baby. Get out of your head and let me pleasure you. I won't do anything you're not comfortable with."

"Okay..." I tell him, trying to relax. "I'm good."

Moments later, he replaces his hand with his mouth. I feel the movements of his jaw rubbing over my panties as he sucks my clit between his lips.

"*Oh my God,*" I mutter, rocking my hips to his rhythm. I want his warm mouth on my skin. "More," I beg as I feel my arousal building.

As if reading my mind, he lowers them and exposes my clit. His tongue wages war over and over, followed by suction. Heat surfaces as I experience sensations like I've never felt before, and all of my insecurities disappear.

"Fuck, you taste like heaven." He kisses along my pussy. "Put your hands on my head and control the pace."

He lowers his mouth back on me, and I do as he says. As soon as my fingers thread in his hair, he growls against me. Lifting my hips, I hold him against my core as the buildup gets more intense.

I try to catch my breath and focus on climbing to the edge. When I glance down at our position, I realize I'm nearly suffocating him with my thighs and pussy.

"I'm so close…" I pant as my eyes roll back. When I use my vibrator, it takes me a good ten to fifteen minutes to climax. With Kane, he nearly has me exploding within five.

Kane hums as he continues his sweet assault, and soon, I'm soaring above us, floating high as the orgasm takes control. My muscles tense, and my back arches before I return to earth.

As soon as I release my grip from his hair, he lifts and wipes his mouth with his forearm. "That was the hottest thing I've ever experienced."

"You're just sayin' that."

Kane slides my panties into place, then settles down next to me.

"I'll prove it to you." Those words are my only warning before he crashes his lips against mine. Slowly, our tongues intertwine as he takes my hand and lowers it to his erection. "See how you taste? How hard your arousal made me? I'd never lie about that."

"I'm just worried I won't be able to fully satisfy you because I'm inexperienced."

"That's the silliest thing I've ever heard."

I chuckle as his cock twitches against my palm. I'm dying to take him into my mouth again.

"The fact that I'm using every ounce of willpower to stop myself from mauling you should speak volumes. You have nothin' to worry about because every touch sets me on fire."

"That's giving me a lot of credit," I say with a half-laugh. "It amazes me someone hasn't already tied you down."

"Believe it or not, I haven't had the best luck in the dating department," he admits. "Girls think they wanna date a cowboy until they realize we work long hours and are rarely home in time for dinner. Our clothes are always dirty, and when we aren't workin' or eatin', we're probably sleepin'. So I hope you understand what you're gettin' yourself into. Otherwise, you better tell me now if you can't handle that before I get my heart broken."

I smile, leaning up on my elbow to face him. "That may all be true, but you're also the most loyal, kind, and sweetest man I know. You'd be worth waitin' for."

CHAPTER FOURTEEN

KANE

Even on my days off, my internal clock has me up before sunrise. But I stay put for a little longer as Ivy sleeps peacefully next to me. After our talk, she started having period cramps and abdominal pain, so I snuggled her into my arms all night. Once she confessed her concerns, I made it my personal mission to prove how wrong she is. I'm committed to making her comfortable and sexually confident in our relationship.

After an hour of listening to her soft breathing, I slide out of bed and decide to find her some feminine items for when she wakes.

Since I have no clue what she'd need besides some Tylenol, I head over to Knox and Hadleigh's house. With the baby and Knox's work schedule, I know they're awake.

"Did you bring me coffee?" Hadleigh asks as soon as she whips open the door.

"Uh, no?" I glance down at my empty hands.

She cocks her hip and blows out a breath. "Then you better have a good reason for being here at the ass crack of dawn."

I hold back a laugh, lingering on her exposed nursing bra and wondering if she realizes she's topless.

"Sorry, I need a favor." I give her my best puppy dog eyes and hope it's enough for her to let me in.

She sighs and steps aside. "Fine. I was just feedin' Hendrix."

"I figured as much."

As soon as my words are out, she glances down, and her cheeks go red. "Jesus. Thanks for tellin' me I was givin' you a free show." She quickly throws her arms across her chest.

"Don't worry, Hads. Nothin' I haven't seen before." I shoot her a wink, which only pisses her off more. She smacks my arm, then shoves me out of her way so she can shut the door.

"Better watch that mouth." Knox enters the living room, shooting me a scowl.

"Damn, you two are *cheerful* in the morning." I chuckle.

"Well, when you're sleep deprived and become a human milk machine, you'll understand." She checks on Hendrix, who's asleep in his bassinet.

"Then what's Knox's excuse?" I taunt.

"That kid has a set of lungs," he tells me. "If he ain't happy, no one is."

"Sounds just like his daddy," I muse, shoving my hands into my pocket.

"Har har. So what're ya doin' here so early anyway?" he asks, walking toward the kitchen.

"I need to ask Hadleigh for some period supplies. Tampons, meds for cramps, a heating pad, if you have one. Typical stuff like that." I swallow down my nerves because I know what's coming. She'll ask who I have over, then I'm gonna have to deflect or lie.

Ivy and I are going slow. We don't want to rush and tell the whole world just yet, especially because of our age gap.

"Are you finally going through puberty and becoming a woman?" Hadleigh gasps with faux excitement. "I'm so happy for you."

I roll my eyes with a smirk. "Yeah, yeah. I have a guest who needs it, okay?"

"So what's her name?" she sing-songs.

"It's private," I retort in the same high-pitched voice she had.

"I'm your best friend! How can you not tell me?"

Knox returns with a half-eaten muffin in his hand. "I knew you were seein' someone. This is proof. Don't give him anything until he confesses," he instructs Hadleigh.

"Why do you care about my love life so much? Need the details of mine to help spice up things in the bedroom?"

"I'd kill for *anything* at this point."

"Oh shut it," Hadleigh groans. "We have a two-month-old, and I'm still trying to lose the baby weight, so—"

"As much as I'm enjoying this front row seat of you chewin' him a new one, do you think you can help me? I wanted to grab some breakfast and bring it back before she wakes up."

"Well, aren't you a sweetheart?" Hadleigh smiles. "Fine. I'll pack some toiletries with all the necessities. Whoever she is, tell her she needs to make one for herself if she's planning on sleeping over ."

I walk over and wrap my arm around her shoulder, careful not to touch anything below the neck. "Thanks, Hads. You're the best." I kiss the top of her head.

"Yeah, yeah. Next time, though, bring a girl some coffee before you ask for favors this early, okay?"

I grin. "Got it."

Hadleigh strolls down the hallway. Knox's still stuffing his face as he glances down at Hendrix.

"You wouldn't know it by lookin' at him, but I swear this kid eats more than I do. No tellin' where it's going, though."

"His diapers!" Hadleigh calls from the bathroom, and we both laugh.

"Oh yeah." Knox laughs.

"Perhaps you should be changin' them more," I quip.

"I do all night long!" he counters. "I clean his butt and then latch him on her boob."

I snort-laugh. "And y'all want more, huh?"

"Of course. Have you seen my wife when she's pregnant? She's insatiable!"

"Dude." I groan. "You need a filter."

He shrugs, shoving the rest of the muffin down his throat.

Hendrix stirs, and I rub the pad of my finger along his little soft cheek.

"Good mornin'. Your favorite uncle is here."

His eyes open, and he kicks his legs around, clearly giving no fucks who I am. All he knows is I'm not his mom who provides the milk.

"Can I pick him up?" I ask Knox.

"Sure, but then you're in charge of changing him."

I scoff, leaning down to pick him up. "Nice try. We both know that's Daddy's job, don't we?" I tell Hendrix.

He looks up at me as I carefully rock him in my arms. "Thank God you got your mama's looks."

"We have the same face, asshole." Knox grunts, and I laugh.

Finally, Hadleigh returns wearing a shirt and carrying a small duffel.

"Okay, I packed Midol and ibuprofen since I don't know her preference. A variety of regular and super tampons, a heating pad along with some face sheet masks and under-eye patches to help with puffiness. I also figured you don't have any girly soaps, so I added some lavender body wash and bath salts. So in case you didn't get my hints...run her a hot bath. You'll get some bonus points, trust me. Oh! I threw in some travel shampoo and conditioner too in case she doesn't wanna use your three-in-one *Old Spice.*"

I smile, exchanging Hendrix for the bag. She's a natural caregiver, and her intentions are pure. If I asked, Hadleigh would give me the shirt off her back. "You're the best, Hads. Thank you."

"And just an FYI...orgasms help with cramping. So if she needs some relief, help her out with that." She waggles her brows.

I bite my tongue so I don't admit to doing that very thing last night.

"Also, I packed a peppermint essential oil roller. It helps reduce pain and stress. Tell her to rub it on her temples and anything that aches."

"Geez, she's gonna think I'm askin' her to move in or something. I'm gonna scare her off with all this stuff."

She scowls, shaking her head. "Or she'll think she found herself a sweet and thoughtful man."

"Wait. Is that actually true about the orgasms?" Knox interjects.

"Of course it is! When a woman orgasms, blood rushes to her uterus and helps relieve cramping. On top of that, it can reduce stress and release endorphins, which helps us relax and sleep better."

"Well, good to know." Knox smirks.

"I haven't had a period in over a year and probably won't until I'm done breastfeeding, so get that smug look off your face. If you want to help me relax, take your child and change him."

Knox swoops Hendrix in one arm, then snakes his other arm around her waist and pulls her in for a kiss. "I can find many more fun ways to help you relax. All you gotta do is ask."

"And that's my cue to leave. Thank you again, Hads. I really appreciate it."

"You're welcome. I better find out who this new woman in your life is soon, though. As your bestie, I deserve all the details. Plus, I'll need to approve of her first."

I hold back a smirk, the irony nearly making me burst out laughing. "One day." I shoot her a smile, hoping I get to keep that promise.

After I fill a to-go box at the B&B with breakfast foods and pastries, I head home and quietly walk in the door. It's silent when I walk in, so I know she's still sleeping. I find her in my bed and take her in. Ivy's curly hair is sprawled out on the pillow, and her soft lips are begging me to kiss them.

"Stop being a creep," she mutters with closed eyes and a smile on her face.

"Can't help myself." I walk over, then climb under the covers next to her. "I could watch you sleep for hours."

"That's weird, Kane. Even for you."

I snicker, then pull her into my chest and bury my face in her neck, nibbling below her ear. "I got some girly things for you and got us breakfast. Are you hungry?"

Ivy snorts and pushes back as her gaze finds mine. "*Girly* things?"

"Period stuff...I wanted to make sure you had what you needed for the day and were comfortable. That way, you wouldn't have to run home."

"You did? Like what?"

I list everything without mentioning that her sister gave me those things. Her eyes light up as I tell her about the bath items and cinnamon rolls I snagged.

"Wow...that was very sweet of you. I was worried I'd have to leave right away and would lay alone in my bed for the next couple of days."

"Stay here. Let me take care of you." I kiss the tip of her nose, then slide out of bed to grab the bag. "Here are the goods. Now it's time for coffee and food."

She sits up and rummages through it while I go to the kitchen. Once I have everything ready, I bring her breakfast in bed.

"Oh my gosh, this smells so good." She takes a bite of the western omelet covered in hot sauce. "And tastes even better."

"Good, I'm glad I guessed right. I thought I heard you liked spicy foods."

"Yep. I eat spicy noodles and hot Cheetos like it's nothin'. Hadleigh teases me about having no taste buds."

I chuckle as we continue eating.

Once we're finished, I put our dishes in the sink, then return and grab the bag.

"Where're ya goin' with that?"

"Gonna run you a hot bath, so get undressed and meet me in there." I flash her a wink, then grab the fluffy pink robe from my closet that Knox gave me as a gag gift. Joke's on him because it's perfect for Ivy. "Put this on."

As the water runs, I set out the soap, shampoo, and conditioner for her. I light a few candles I found stashed in the linen closet, then I toss in some petals from the rose bush I plucked from the B&B.

"This looks like a spa," Ivy says when she enters and glances around the dimly lit room. "I can't believe you did this for me."

Grabbing her waist, I pull her body into mine, then press my lips to her forehead. "I wanted to help you feel as comfortable as possible."

She narrows her eyes, then pinches my arm.

"Ow, what was that for?" I chuckle.

"Had to double-check that you're real." She grins.

I lower my mouth to hers as I tilt her chin upward. "Get in, sassy girl."

Out of respect, I look away so she can dispose of her tampon.

Once she drops the robe and settles underneath the bubbles, I bring over a washcloth and the body wash.

"Close your eyes," I tell her, then kneel outside the tub. "No peeking."

"Is this one of those *happy ending* spas?" Her taunting voice has me smiling wide while I carefully place the under-eye patches on her face.

"I'm a professional," I say with mock humor. "Eyes and hands above the neck at all times."

"Well, that's boring. What if I offer a big tip?"

I smirk, although she can't see me, but play along as I lay the sheet mask on top and smooth it out with my fingers. "Depends. What are you offering in exchange?"

She reaches for me and grabs my wrist, then lowers my hand to her chest. I hold my breath as I cup her bare breast.

"Ivy..." I swallow down the lump in my throat. I've been trying to go slow and didn't want her to feel pressured to do anything she wasn't ready for, but fuck me. Touching her is testing my willpower.

"I think the other is jealous..."

I chuckle, amused by her eagerness. I flick her nipple, loving how hard it is. Then I massage the other one.

"Your tits are so goddamn sexy," I murmur, nearly growling at how worked up she's making me.

"Sorry they aren't bigger. I'm sure you're used to—"

I slide off her mask and slam my mouth against hers. I want to erase any negative thoughts spiraling through her mind because there isn't anything I don't love about her. Every inch is pure perfection.

"Give me your hand," I order, then take it in mine and press it to my hard cock. "Do you feel what you're doing to me right now? How much I want you?"

She looks up at me through dark lashes, biting down on her plump lower lip.

"There's no one before you, Ivy. I've erased them from my mind because all that matters is how I feel about *you*. I want to experience all your firsts and anything else you'll give me. So don't think for one second that you're not enough or that I won't like your body because trust me, I'm using all my strength to be a gentleman around you."

She pushes into my erection, and I groan. "How gentlemanly are we talkin'?"

"Goddammit." I laugh. "Let me take care of you now. *No touching.*"

She playfully pouts when I remove her hand. The bubbles float up to her neck, and she closes her eyes as I clean her. I glide the washcloth over every inch of her, sliding down between her legs and being extra gentle. Then I prop each foot on the edge of the tub and massage each toe.

"You're gonna make me fall asleep," she hums.

I grin, kneading my thumbs into her calves and up her legs. "I'd carry you back to bed, don't worry."

"I'm convinced you were written by a woman."

"Well, my mama did raise a Southern *gentleman*." I smirk, then add, "And one devious hellion."

"Pretty sure my sister would agree."

"Want me to shampoo and condition your hair in the shower?"

"Sure."

"Speaking of books, are you gonna read me more of the smutty dragon beast one?" I ask, draining the tub.

"Sure, I brought it with me."

"Good. I love listening to you." I smile, helping her to her feet.

"Thank you. I know I sometimes sound like a nervous teenager who can't get their words out when they finally meet their favorite boy band. It's embarrassing, but I still like reading to you."

I don't mind her stammering at all. It's a part of who she is, and I love that she feels comfortable enough to expose herself to me in such a vulnerable way.

"If it makes you feel any better, I've had my fair share of embarrassing things happen."

"Oh, do tell." She chuckles as I rinse out the suds at the bottom.

"When I was thirteen, I had a crush on one of my teachers and had a sex dream about it. The next day in class, she called on me to come write on the board, and I couldn't stop thinking about the dream during class, which means..."

"You walked up there with an erection?" She bursts out laughing.

"Sadly, yes. I walked up covering my junk, and of course my asshole brother noticed, so he was loud as fuck and pointed it out. Could never look Miss Haise in the eye again."

"You remembered her name."

"I was traumatized. *For life*. Now, I can't think about geography without getting a boner."

"Wow...I've never been more attracted to you," she deadpans.

I turn on the shower and playfully splash her face. "Get under the water, smart-ass."

She steps underneath it, then looks back and catches me staring at her ass.

"You washin' my hair from there, or are ya gonna come in and join me?"

I hadn't really thought this through, but I guess it makes the most sense to be in there *with* her.

"Alright, if you think you can keep your hands off. I'd hate to have to file a harassment claim with HR."

"I think we passed that point when I caught you drooling at my backside."

I chuckle, then remove my clothes. "Your tits too."

When I step in behind her, I wet my hands, then squeeze some shampoo into my palms. Luckily, I'm a foot taller, so I can easily massage it into her scalp. Once I'm done, I spin her around so I can rinse it out.

"Oh my God, that feels amazing." She releases a moan and leans her head back.

"Better stop making those little whimpers," I murmur while I tenderly caress her head.

"Should I start naming off the state capitals? I can do them alphabetically." She snickers, then adds, "Or is it only *world geography* that gets you aroused?"

I snake my arm around her waist, pulling her flush against my front so the water doesn't splash on her face. My palm rests on her lower back as my mouth goes to her ear. "Very funny, but if you must know, it's *human geography* that entices me the most."

"Mmm. Show me."

I turn her back around so I can continue with the conditioner. "Ivy...I wanted to take care of you and help you relax. Let me finish." Gripping her hips, I hold her in place.

"Or you could slide your hand a little lower, and we could both *finish*."

Swallowing hard, I shake my head, trying to fight the urge to do just that. I want to take care of her without her thinking she needs to reciprocate. Although I'm learning Ivy has something I hadn't expected—*a mischievous side*.

It's been tempting me since this secret relationship started.

"Kane. I'm not opposed to beggin'."

I smile against the base of her neck as my fingers move between her thighs. Most women aren't comfortable being touched during their cycles, and I think that's what shocks me the most—her unpredictability.

"I kinda like the idea of you beggin' for me..." I taunt as I suck the skin between her neck and shoulder.

The pads of my fingers rub circles over her clit, and her breath hitches. "Tell me what you want, sweetheart. And I just might do it."

"Go lower. I-I want your fingers *inside* me," she finally admits, her chest rapidly rising and falling. "I wanna know how it feels."

Fuck.

Ivy's so innocent. It almost feels wrong to corrupt her this way.

Almost.

She might be inexperienced, but I know her mind is anything but pure.

"If I claim this cunt, it means you're mine, Ivy."

"God, yes. I want to be only yours."

I groan at the sound of her admission. "Just relax...spread your legs for me."

Reaching up, I move the showerhead to the side so it's not directly on us. Then I slide one finger down her slit, coating it with warm water and her arousal. She leans back against my chest, fully relaxing. I cup her chin with my other hand and press my mouth to hers.

"It might hurt at first," I warn.

"I know."

Although she's used a vibrator, she's only used it for clit stimulation.

Slowly, I sink my finger between her folds and nearly growl at how tight her pussy squeezes me. She's warm and wet as I carefully thrust, allowing her body to get used to the intrusion.

"Let me know if it's too painful, and I'll stop," I whisper.

"No, keep going. I can take it."

"Your confidence is so damn attractive, baby. Hell, everything about you is. But I especially love how you aren't afraid to express what you want."

"You make me feel like I'm good enough."

"You're more than good enough."

I thrust in deeper, and she gasps, pressing her palms against the shower wall for support. Not wanting to hurt her, I move slowly and test how much she can handle. Her breathing staggers, and I know she's enjoying this as much as I am.

"I'm gonna add another finger. Let me know if it's—"

"Shut up and do it already," she blurts out, and I fight back the urge to laugh.

Without warning, I slide two digits inside her tight cunt, and she sinks down onto me.

"Fuck, baby. Your pussy is like a vise grip."

"Make me come, *please*."

I pull out, rinse off my hand, then thrust back in. She gasps, then spreads her legs wider. My dick is so goddamn hard, it's branding an imprint on her lower back, but all I care about is giving Ivy exactly what she wants.

As I work her pussy and rub her clit, I whisper in her ear.

"You're so beautiful."

"God, you take my fingers so damn good."

"Take it, Ivy. Ride my hand."

"Such a good girl."

"Use me to make yourself come, baby."

She shatters against me with shaky legs. Her back arches as she cries out her release. Keeping her upright, I kiss her jawline while holding her in place.

"That was the hottest fucking thing I've ever seen."

"I don't know how I'll ever go back to Winston after that."

Laughing, I wash my hands again, then spin her around to face me.

"You only need him if I'm not around. Otherwise, I've got it covered." I flash her a wink.

She cups my face and drags her mouth across mine. "Thank you."

"Are you thanking me for the orgasm?" I ask against her lips, my brows rising in amusement.

"No. Well, maybe. But for making me feel wanted. I've read

about *that feeling* countless times but never thought I'd actually experience it. That feeling of complete trust with your partner."

I palm her cheeks, bringing our foreheads together. "What we have is the real deal. You make me feel things I've never felt before too, sweetheart. My job as your boyfriend is to make sure you're the best version of yourself and to comfort you at your worst. There will never be a time when you can't be upfront with me or tell me what you want or need from me. I will always want to give you anything and everything."

"My *boyfriend*, huh?"

"Out of everything I said, you fixate on *that*?"

I almost worry I spoke too soon, but then she bursts out laughing. "I'm sorry, but I've never had a boyfriend before. Hearing it makes me feel like a giddy thirteen-year-old."

I smirk, kissing her. "Will you stay the night?"

"You'd have to get HR in here to remove me at this point."

Chuckling, I continue with her hair, and once we're both clean, we rinse off. After we're done, I give her privacy to get dressed.

"So there's something we should talk about," I tell her as we get comfortable in bed and snuggle underneath the sheets. It's only late morning, but we're both sleepy.

"You have another weird school subject fetish? Is it math?"

I shake my head at her snarky remark. "I'm starting to remember why Hadleigh always called you an annoying little brat."

Her eyes widen. "You're lying!" She throws a pillow at me but misses, and it falls to the floor. "She *adored* me."

I snicker, capturing her wrists and towering over her until she's flat against the mattress.

"I think you may have selective memory because I recall a lot of complainin' when it came to you."

She wiggles beneath me, but I nudge my knee between her thighs and push my weight on top of her.

"Dammit, you're too strong."

Chuckling, I lower my mouth to her ear. "Are you gonna play nice, or do I need to punish you?"

"Is that supposed to be a threat?"

"I'm startin' to think you antagonize me on purpose."

"Perhaps you would've caught on a lot sooner if you'd paid attention in school and hadn't been getting boners for your teachers."

"Don't be jealous, sweetheart." I push my hips into her, letting her feel how hard I am right now. "I'm not into cougars anymore."

She tries not to smile but can't stop herself. Then she bursts out laughing. "Fine. What do you want to talk about?"

I settle in next to her. "Your sister. I'm a little concerned about what her reaction will be so we should probably discuss how we want to handle it."

"Well, it's only been a couple of weeks, so even if she were to find out, we could just tell her the truth. We weren't rushing things and wanted to see where they went before we announced it."

"Right. I don't want her to assume I'm using you or treating you like a rebound because of Raelyn. That's not the case," I explain honestly. Raelyn and I dated for a couple of months, but there's no comparison to how I feel about Ivy.

"I don't think Hadleigh would think that. She's pretty reasonable."

"I'd like to assume she'd think the best about me and my intentions, but she's fiercely protective when it comes to you. Doesn't matter that I've been her best friend our entire lives, she won't think twice about taking a bat to my balls if she thinks I'll hurt you."

She snorts. "So maybe we should wait..."

"I kinda like being able to focus on us without the pressure of everyone's opinions and interrogations," I admit. "Mainly from my grandmother and family. I already know they're going to lose their fucking minds."

"Not to mention, sneaking around is kinda hot. I like spending time with you."

"Same here. At least for now. We can't hide forever. Eventually, it'll catch up with us."

"I know, but in the meantime, it's nice being able to figure this out together and not have to answer everyone's questions. Like with Winston. My current *lover*." She snorts. "Maybe I should have an imaginary breakup so I'm not adding more lies."

I brush damp strands of hair off her cheek and tuck them behind her ear. I smile at how hard and fast I'm falling for her. "Out of respect for Hadleigh's and my friendship, I'll have to come clean eventually. But for now, I like sneaking you into my bed."

"Like a dirty little secret, huh?" She waggles her brows.

"Don't get any ideas. You promised to read to me."

"I will. But maybe after a nap." She yawns, snuggling in closer.

"Sounds like heaven."

A moment passes, and then she meets my eyes. "Hadleigh loves you. When we're ready, we'll tell her. She'll approve or she'll freak the fuck out, but either way, we'll be together."

"And that's all that really matters." I kiss her softly. "But just in case, I'm gonna wear a cup that day."

CHAPTER FIFTEEN

IVY

It's been two days since Kane called me his girlfriend and finger-fucked me in the shower. Everything we talked about still has me on cloud nine. We're *official* now, even if we're hiding it, but that still has my inner teenage self all giddy.

I'd typically feel guilty for calling into work yesterday, but honestly, I'm too happy to care. We were completely caught up with orders, so Harper would survive without me for one day. If she desperately needed help, she'd call Hadleigh since she's still on maternity leave. Either way, I enjoyed a lazy Sunday off with Kane.

Between sleeping with a heating pad, Kane feeding me and giving me foot massages, I barely had a reason to get out of bed. I read him a few more chapters of my book, then he showed me a new leather engraving technique he figured out. It was one of the best weekends I've had in years, even if it was during one of the worst weeks of the month.

But now it's Monday, and I begrudgingly get ready for work. I stopped at my house yesterday to pack an overnight bag and show my mom I'm still alive.

"Good mornin'," I call out when I see Harper and my sister in the warehouse. I'm surprised to see Hadleigh here so bright and early, but it's not unusual.

"Mornin'! How are ya feelin'?" Hadleigh gives me a side hug, careful not to squish Hendrix. He's snug inside the baby wrap she's wearing.

"Yeah, I was worried about you," Harper adds.

Considering I've *never* called in before, I can see why they'd be concerned.

"I'm better. I just started my period, and it was really bad. Worse than usual," I say, which isn't a complete lie. The cramps were painful, but Kane definitely helped me feel better.

Hadleigh narrows her eyes as if she's contemplating something. "You did?" she asks. "We used to be synced up like a ventriloquist dummy."

I laugh, remembering that before she got pregnant, we were only a day apart.

"Yeah, and it's brutal."

"Maybe yours are so bad because you're getting period sympathy pains since Aunt Flo hasn't visited Hadleigh in over a year," Harper says with a snort. "Kinda like sympathy pregnancy symptoms."

"Oh my God, please no one give me those," I beg, grabbing some packaging supplies.

Before I get to work, I say hi to Hayden and Hailey-Mae, remembering my promise to play with them during my lunch break. Then I grab the order list I need.

"So give me the 411 on Winston. Did you see him this weekend?" Hadleigh asks while pulling some soaps off the shelves.

I think back to the conversation I had with Kane about that story. I clear my throat and prepare myself for the million questions she'll throw my way.

"Actually, we decided to take a break."

"*What?*" Hadleigh and Harper gasp at the same time.

"Already? What happened?" my sister asks.

I shrug casually, keeping my eyes on the table as I work. "Nothing really. We just have opposite schedules and couldn't make time to hang out. Decided to wait until we're back in school and go from there."

"Aw...are you okay?" Hadleigh's tone softens.

"I'm fine. We weren't serious or anything."

"Well, maybe that's for the best, especially if you're not even able to see each other. Now you can have a *hot girl summer*!"

I snort at Hadleigh's excitement.

"This is almost too perfect!" Harper beams. "My mom's friend mentioned her newly single son and had asked if she knew of any available ladies in the area. I told her I'd ask around, and we'd plan a double date or something, so—"

"No, no, no. I don't go on blind dates," I quickly interject. That's the last thing I want to do.

"It'll be totally casual. Just have some drinks or something. No pressure."

"I dunno..." I say, hoping she'll hear my uncertainty.

"What if Knox and I go? We can triple date, and I can vet him for you," Hadleigh adds.

"That'd be perfect!" Harper exclaims. "Just a fun, casual vibe with three couples hangin' out."

I narrow my eyes at them. "You really think I should go out with another guy right after ending a relationship?"

"Yes!" they say in unison.

"The fastest way to get over a guy is to get under another one." Hadleigh waggles her brows.

"I wasn't even *under* Winston..." I mutter.

"Rhett's a few years older than you. He's fresh out of college and isn't looking for a wife to pop out his babies right away. I bet you two would have fun and totally hit it off!" Harper smiles eagerly as she waits for my response.

I don't know how I'm going to get out of this. She and my

sister look so excited, and I don't want to let them down. The peer pressure nearly eats me alive.

"Yes! He sounds great. And since you're *newly single*, why not see who else is out there?" There is a hint of uncertainty as if she knows the truth. Ever since I mentioned my period, she's been giving me weird looks.

I swallow, then say firmly, "I'll *think* about it."

"Perfect! I'll text his mom and ask when he's available. You'll have until then to make up your mind."

How the hell am I supposed to tell my boyfriend I agreed to a blind date simply because we're hiding our relationship? It would be too suspicious if I said no.

Fuck me.

By the end of the work day, they'd planned everything—drinks at the Circle B Saloon on Friday night. I agreed to something casual, but I didn't expect it to be at the Bishops' bar. I can't even legally drink, but they assured me it wouldn't be an issue since I'm considered family. As long as I don't order alcohol, of course. Although I almost wished I could, then maybe I'd get through the awkwardness.

After work, I head over to Kane's and read while I wait for him to finish with work. I'm in the middle of a smutty scene when he walks in, smiling and looking as handsome as ever. Although his jeans are full of dirt and dried mud, I'm ready to jump him.

"I could get used to comin' home to you." He pulls me into his arms, then presses his lips to mine. "How was your day?"

"Just got a million times better, actually." He takes off his hat and throws it on the couch.

His warm smile gives me butterflies. "So did mine."

I melt into his body, massaging my tongue against his, and then he lifts me until my legs wrap around his waist.

"I need a shower, but I don't wanna let you go," he murmurs.

"So take me with you."

He walks us toward the bathroom. Once we're inside, he sets me down on the counter and stands between my legs.

"I want to devour your pussy so goddamn bad." His mouth moves down my jawline and settles on my neck.

I'm ready for all of him, but too bad Mother Nature's still lingering.

"I wish you could," I admit. "Just a couple more days."

"Thank God, because I have something special planned for you this weekend."

I sit up straighter so I can meet his gaze. "You do?"

"Yeah, I wanted to take you on a real date where no one will see us. You'll need to pack a bag and stay the night."

"Oh, what a hardship," I deadpan with a smile. "Except, umm...shit. I kinda have to tell you something."

He lifts a brow.

"I told Hadleigh and Harper that I ended things with Winston, and now they've set me up on a blind date."

He rolls his eyes with a laugh. "Of course they would. Are you going?"

I wince as I nod. "They wouldn't let it go and kept telling me how casual it'd be, so there was no reason for me not to. Though, I think Hadleigh's onto me. Seriously. She kept giving me weird looks all day, especially after I explained why I called in yesterday."

"Why would...?" He pauses, then smacks his forehead. "*Shit.* I asked her for the period supplies, so she might think it's a coincidence, or maybe she's put the pieces together."

"What?" My eyes widen as I gasp loudly. "Kane! You have to tell me these things. I would've given her a different excuse had I known. Shit, she'll be overly suspicious if I bail on Friday."

"Sorry, I didn't think about that." He lets out a deep breath. "So who's the guy? Do you know him?"

"No. His name is Rhett, and his mom is friends with Harper's mom. He just got out of a relationship and—"

"Great, so he's looking for a rebound." He aggressively brushes a hand through his messy hair. "You gotta get out of it."

"I'd love to. Tell me how."

"Tell them you're sick, not over fake Winston, then decided you're a lesbian. I don't know. But there's *no way*—"

"Wait a minute...are you gettin' all possessive?" I sing-song, thinking back to the books I've read where the hero goes apeshit for his girl. "Because not gonna lie, I'm super turned on right now."

He huffs out a laugh, caging me on the counter between his arms. "Ivy. I'm serious."

"So am I. Take off your pants, Cowboy."

"*Ivy.*"

"What're ya so worried about? That I'm gonna magically fall head over heels for this Rhett guy? Because I doubt it. Not when I'm already head over heels for you and have been for years."

He shrugs with a heartfelt smile. "That's very sweet of you to say, but that's not a risk I'm willing to take."

I scoff. "Don't you trust me?"

"Of course. But *him*? Not so much."

"Well, I won't let anything inappropriate happen. I'll be nice and make small talk to get my sister and Harper off my back, and then I'll sneak over here afterward. Then on Monday, I'll tell them I just didn't feel a connection, and they'll drop it."

"Or maybe I'll have to kidnap you instead." One side of his

mouth tilts up in a cocky smirk. "Hope this kid knows I can bench three fifty."

I snort. "I'll be sure to bring it up in our convo. That won't tip off my sister or anything. *Oh hey, did you know this random guy I'm not supposed to be hanging out with can bench twice your weight? Just thought I'd let ya know for absolutely no reason,*" I say in a mocking tone.

"You're gonna pay for that sassy little mouth of yours," he taunts, sliding his hand up my inner thigh and rubbing over my pussy.

"Oh yeah? Going to punish me with an orgasm?" I waggle my brows.

"You wish, sweetheart." He backs up, slowly stripping off his clothes. I'm mesmerized by every hard inch of him. The tattoos over his chest and arm, his length and piercings, his thick quads—everything about him screams *fuck me*. He'd probably thrust me into next weekend so I'd skip the blind date altogether.

He turns on the shower, leaving the door open, then stands underneath the stream of water.

"Are you gonna invite me in?" I ask impatiently.

"Nope. That's your punishment. Sit there and *only* watch."

I cross my arms and pout but keep my focus on him. Kane's a masterpiece like I've never seen in real life. Hell, not even on paper. Every solid inch is screaming to be touched and licked.

Just when I thought he couldn't top his seductive torture, he lowers his hand to his dick and strokes it.

"*Fuck*," he curses, jerking faster. His cock springs to life, growing hard and thick. "I bet you want this, don't you, baby?"

"You're so cruel," I hiss, narrowing my eyes.

To add to my torment, he moans and curses under his breath as his beating goes frantic and fast. The thick veins bulge out as he simultaneously teases himself and me. My body begs for him, but I force myself to stay planted. "Tell me what you wanna do to me, and I just might let you..." he taunts, his voice deep and hoarse.

"I think you already know..." I respond, my mouth watering at the sight of him. I've only sucked him off once, but I've been dying to do it again.

"Say the words, Ivy. I want you to tell me."

"I wanna lick and choke on your dick, then swallow down every drop of your come."

"Jesus fucking Christ," he hisses between gritted teeth, pumping harder.

"I'm so wet right now," I add, hoping he'll cave and let me touch him soon.

"I bet you are, sweet girl. That sexy clit is needy for my tongue, isn't it?"

"Not as needy as I am for your cock."

"Ivy...shit, I'm so close."

This little game is turning me on so damn much that I squeeze my thighs together for some friction.

"Get your ass in here right now," he demands. "On your knees."

I've never moved so fast in my life than I do now as I jump off the counter. I don't even care that I'm fully dressed. I obey as soon as I'm in front of him. The water pounds against his back, protecting me from getting drenched.

"Open up."

As soon as I do, he smacks the crown on my tongue, and I take my time teasing the tip. His head falls back with a groan when I linger around his piercings.

"Take all of me, Ivy. Down your throat."

I wrap my fingers around his shaft and go torturously slow into my mouth. When his eyes lock with mine, I smile around him.

"You're being defiant."

Pulling him out with a pop, I say, "I'm not the only one who should be punished."

He arches a brow with his hands on his hips. "Explain."

"For tormenting me with what I couldn't have."

His fingers brush along my cheek. "I thought you liked it when I teased you. Especially that clit."

"I'm talking about the years you didn't notice me."

"Trust me...I notice you now."

The butterflies resurface as my heart flutters. I know it would've been inappropriate for him to pursue me in high school, but I can't help thinking about what could've been.

I wrap my mouth around him again, hollowing my cheeks and sucking hard. As I force him down as far as I can handle, Kane grabs a fistful of my hair, jerking my head up until our eyes meet.

"Just like that, baby. So fuckin' good."

My head bobs fast, and I'm eager to please him. I feel his shaft tense against my tongue, and when his body stiffens, I know he's close.

Kane grunts and groans, his body convulsing as he releases in my mouth. I breathe out of my nose and keep his come inside, knowing he doesn't want me to swallow it right away.

As soon as he finishes, he pulls back, and I open wide, showing him.

"So goddamn beautiful." He bends down and captures my mouth with his, sliding his tongue in and tasting his pleasure. Clearly, nothing is off-limits to him, and that turns me on even more.

"Can I ask you something?" I ask when we're dry and sitting on his couch with my book. Since my clothes got wet, he lent me a pair of his boxers and a T-shirt that I'm currently swimming in.

"Of course."

"Don't take this the wrong way, but why do you like swallowing your own come?"

"I only like it once it's been in your mouth. My pleasure combined with your tongue is what I like. Does it weird you out?"

"Surprisingly, no. But it does make me wonder what I taste like."

"You've never licked your fingers or vibrator afterward?"

"No, I never really thought about it until you. You're teaching me all kinds of new kinky things." I smirk.

"Wait until you experience edging." He flashes me a wink, holding me in his arms.

"I've heard of it but not really sure what it entails," I tell him truthfully. "Like where you almost get off, right?"

"Yeah, build you up to the brink of an orgasm, then stop. Then do it over and over again until you can't take it any longer. When you finally combust, it's out of this world."

Just the thought of that makes me squirm. "Sounds torturous, if I'm being honest."

"A painful pleasure, maybe, but trust me, you'll like it. You'll beg for me to let you come, and I'll keep edging you closer and closer until I finally give you what you want."

"Oh my God...stop it." I moan, nearly melting against him. "Don't tease me. I'm already dying here."

Stupid Aunt Flo.

"How about you keep reading, and I'll give you a little preview?"

"Of what?"

He flashes me a wink. "Lie back on the pillow."

I do as he says, bringing my book with me and getting comfortable against the arm of the sofa. Then he sits up and pushes his knee between my legs.

"Keep reading," he orders. "I need to know what happens."

I smirk because he's been totally invested in the heroine's story, which I love since it's one of my favorite books.

He lowers himself between my thighs and cups my pussy

with his mouth over the boxers. Although he's not touching bare skin, the fabric is thin enough to feel everything.

"Oh my God...I can't focus when you do that." My head falls back, and I arch my hips to greet him.

"You stop reading, then I stop eating. So keep going."

"You don't play fair," I grit out.

"Read, Ivy."

He brings his face back to my pussy, rubbing and creating the best friction with his lips on my most sensitive spot. As I speak with shallow breaths, I focus on the pleasure he's creating between my legs and how badly I wish his tongue was inside me. But I'm not complaining.

"Your cunt is so needy, sweet girl. I can't stay away." Those words are my only warning before he lowers the boxers to expose my clit. He doesn't push them all the way down, just enough to reveal what he wants.

"I-I..." My eyes flutter closed, unable to make out the blurry sentences on the pages.

Kane twirls his tongue, then backs away. A quick slap against my pussy jolts me upward.

"I don't hear you," he states calmly, then flicks my clit again.

How the hell can I concentrate on words when I can barely concentrate enough to breathe?

Somehow, I continue reading while he continues with his delicious assault on my sensitive bud. I grow closer and closer, and then as promised, he backs away, leaving me frustrated and horny as fuck.

"Kane, *please*," I beg, nearly shoving my cunt in his face to finish me off. "Don't stop."

"I think you were about to read me a naughty scene," he taunts when my speech slows. He's not wrong, but it's not a real one. She's having a sex dream.

"Why do I need to read it when I'm living it right now?"

"Follow my rules, sweet girl, or you won't get to finish."

"That's cruel," I hiss. "I'll just finish myself off then." Considering I spent years doing it on my own, I know it wouldn't take long to find my release.

"C'mon, tell me what he does to her. How badly does she want it? Don't leave me hanging."

I groan out with frustration, then he lowers the boxers another inch, getting a bit too close to where my tampon is.

"Kane, I have—"

"Doesn't bother me," he says casually. "Your skin tastes so damn sweet. I need more of it."

I blink hard, trying to comprehend what he's saying, but I can barely think. I stutter my way through another paragraph, feeling self-conscious about how close his tongue is getting.

"Relax, baby. I'm here to make you feel good. Don't be nervous with me," he tells me softly. Kane's awareness of what I'm thinking and feeling is the hottest turn-on ever.

I focus on the pages while his tongue slides up and down my slit, then sucks on my clit. He brings me closer and closer to the edge until I'm panting.

"Get ready, sweet girl. This time, I'm not stopping."

His mouth latches on, and he sucks and teases until every nerve in my body explodes with pleasure. The book falls to the floor, and my hips jolt as I scream out my release. My hands cling to his hair, squeezing tightly as I ride out the wave.

"Holy shit, that was intense," I whisper, sinking into the couch as stars consume my vision.

"You thought that was good? I'm going to blow your goddamn mind this weekend."

CHAPTER SIXTEEN

KANE

I'VE BEEN DREADING this day all fucking week.

I know Ivy's blind date isn't real, and she's only doing it to amuse her sister, but I'm still not happy. Though I've never been the possessive type with any other woman, not even Hadleigh, Ivy brings it out in me.

Not only do I not want any other man getting the idea he can touch her, but I can't even stand the thought of him sitting next to her. It fills me with a rage I haven't felt in a long-ass time. Ivy's so fucking special to me and sweet that I can't risk losing her to some country club boy who's never gotten his hands dirty.

Not when I'm falling hard and fast.

It's why I'm bribing my little sister to meet me at the bar tonight. It'd be suspicious if I showed up alone, so I need a wingman. Or rather, wingwoman.

I told her to invite Payton too, so now it looks like we're just three people getting together for an after-work drink.

In reality, I'm keeping my eyes on this fucking guy. If he even touches her fingernail, I'm going to lose my goddamn mind.

Of course, I didn't warn Ivy I'd be there. I knew she'd try to talk me out of it or even make me promise I wouldn't, and since I don't want to lie, I didn't fill her in. She'll soon find out anyway.

"Why are you so tense?" Kaitlyn asks as I drive us into town. "You look like you're ready to murder someone."

I try to relax my shoulders, not wanting to give myself away, especially to my gossipy loud-mouth sister.

"Just a long week at work, I guess."

"Hopefully, a few beers will relax you, geez. Your face says you're ready to fuck someone up."

Well, she's not wrong.

I force a smile. "Nah, I'm good. Just had a rough day. How was your week?" I change the subject.

She goes on for ten minutes about anything and everything. The horse shows she's preparing for, the drama between two customers competing against each other, and how she had to call Payton to separate them. I'm actually surprised I didn't hear about that from the ranch hands, but I've kept myself occupied. Ivy comes over after work, we eat dinner and fool around, and then she either sleeps over or leaves late at night.

Once we arrive at the saloon, Kaitlyn finds Payton at the bar. He smiles as soon as she approaches, and I shake my head. It's obvious to everyone—but her—how much he likes her. Only God knows why he doesn't say anything, but I'm not one to talk. I hid my crush on Hadleigh for a decade.

Before I order a beer, I find the table of six where Ivy's sitting with everyone—Hadleigh and Knox, Harper and Ethan, and her *date*, Rhett. My heart hammers as I briefly watch them. She's laughing and smiling as they chat and drink, except she doesn't have alcohol. Since the saloon is also considered a restaurant, she's allowed to be here.

I walk discreetly to the office that I know is empty since both bartenders are serving drinks. It's the evening rush, so they'll be occupied by chaos for a while.

Once I'm inside with the door shut, I pull out my phone to text Ivy but see she's already sent me a message.

Ivy: What're you doing here?

Kane: Tell them you have to use the bathroom and meet me in the office.

Ivy: Are you crazy?

Kane: Only for you.

Ivy: They'll know something is up if I'm gone too long.

Kane: I'll be fast. Now get your sexy ass in here.

Ivy: Give me a minute.

A few moments pass, and when the door finally opens, I scoop Ivy into my arms and pull her to my chest.
"Fuck, you look too damn good tonight."
"What're you doing, Kane?" she whisper-hisses as I cage her against the door, then lock it.
I press my face into her neck and kiss her soft skin. "I came to make sure that bastard was keeping his hands to himself. Is he?"
She finally relaxes and wraps her arms around me. "Yes. He's been a perfect gentleman, so stop worrying."
"Not happenin'. Tell 'em you aren't feeling well and come home with me."
"Kane..." She whimpers as I suck on her collarbone. "I can't bail after twenty minutes of being here. You're just gonna have to trust me."
"I don't like the idea of another man being on a date with my

girlfriend," I say harshly. "I'll go out there right now and tell Hadleigh."

She freezes. "Really? You're going to admit we've been sneaking around?"

"Is that what you want?" I ask.

She swallows hard. "I don't know. As much as I hate being deceptive, I don't want the interrogations and judgments right now. Blindsiding everyone in public isn't right. I don't want her to be mad at you or hate me. You two have a *history,* and I'm not sure how she'll take us being together."

I cup her cheek, softly bringing my lips to hers. "I won't do anything that makes you feel uncomfortable. But just know, tomorrow night, you're mine. Tonight is the last time I'll ever share you."

"You aren't sharing me because nothing's happening with him," she assures me. "If he so much as wraps his arm around me, I will scream bloody murder. Happy?"

I lower my arm and smack her ass. "Sassy girl."

She smirks, then grabs my face and meets my gaze. "Stop worrying. Rhett does nothing for me. You're all I think about, okay? Like annoyingly so. Thoughts of you consume me. Day and night. Sometimes I just beg for a break so I can focus at work."

I chuckle, unable to contain the smile that takes over my face. "Good, then you know exactly how I feel."

Leaning in, I capture her mouth and slide my tongue between her lips. "I won't bother you again, but I'll be at the bar in case you need me."

"Behave yourself," she warns.

I flash her a wink. "Just for tonight, sweetheart. Tomorrow, you'll be begging for more."

IVY

After I return to the table, I rejoin the conversation and watch Kane walk to the bar out of the corner of my eye. He sits next to Payton and his sister, then orders a drink.

I do my best to participate in the conversation, but I can't stop my eyes from lingering on Kane and the blonde who just approached him. Though I understood why he wouldn't want me going on a date, I didn't consider how it'd feel to sit on the sidelines while another woman flirts with him.

A woman his age who looks more experienced and mature than me.

He barely gives her any attention, but apparently, this chick likes that because she's not giving up. She leans into his ear, and he dismisses her, which fills me with pride.

Still, this woman continues to chat, and when she licks his ear, I snap. The glass I was holding tips over and spills onto the table. Luckily, it only had a third left, but it's everywhere.

"Oh shit, I'm so sorry," I blurt out as everyone quickly gathers napkins.

"Did any get on you?" Rhett asks.

"No. How about you?"

"Nah, I'm good. But let me get you another drink."

He's up and heading to the bar before I can stop him.

Fuck.

Hadleigh and Harper move the basket of fries out of the way and continue wiping the table. Harper started drinking when we got here and has been super bubbly and chatty.

Rhett stands on the other side of the blonde. Kane looks over at him, then he glances over his shoulder at me. I shake my head, begging him with my eyes not to do anything stupid. He smirks before quickly turning toward the blonde and Rhett.

"Is that Kane?" Hadleigh asks, just now noticing him.

"Yeah, Kaitlyn and Payton too," I respond as casually as I can.

"Oh my God, we should invite them over," Harper announces.

"There's no room," I quickly remind her.

"Plus, it looks like Kane's gonna get lucky tonight. Don't wanna interrupt," Knox says with a laugh, and my jaw tightens.

"Looks more like Rhett is with the way Kane's ignoring her," Ethan mutters. "I don't think he's interested."

"Trust me, he *is*. He's on the rebound playin' like he isn't because he knows it drives chicks wild," Knox remarks confidently. "He was hookin' up with someone the other week, so he's gotta be playin' the field after Raelyn."

I keep my eyes down so no one notices my rage, but as soon as I look up, Hadleigh's gaze zeroes in on me.

"So do you think Rhett likes me?" I blurt out, needing something to steer the conversation away from Kane. "I've never been on a blind date before, so I'm not sure how things are going."

"Rhett's *totally* into you!" Harper gushes, but Hadleigh stays quiet. "He's a catch. Has a great job, a good head on his shoulders, and Southern morals. I wouldn't be surprised if he asks for your number before the night's over."

"If he does, would you give it to him?" Hadleigh asks curiously.

"Sure, yeah, of course." I shrug with a smile. "Doesn't hurt to see where things could go."

Rhett finally returns with my soda, and I thank him. Considering Hadleigh's watching me, I need to lay the flirting on a little thicker. As much as I don't want to, I have to act interested in him and *not* her best friend.

"So you wanna play pool or darts with me?" I ask, leaning in closer.

"Yeah, I'd love to. Let's start with a game of pool, but fair warning, I'm not the best."

I smile wide. "Don't worry, I'm not either."

We grab our drinks and stand, my eyes quickly scanning for

Kane. He spots me, and I give him a look to *stay there*. I'll explain to him later what I'm doing because now is not the time.

"Ladies first," Rhett says once he removes the triangle. "You good to break?"

I shrug because I've never done it. "Sure, I'll give it a try."

Leaning down, I narrow my gaze to the tip of the pool stick and the white ball in front of me. Then with as much strength as I can, I take my shot.

Balls go flying all across the table, including a few that bounce off and onto the floor. "Oh my gosh." I palm my forehead. "I'm so sorry."

Rhett chuckles while chasing them and then sets each one back on the table. "Nah, don't worry about it. You wanna be solids or stripes?"

"I'll pick solids. Maybe it'll be easier for me to see them," I say with a laugh.

Rhett gets into position to take his turn. He's dressed differently than most of the men in here. The Circle B Saloon is usually filled with ranchers and blue-collar workers from town, but he's wearing a polo and khakis like he just finished a round of golf. It's comical that Harper's mom thought he'd be my type. While he's a nice enough guy, he's not someone I'd be interested in romantically, even if I was single.

One of the striped balls goes in, and as he takes another shot, Kaitlyn walks over.

"Ivy! What're you doin' here?" She greets me with a hug.

"I'm with the foursome over there." I jerk my chin toward my sister and Harper, who are currently staring at me so hard, it's a wonder they haven't burned a hole in the back of my head.

"And who's this?"

"Rhett Fields," he answers, holding out his hand.

"Very gentlemanly," she sing-songs and shakes it. "Nice to meet you, *Rhett Fields*. I'm Kaitlyn."

"Pleasure's all mine." He flashes a bright smile, then kisses her knuckles.

Kaitlyn looks at me with wide eyes as if she's ready to get down on one knee and propose to *him*.

"How old are you, Rhett?" she asks.

"Twenty-four."

"Dammit," she mutters under her breath, and I sniffle a laugh. Kaitlyn's in her late twenties and isn't looking for a man-child. "Well, you two *kids* have fun. Kane's over there gettin' a dental exam from Malibu Barbie, so I dipped for a minute."

My throat stings as I chance a look at Payton and Kane, who are talking to her. He glances over his shoulder, and our gazes lock. My lips turn into a firm scowl as he arches a confused brow. I roll my eyes, then turn back to Rhett.

"Do you think you could help me with my next shot?" I ask innocently. I shouldn't be baiting Kane, but then again, he shouldn't be here spying in the first place. If he came to keep tabs on me, I might as well give him something worth watching.

CHAPTER SEVENTEEN

KANE

My teeth grind as I watch Ivy flirt with Rhett. Kaitlyn hung out with them for a few minutes, then walked off. I wished she'd stay over there, but I couldn't ask her to watch them without her asking questions. Andrea's been talking my ear off for the past thirty minutes, and although I've tried to give her subtle hints that I'm not interested, she hasn't moved. Then Payton chimed into the conversation, and she's been glued to my side ever since.

If I didn't know any better, I'd say Ivy's testing my willpower. The moment she bends over the table and Rhett comes up behind her, I nearly lose my shit.

He wraps his arms around her back and grabs the stick, then guides her on how to aim and shoot. My jaw nearly snaps in half when I catch him glancing at her ass.

I watch as he says something to her, and whatever it is, it makes Ivy giddy with a smile. Then she leans over again, but this time, the fucker doesn't touch her. Instead, he's staring at her bare legs like they're his next meal.

I tightly grip my chair as I obsessively watch them play, and every time he gets too close, I'm seconds from stepping between them.

Andrea and Payton keep chatting, but I've blacked out their entire conversation. Kaitlyn orders another round and talks to the bartender. Meanwhile, my eyes are fixated on Rhett, who's mere inches from Ivy.

I'm ready to do something really fucking stupid.

His hand rests on her lower back as he leans in and whispers something in her ear. I can tell she's uncomfortable by the way her body stiffens. She takes a step away, but the idiot is too stupid to understand. Instead, he closes the gap between them, and when his mouth lowers, I see *red*.

"Hey!" I shout as I stalk over there.

Ivy immediately spins around and looks at me with aggressive wide eyes. Rhett removes his hands from her and steps back.

"You okay?" I ask, ignoring Rhett's death glare.

"I'm *fine*," she grits out between her teeth. "What're you doin'?"

"You were tryin' to get away from him, and he wasn't takin' the hint," I say, then narrow my gaze to Rhett. "You were gettin' too close."

"I was leaning in so she could hear me over the music and everyone talkin'. Who are you anyway? Her older brother or something?"

Just as I'm about to blow my cover, Hadleigh walks over and nudges me. "What's goin' on?"

I explain the situation and how I thought Ivy looked uncomfortable. Ivy claims everything's just fine, and Hadleigh gives me a suspicious look while crossing her arms.

"Is there something goin' on between you two?" She waves a finger back and forth between Ivy and me.

"What?" I ask stupidly.

"You're actin' like either a jealous lover or an overbearing older brother. So which one is it?"

"An *obnoxious and annoying* older brother," Ivy blurts out. "So glad Mom only had us girls. That behavior is too much."

"*Protective*," I counter. "There's a difference. We don't know this guy, and she looked like she was going home with him. He could be a serial killer for all we know."

"Um…I could sleep with every guy in this bar if I wanted, and it wouldn't be any of your damn business," Ivy hisses, narrowing her eyes at me, and now I'm wondering if she's putting on a show or if she's really mad at me for interjecting.

"Okay, maybe y'all should give each other some space. Kane, you go back to the bar with Payton, and Ivy, you stay at the pool table. As much as I appreciate you lookin' out for her…" She pauses and studies my face. "I'm watching them, so you don't have to worry."

"I'm nineteen!" Ivy states. "Y'all don't need to babysit me. Jesus. In case you forgot, I'm not twelve anymore." She shifts her gaze to mine and glares.

Yep, she's definitely mad at me.

"You could be thirty, and I'll still wanna protect you," Hadleigh tells her. "Kane knows how important you are to me, so he's just makin' sure you're safe."

"Maybe Kane should worry about his own sister." Ivy juts her chin, and we turn to see Kaitlyn giving Andrea a mouthful.

"Jesus Christ," I mutter, shaking my head and pinching the bridge of my nose. "This is why I don't go out anymore. Y'all start trouble."

I walk away before Ivy can rip me a new one.

"Stay away. Payton doesn't do one-night stands, so go find someone else," Kaitlyn shouts in her face.

I grab my sister's arm, pulling her back before I have to physically remove her. "Have you lost your mind? We're in the saloon," I remind her. It's one thing to start a fight in a random bar, but one in our family's establishment would be a bad look for us.

"Then tell this chick to quit touching Payton inappropriately. He's already told her *no* three times. He's not interested, *sweetie*."

"Only because you're tellin' him to say that. Who are you, *his wife*?" Andrea mocks.

"It's time you leave," I explain, already at my max level of annoyance for one night. "Pay your tab and go."

"You can't kick me out," she argues.

"My family owns this bar, so yes, I can. You can either walk out on your feet, or I can escort you out over my shoulder. I'll let you decide."

The bartender brings Andrea her receipt and card. With an eye roll, she signs it and storms off with a huff.

"I could've taken care of her," Payton finally speaks up.

"Who? Andrea or Kaitlyn?" I ask with a laugh, then grab my beer.

"She asked Payton to take her home several times, and he specifically said, *no thank you*. Like...was she hard of hearing or just didn't like what he was saying? Either way, I had enough of it." Kaitlyn shrugs, then chugs the last of her drink.

Once my beer is empty, I set it down, then look around for Ivy. She's sitting at the table without Rhett, so hopefully, he took the hint and left.

Just as those thoughts surface, I turn and see the asshole at my side ordering more drinks.

"You like her, don't you?" Rhett asks only loud enough for me to hear. "You weren't just being overprotective as a brother. You're in love with her."

"What the fuck are you talkin' about, man?" I scowl, ready to haul this guy out on his ass.

"She's a nice girl, but I'm not interested in her that way, so don't worry. My mom's friends with Harper's mom, and I didn't want to be rude and say no when they fixed us up. Truthfully, I'm already seeing someone, but I know my parents wouldn't approve, so I haven't told them."

"You're serious?"

"Yeah. I just thought you should know. I have no intentions with Ivy."

"Alright, I believe ya."

He blows out a breath and smiles.

"So who's this girl you're sneaking around with?" I ask, making conversation while he waits for his order.

"The one you just kicked outta here." He smirks and shrugs. "She wasn't happy when I told her about tonight and showed up unannounced. I didn't want to make a scene with the group I'm with, so I didn't pay her any attention. That's why she was trying so hard. She wanted to make me jealous, and hell, I was. I'm gonna pay for this later."

I blow out a breath and laugh. "Holy shit. The plot thickens. Not gonna lie, she sounds like a handful, bro."

"Yeah, she is, but I'm crazy about her." He shakes his head, then adds, "I'm sorry about the trouble, man."

"I appreciate you tellin' me. Now I won't have to bash your face in behind the parking lot." I flash him a smug grin. I'd only hit him if he deserved it.

"And I appreciate you not. But I'm gonna have to leave soon to catch up with Andrea, so if you're able to give Ivy a lift home, it'll give you the chance to apologize."

"Absolutely."

I'm tempted to tell him he's right, that I am with Ivy and we're in the same situation, but I don't trust small-town gossip. You tell one person, and soon, everyone knows.

Rhett takes the two drinks, and I closely watch as he delivers them. Ivy avoids looking my way, and I know I'm gonna have to do some damage control later. I'm not above groveling, but she pushed it a tad too far when she allowed him to be so damn close. Having insight into Rhett's dilemma makes me relax, but in the heat of the moment, it pissed me off. Once Rhett leaves, I take his seat. I stopped drinking after my last beer, so I'm fine to drive us to my house.

"Hello, am I allowed to sit here?" I ask with amusement.

"Only if you're going to behave," Hadleigh states.

"And they call *me* the wild twin," Knox says with a laugh.

"Don't worry, you still proudly hold that title." I smirk.

"I think we're gonna head out so we can get back to the kids," Harper announces as Ethan stands and helps her up.

"Us too. I need to pump before I pass out," Hadleigh says.

"Wow, you scold me for being *too young,* and here y'all are, actin' like you're in your fifties." Ivy snickers.

"You just wait, lady. Kids and marriage take like ten years off you and then add another ten for each child," Harper teases, then continues, "But I wouldn't trade it for the world. So hurry up and get married and make babies."

"No!" Hadleigh interjects. "Not yet. She's my baby sister."

"Who *isn't* a baby," Ivy clarifies.

"You better not get pregnant before me." Kaitlyn stalks over. "Because I swear to God, if I have to go to one more baby shower or wedding and be asked, *"Kaitlyn, sweetie, when is it your turn?"* she mocks in an elderly woman's voice filled with pain, then shouts, "I don't know, *Karen*! You have any single grandsons who aren't cheating bastards?"

The table falls silent as Kaitlyn has an emotional breakdown. I know she's eager to start a family, but I hadn't realized it was a trigger.

"Don't worry, I'm not planning to pop anything out of my vag for a *very* long time," Ivy comforts her.

"Well, at this rate, I'll be going to a sperm bank before I find a decent man."

"You will not!" Harper scolds. "Go ask Payton. I'm sure he'll make a baby with you." She waves her arm toward him after casually suggesting she sleep with her best friend and have kids.

Kaitlyn groans with an eye roll. "Yeah, we'll call that plan C."

Hadleigh snorts. "I'm afraid to ask what plans A and B are."

"Well, plan A was to find a man before I was twenty-five. Plan B is to find a man before I'm thirty. Seeing as I turn twenty-nine this year, plan C might become a reality."

"You still have eighteen months." Hadleigh smirks. "That's like five years for the Bishops."

We all laugh because it's true. Almost everyone in our family gets engaged, married, and pregnant within that timeframe. There's no such thing as taking it slow.

When we know we've found *the one*, we know.

I glance at Ivy, hoping she won't argue with what I'm about to ask her.

"So can I take you home since they're all leaving and your ride left?"

She doesn't look at me as she shrugs, then responds, "Sure, I *guess*."

"You two play nice," Hadleigh scolds, then meets my eyes. "I appreciate you driving her."

Ivy stands and grabs her purse. I wait while they hug goodbye, and then I remember I need to pay my tab.

"Be right back," I tell Ivy.

Once I sign my receipt, I tell Payton and Kaitlyn good night. Then just for shits and giggles, I give Payton a hard time.

I pat his shoulder and say, "If I were you, I'd stock up on condoms." He throws me a confused expression, and then I'm greeted with a smack from Kaitlyn.

"What was that for?" I rub the spot on my arm even though it barely stung.

"For breathing my air," she mocks.

I chuckle, then meet Ivy at the door. "Ready?"

"To go home, yep." She whips open the door, and I follow.

"Really? I was hoping you'd like to come home with me."

"You're nuts if you thought I would."

"*Ivy*."

She stands against the passenger door of my truck, neither of us making a move to open it.

"You embarrassed me tonight, so you really think I wanna go anywhere with you? You acted like a jealous caveman!" she shouts. Although the parking lot is nearly empty, I don't need Kaitlyn and Payton coming outside and overhearing us.

"Ivy, calm the fuck down." I wedge my shoe between her feet and cup her cheeks as my knee rubs against her thighs.

Her eyes widen in anger as her jaw drops. "Don't you dare tell me to—"

Before she can continue yelling at me, I crash my mouth against hers. She relaxes and wraps her arms around my waist, letting me slide my tongue between her soft lips.

"Don't think you can kiss me and I'll just forget everything," she murmurs as I slide up her jawline and to her ear.

"What if I do *more* than just kissing? Then will I earn your forgiveness?" I ask with amusement as my hand glides between her legs. "I can kiss you here instead."

"Kane...what if someone sees us?" she asks in an airy tone as her back rests against the cool metal of my truck.

"Afraid of givin' drunk people a show?" I tease, feathering my fingers along the top of her jean shorts. "That might be a risk we take."

Kaitlyn and Payton are the only ones left inside, but I'm not worried about them. They'll probably stay another thirty minutes, so that means I have until then to give Ivy an orgasm.

Once I slide under her panties, her head falls back with a gasp, and she's no longer worried about getting caught. I suck on her neck as the pad of my middle finger rubs circles on her clit.

"Do you forgive me yet?" I tease as her breath hitches.

"No..." she whimpers.

I move lower, down her slit, and thrust a finger inside.

"*Kane*." She moans, arching her hips into me.

"How about now?" I pull out and push back in, harder this time.

"You can't just act like a jerk and think touching me will make it all better," she counters, fisting my shirt as she seeks out her pleasure.

"Then let me make it up to you. Use me, baby. Let me make you feel good."

Her walls crumble as she spreads her legs wider, allowing me to go deeper.

"Take what you need. Ride my hand until you come."

"I can take more," she tells me eagerly. "*Please.*"

My dick is so goddamn hard, I can hardly stand it, but I want nothing more than to taste her sweet release.

Instead of shoving a second finger inside, I remove my hand and open the door.

"What are you doin'?"

"Giving you what you asked for, sweetheart." I spin her around so she faces the inside of my truck. "Lean over the seats with your arms stretched forward."

Once she's in position, I lower her shorts and panties down her legs, then help her take one foot out of them so I can spread her wide.

"Fuck me, you look so goddamn sexy, baby." I smack her ass cheek, and she yelps.

"What if someone—?"

"Don't worry, I'm not gonna let anyone see what's mine." I kneel between her feet and spread her open. "Your pussy's so wet for me. You're practically dripping."

"Kane...*please.*"

"Please what, my sweet girl? What do you need?"

"I wanna come so badly," she pleads, sticking her ass out farther.

"Say you forgive me first."

"Damn you," she hisses, and I smirk. I shouldn't be taunting her while touching her, but I can't help myself. I've fallen too hard for her.

"Say it, Ivy. Say you forgive me for not being able to control myself when it comes to you." I blow air against her clit, knowing it'll drive her insane. Then I tease her slightly with the tip of my tongue.

"Fine, you sadist! I'll forgive you this one time. You act like a caveman again, it's gonna take more than oral for me to drop it."

I smirk. "I'll do whatever I need to protect what's mine, sweetheart."

With her bare pussy in front of me, I grip her thighs, then dive in. As I lick, suck, and play with her cunt, I bring her closer to the edge. I know she's almost there when her breathing grows erratic, and she begs me not to stop.

Her legs shake when I stick my thumb inside her wet pussy. The next time my tongue circles her swollen bud, she screams in ecstasy as her sweetness coats my lips.

"*Oh my God*, that's so good." She moans as I lap up her juices.

"Fuck, you taste amazin'." I wipe my chin, then lean down and press one more kiss on her soft skin.

Once I help get her clothes back on, I pull her into my arms and sigh. "I hope you know now that I've fully tasted you, I'm gonna be like an addict, always craving my next hit and wanting more."

"You're lucky you're good at it, or I'd be kneeing you in the junk right now."

I chuckle in amusement at the serious look she's trying to maintain. "If you think I'd *ever* be okay with another man touching you, you've forgotten exactly who you're dating."

"You knew I was only here to keep our cover! I wasn't even interested in him, and you still overstepped the boundaries."

"You allowed him to *help you shoot pool* and touch you."

"I did that because you had Malibu Barbie undressing you

with her eyes! Plus, I had to act like I was interested in my date because Hadleigh was eyeing me. You didn't have an excuse."

"So you *were* testing me." The side of my mouth tilts up. "You were jealous."

"*No*. I was annoyed that you showed up."

I inch closer, cupping her cheek and leaning over her. "It's okay for you to admit you didn't like seeing another woman all over me. Because I can tell you right now, if we weren't being secretive, I wouldn't have thought twice about physically removing Rhett's hands from you. That goes for *any* man flirting with you."

"You can't just go around punching guys in the face who talk to me."

"I beg to differ." I won't deny that I can be hotheaded, but I've never felt so tempted to destroy someone for simply looking at Ivy.

She rolls her eyes and tries to stay mad, but I see the way her lips curl up into a smile.

"Isn't that what your book boyfriends would do? The ones you find so sexy."

"They're fictional. That's different."

"Not for me." I crush my mouth to hers, seeking her tongue.

She gives in, wrapping her arms around me and humming into my mouth.

"Are you done being mad at me yet?" I taunt, twirling a piece of hair behind her ear. "Because I still have an amazin' date planned for us tomorrow evening."

She contemplates her answer, making me sweat as I await her response. "Yes...*for now*."

I grin. "Good enough for me."

CHAPTER EIGHTEEN

KANE

Last night, I brought Ivy home with me, and this morning, I woke up with her in my arms. During my break, I brought her to her house so she could shower and get ready for our date tonight. It's all I've been thinking about at work.

"Big plans tonight?" Payton asks while we load a mare into a trailer.

I can usually bullshit my way out of lying and just explain I'm lying low or going to bed early.

"Not sure yet, might chill, maybe go on a drive." It's not a lie since I'm taking Ivy out. I've been planning it for days and can't fucking wait. "How 'bout you?" I ask, so he won't pry.

"Jerkin' off in the shower, drinkin' a six-pack, and watching anime porn."

"So a typical Saturday night for ya?"

He nods.

I chuckle at his humorless expression. Payton will probably hang out with my sister or meet some of the ranch hands at the bar.

After I've gotten Mr. Wilton to sign all the paperwork for Sophie and pay the final boarding fees, I send him on his way with a handshake. Knox left early to help Hadleigh with something, so it's just us for the rest of the shift.

"You don't ever go home, do you?" I ask Payton when we head back to the barn. "To see your family," I clarify when he gives me a weird look.

His eyes lower as he cracks his knuckles. "No, not in years."

"May I ask why?"

"Never had a good relationship with my stepdad," he states in a firm finality, obviously not wanting to discuss it.

Once we've cleaned the stables and fed the horses, we say goodbye and part ways.

As soon as I'm in my truck, I check my phone and smile when I see Ivy's name pop up.

Ivy: What should I wear tonight, Cowboy?

Kane: Preferably nothing. But if you must pick something, whatever goes with boots.

Ivy: So...only boots, then?

I growl as I imagine her naked body.

Kane: Don't tease me, woman.

Ivy: Where's the fun in that?

She sends an upside-down smiley emoji, and I laugh.

Kane: I'm on my way home now. Gimme an hour, then I'll come get ya.

Ivy: I'll be ready and waiting!

Once I'm home, I quickly clean the house, then take a shower. I throw on some ripped jeans, a gray sweater, and boots, then put on my cowboy hat. Before heading out, I grab the bouquet I ordered for her. Before I can get Ivy, I have to stop at my grandparents'. Thankfully, I already packed my truck with everything we needed for our date this morning.

As soon as I pull into their driveway, I'm greeted at the door.

"Well, don't you look super pretty." I lean down and kiss my grandma's cheek.

"Save some of that charm for your date," she taunts.

"I always have some set aside for you." I flash her a wink.

Smiling, she leads me into the kitchen, where I see the barbecue pulled pork sandwiches and coleslaw.

"Grams, this smells so good."

"And if ya want it, you better tell me who I made this for." She arches a brow with a hand on her hip. Should've figured she'd try to blackmail me.

"You know I can't do that."

"Says who?" she snaps.

"Secrets are more fun, didn't ya know that?" I smirk, hoping she'll drop it.

I wanted tonight to be special but knew I wouldn't have time to cook a meal, so I asked Grandma to make a Bishop specialty.

"Alright, I'll make ya a deal. Since I worked so hard to make one of your favorites, you'll make sure I'm the first to know who she is when you decide to announce it. Got it?" Her stern tone nearly has me cracking up.

"You got yourself a deal." I smirk, knowing news spreads fast around here.

After she neatly packs our dinner and dessert in a wicker picnic basket for me, I kiss her cheek again and thank her. Then I head to Ivy's.

My heart races when I turn onto her road. Even though we've been official for a few weeks, my nerves still get the best of me.

The closer we grow, the harder I fall. This is a night I want us to remember forever.

I park across the street from her house and shoot her a text.

Kane: I'm here.

Ivy: Almost ready. You can come to the door.

Looking over, I notice her mom's car is parked in the driveway.

Taking a deep breath, I grab the flowers from the passenger side, then get out of the truck. I walk down the sidewalk, and before I can even knock, the door swings open, and her mother stares me down.

Nervously, I clear my throat. "Hello, Ms. Callaway. It's nice to see you."

"Hi, Kane. Haven't seen you in a while."

"I know. How're you doin'?"

"Stayin' busy at work. I assume you're here for Ivy?"

I swallow hard as she eyes the bouquet in my hand. "Yes, ma'am."

She nods, then motions for me to come inside. "She's still getting ready. Can I offer you any water or lemonade?"

"No, thank you."

The awkward silence lingers, and I'm not sure how much Ivy's told her mom, if anything.

"Where are you takin' her tonight?" she asks.

"We'll be on the ranch, but I haven't told her yet. I wanted it to be a surprise," I admit.

She nods in approval. "You know she's only nineteen. No alcohol."

"Of course, ma'am. I brought sparkling cider."

"Mom, stop barraging him," Ivy mutters from the top of the stairs. I look up and find her in a knee-length summer dress with brown and pink cowboy boots. Her naturally curly hair has been straightened and now reaches to her erect nipples. Everything about her is so goddamn sexy.

"She wasn't," I confirm.

Ivy's lips widen as she walks down the steps.

"You look lovely."

"Thanks. You look quite handsome yourself." Her approving stare makes me hot.

"These are for you."

"Wow, they're beautiful, Kane," she says as I hand them to her.

She inhales the flowery scent. "I love how you always get me red roses. They smell so sweet."

"Just like you." I rake my eyes down her body, but quickly remember her mom is watching. Flashing her a quick wink, I add, "Ready?"

"Yep, I just need to grab my overnight bag. Be right back."

She shimmies off, leaving me alone with her mother again.

"I'm happy to see Ivy get out of the house and experience life outside of her books and work, but not at the expense of getting her heart broken," Ms. Callaway warns. "I have faith that I can trust you."

"You have my word," I reassure her confidently. "She means a lot to me."

She nods. "Good. I know you were in love with Hadleigh through high school and that you were always a good friend. But Ivy's my baby, and we're all very protective of her."

"I understand. I am too," I admit.

"Okay, ready!" Ivy beams. "I'll be home sometime tomorrow, Ma."

I watch as they exchange hugs, then I wave goodbye and escort Ivy out the door with her bag in my other hand.

"Sorry about that. I should've warned you," Ivy says softly as I lead her to my truck while she carries the flowers.

"Yeah, umm, I wasn't expecting that, to be honest."

Before I can open the passenger door, she spins around. "You're not mad, are you?"

"Of course not." I cup her face with my free hand, stealing a kiss.

"She asked if I was seeing someone, and I couldn't lie. I think she heard you sneaking out one time, and with me not coming home, she put two and two together."

"Does she approve?"

"For the most part, yes, but she's skeptical of all men. Hasn't remarried since my dad left. But she'll warm up to you. Mom knows you're not a bad guy."

"I hope so." I press my lips to hers once more. "I can't wait to show you what I've planned for you."

She smiles wide. "I can't wait!"

Once she's buckled in, I place her duffel and roses in the back, then drive us to the ranch. "Radio's all yours. Lady's choice," I tell her once we're out of town.

"Actually, I had a different idea..." Her seductive voice lingers, and when I catch her unbuckling, I arch a brow.

"Ivy, what are you...?"

She scoots closer, rubbing her hand over my thigh and groin. "Something I've always wanted to try."

My eyes widen. *Right now?*

"Well, it's not called road head for nothing," she sasses.

"That sounds dangerous," I admit, gripping the steering wheel with one hand.

"Then you better pay extra attention, Cowboy."

Instinctively, I part my legs to give her better access. As soon as she frees my dick, it springs alive.

"Jesus Christ, this is a bad idea," I mutter, desperately trying to keep my eyes open as she strokes my length.

When Ivy tightens her grip around my shaft, I inhale sharply. "*Fuck*, that feels good."

Then she leans over, repositioning herself, and deep throats my cock.

"Holy shit, Ivy." My head leans against the headrest, and I fight the urge to pull over. Carefully, I slide my hand up her back and neck, and fist her silky hair. "God, you're so good at that."

She releases me with a pop, then spits on the tip, circling the pad of her thumb over my piercings. Ivy knows that's a fucking sensitive spot.

As I fight like hell to concentrate on the road, Ivy continues to suck and lick like a pro. She strokes and plays with my balls, but then I nearly lose it when she increases her pace and starts choking.

"Fuck, I'm so close," I warn. We're only a couple of minutes from the ranch.

She squeezes my thigh with one hand while she gags on every inch of me.

My balls tighten, and moments later, I release inside her wet, warm mouth. Ivy's long, hungry moans encourage every drop to spill out of me.

I release my hold on her and wipe my forehead. "Shit, you got me sweatin' over here."

She sits upright and gives me a mischievous grin. Proudly, she opens her mouth and shows off her handiwork.

"Don't swallow," I order, trying to put my dick back inside my pants so I can pull over. "Get over here."

I pull her into my lap and slam my mouth against hers, tasting all the pleasure she gave me.

"That was the fucking best road head ever," I tell her between kisses. "Glad I experienced that first with you."

She pulls back with a curved brow. "Really? I got a first of *yours*?"

"Just you, baby." I press my lips to hers again. "We'll continue this in just a minute. We're almost there."

I veer onto the road, and once we're at the ranch, I turn onto a dirt trail. It's a bouncy ride as I put it in four-wheel drive and climb over some hills and weave through the trees.

"Where in the heck are you takin' me?" She looks around, but with the sun setting, the visibility is low. "It's givin' me serial killer in the woods, *Texas Chainsaw Massacre* vibes."

I chuckle. "This is what's known as the Bishop spot. There's a massive firepit, and the history of it started with my father and uncles. They all brought their ladies here."

"Ohh, I see, so it's a *gettin' lucky* spot."

I burst out laughing as I park six feet from the firepit with the tailgate facing it. "Sorta, but it's more special than that. They ended up marrying the women they brought here."

"Are you messin' with me? Is that *actually* true?"

"I swear! You can ask Rowan and Diesel. When they were sneakin' around, this was one of the places he took her."

"Oh, so it's a *sneakin' around* spot."

I shrug with a grin. "It's private...and *romantic*. Now wait in here while I set up."

"Set up?" she asks as I jump out of the truck.

I respond with a wink, then walk to the back of my truck and fold up the truck cover, revealing the twin air mattress, pillows, and blankets. I wanted our first date to be as romantic for her as possible, so I got the same fairy lights she has in her bedroom and decorated the inside.

I grab the basket of food from the back seat and swipe one of the roses from her bouquet.

"Almost done," I quickly tell her before closing the door. She smiles wide.

Thankfully, Grandma stocked it with plates, silverware, napkins, and cups. I set out the dishes, then grab the bottle of sparkling cider.

Quickly, I pluck some rose petals, then sprinkle them around the bed. Once I'm satisfied with how it all turned out, I start the fire.

"Ready?" I open her door, then hold out my hand and help her out.

She looks around, but I quickly cover her eyes. "Hold on, no peeking."

Ivy giggles as I lead her to the back of the truck.

"Can I look now?"

"Yep." I remove my hands and press my body to hers as I wait for her reaction.

"Oh my gosh, Kane..." She turns and looks at me in awe. "I can't believe you did this."

"Do you like it?"

She spins and wraps her arms around my waist, gazing up at me. "I love it."

I bring my mouth to hers, tasting her warm lips, and smiling. "Good. I wanted it to be perfect."

"Is it pathetic that I'm nineteen and only now experiencing a date?"

"Hell no. You were just waitin' for me," I quip, squeezing her tighter.

"Did you read one of my romance novels? This is totally something a swoony hero would do."

"Nope." I chuckle. "Just the smutty *Beauty and the Beast* one you're reading to me."

Ivy eagerly removes her cowboy boots, and I help her up onto the mattress. Then I present tonight's dinner.

"Grandma Bishop is a queen in the kitchen," she hums as she looks at the spread.

I pour two glasses of the cider, then sit next to her on top of the blankets.

Once our food is plated and we dig in, Ivy stares at the crackling fire and night sky.

"It's crystal clear out here. You can see a thousand stars. No wonder y'all love it here so much."

"It's one of the reasons I couldn't see myself living anywhere else," I say honestly. "What about you? Do you see yourself wanting to stay livin' in town?"

"If I had a choice..." She grins as she glances at me. "I'd pick ranch life, hands down."

My smile widens at her admission. There's nothing I'd love more than having Ivy live with me someday. Of course, when we're further into our relationship and no longer hiding it.

"That barbecue was top-notch," Ivy says once we finished our sandwiches. "Even the coleslaw was somehow better than I've ever had."

Chuckling, I nod, then place our empty plates in the basket. We decide to wait on dessert until our dinner has settled.

"She's a master and will teach anyone who wants to learn."

"Must be why Maize is so skilled. Runs in the family."

"Oh yeah, and she'll probably pass it onto her kids, and then their kids, and so on. The tradition will never die."

"Are you hoping to have kids someday?" she asks as we settle underneath the light blankets.

I wrap my arm around her as our heads hit the pillows. "Yeah, I'd love some rug rats to raise on the ranch. I'd teach them about the generations of Bishops that paved the way for us and this lifestyle. You?"

"Oh yeah, I've always wanted a big family because it was just my mom and me once Hadleigh left. I always thought it'd be fun to have siblings around my age, basically a built-in best friend."

"Trust me, close in age doesn't mean you're gonna like 'em," I taunt, referring to Knox and me. "But it's pretty cool having someone to pick on."

Ivy chuckles, snuggling in and wrapping her arm over my stomach.

"You and Hads were always close, though, right?"

"Yeah, but she was sometimes more like a mother figure than a sister. I love her to death, but she's overprotective and was always in a different part of her life than me."

"I can understand that. Sounds like my siblings and me with our cousins. We're the three youngest, and even by the time Knox and Hadleigh got married, the others had several babies and a few wedding anniversaries before then. Riley graduated high school when I was in seventh grade, and he got married when I was eighteen. I was nowhere near that milestone."

"But you're close to some of your other cousins, aren't you?"

"Kinda. I grew up mostly hanging out with Knox and Ethan. The three of us got into so much trouble, though."

"I don't doubt that for a second."

"And of course, we had to tease Kaitlyn as much as possible. Baby of the family and the youngest grandkid. Now she's havin' some kind of life crisis because she's gettin' older."

Ivy snickers, lowering her hand to my cock. "Mm-hmm."

I blink over at her, grabbing her wrist. "You're not even listenin', are you?"

"Sure I am, just multitasking. I can give you a hand job and hear you at the same time."

"Jesus Christ, woman." I roll over, pinning her beneath me and pressing my hips into hers so she feels how hard I am already. "I'm the one who owes you. Spread your legs for me."

She obeys, and I push off the covers before sinking between her thighs. As I slide her dress up, I kiss along her smooth skin.

"Fuck, I can smell your arousal already."

"I'm so wet," she breathes out.

"Want me to taste this sweet pussy of yours?"

"God, yes."

I hook my hands around her thighs, dragging her closer as her legs settle around my shoulders. Her panties are still in place, but I plan to tease her over them first.

"Kane..." She drawls out a long moan as soon as I add pressure to her clit with my lips.

I feather kisses along the outside of her underwear, taunting her until she hisses with frustration.

"Please, I need *more*."

Smirking against her bare flesh, I lap up her slit and suck.

"You want my fingers and tongue inside you, baby?"

"Yes. *Now*."

Without hesitation, I sit up briefly and remove her panties. Then she tells me to take off her dress.

As soon as I do, I'm greeted with the sexiest view I've ever laid eyes on. Ivy in a lacy black bra with hard nipples begging for attention.

"Fuck..." I shake my head. "How am I goin' to resist you lookin' like this?"

"You can't," she quips. "And I don't want you to."

My mouth finds its way back between her thighs, and I give her everything I can. She moans and gasps for air as I finger-fuck her tight cunt and suck on her swollen clit. Everything about her drives me insane, and there's no way I can stop now, not when she's giving me every sign she wants us to move to the next level.

"I'm so close, oh my God. Yes, right there..." Her hips buck wildly as I devour her. My hands hold her steady before the violent buildup pours over.

Moments later, Ivy throws her head back and screams as the orgasm rips through her. Sweet juices coat my mouth and chin, and I can't get enough.

"That...was so intense." Her body relaxes, and I lie next to her, cupping her face.

"Nothing is sexier than you coming all over my tongue." I capture her lips so she can taste herself, then add, "You taste like mine, Ivy. So goddamn good."

"I love the sound of that," she purrs.

My palm finds her breast, carefully massaging it before I pinch the nipple between my finger and thumb. "Did you wear this sexy little piece for me?"

"Yes, but only because I was hoping you'd be takin' it off."

"You know we don't have to rush," I remind her. The way she lets me touch her perfect body is more than enough.

"I want all of you," she whispers, almost as if she's too embarrassed to say it.

Fuck me.

Our foreheads press together as I breathe deeply. "You've got me, baby. Every ounce of me is yours."

"Do you want me?"

I pull back, gazing into her deep brown eyes. "Of course, I do. I can barely take my hands off you," I say, caressing her other breast and squeezing.

"Then be my first...please. I don't want to wait any longer when I already know you're the man I want."

Without another word, I slam my mouth down on hers, sliding my tongue between her eager lips and breathing heavily.

"I don't wanna hurt you, but I know it will."

"I'll be okay," she reassures me. "If there's anyone I trust to make it special and be gentle, it's you. It's always been you."

Her confession has my heart slamming into my chest, and I can barely hold it together. There's nothing more in the world I want right now than to give her exactly what she wants.

"Christ, you give me too much credit, baby."

"Or you just don't give yourself enough."

My dick is hard as fuck, pressing against her nearly naked body.

"You sure you want to do this out here?" I ask.

"Absolutely. Whether I'm on top or bottom, I'll be seeing stars."

"Jesus fuck," I choke-laugh. *She's killing me.*

"Teach me what to do," she pleads.

"Touch me. Take my cock out and get it wet."

I lie back as Ivy takes control, undoing my jeans and lowering my boxers. Lifting my hips, I help her remove them completely along with my boots. Then I take off my shirt so I'm completely bare.

"Sweet Jesus, you should be on a romance book cover."

"Stop droolin', woman," I taunt as she crawls over me.

"I can't help it. You're tall, inked, pierced, and *older*. I'm surprised I've only had to witness one woman hangin' all over you."

I laugh at the memory. She doesn't know Andrea was only there to spy on Rhett, but it's neither here nor there.

All that matters is Ivy and giving her exactly what she needs.

CHAPTER NINETEEN

IVY

"Put your mouth on me and suck," Kane demands.

My heart races a thousand beats per minute because I'm finally going to lose my pesky V-card. I'm giving myself to the only guy I've ever wanted. And that's surreal.

But I'm ready. More than ready to have sex with Kane Bishop.

I position myself and grip his shaft, then bob up and down his thick length. His piercings clank against my teeth as I increase my pace.

"Shit, baby. Slow down."

I moan around his dick, shaking my head. I want him as worked up as I am.

He chuckles darkly. "Be a good girl, and I'll reward you like one."

Peeking up at him, I grin. I smack his cock against my tongue before lapping around the tip.

"Get up here," he orders. "Bra off."

I quickly unhook it, and my breasts fall in his palms. Dipping his tongue between them, he cups both in his hands.

"I've envisioned your tits bouncing in my face as I bury myself deep inside your cunt. Ivy, you're makin' me crazy." His gravelly admission sets my body on fire. The way he craves and touches me makes it impossible to hold back.

Grinding on top of him, I feel his erection sliding between my pussy folds. It would only take a little maneuvering for him to be inside me.

"Shit, that feels too goddamn good," he groans, then smacks my ass cheek. "Sit up a little so I can reach between us."

I do as he says and watch him palm his shaft. As he glides it through my wetness, I suddenly worry how it will feel with his piercings.

"It's important you stay relaxed, okay? Once I'm inside, control the pace to whatever you can take," he explains. "Got it?"

I nod, leaning forward against his chest and giving him more access to thrust in. Concentrating, I try to calm myself when I feel the intrusion.

"Deep breath," he whispers.

His free hand grabs my hip, guiding me down on him.

"You're doing so good, sweet girl. So goddamn tight, it feels amazin' already."

His praises make me so wet that I nearly take all of his cock.

"Ahh," I groan at the foreign feeling of being so full. A mixture of pain and pleasure.

"Widen your legs and relax, baby."

As soon as I do, he slams inside me. "Fuck, are you okay?"

"Yeah, it hurts a little but not as bad as I anticipated," I admit.

"Okay, good. Put your hands on my chest and move when you're ready."

Kane grips my thighs as he patiently waits. When I finally slide up and down his length a few times, the painful sensation disappears.

"It feels..." I can't even finish my sentence. Kane's thumb rubs over my clit, and my head falls back.

"Eyes on me, baby."

I obey, though it's a struggle with the sensations powering through me.

"Tell me how it feels," he says softly.

"Intense. But so good, like I can't get enough, even if it's too much," I admit, increasing my pace.

He nods, adding pressure to my core. "Bounce a little so I can hit your G-spot."

I blink hard, not sure I can take any more. My heart's already beating out of control, and every nerve in my body is blazing hot.

As soon as I do, he captures one of my breasts and pulls it into his mouth. While I focus on keeping a rhythm, he teases my nipple with his tongue. The tightness is so overwhelming that it won't take long before my body succumbs.

"Kane," I drawl out on a long ragged moan.

"Your clit is so needy. Ready to come all over my cock?"

Those words shoot waves of ecstasy down my spine as he slowly circles my clit. Just the right amount of pressure to push me over the edge.

"Oh my God..." I throw my head back as my pussy clenches.

And then an eruption like I've never felt before explodes throughout my body.

I open my mouth to scream, moan, or *something*—but nothing comes out. Every part of me shakes with aftershocks.

Kane releases a guttural groan as my pussy soaks his cock. "Fuck, baby. You comin' all over me is makin' me lose my goddamn mind."

He sits up and slams his mouth on mine. "Lie on the bed."

As soon as I do, he settles between my thighs and laps up my release. With every swipe of his tongue, my body begs for more.

"You want me back inside your tight cunt?" he asks, kissing up my stomach and between my breasts.

"Yes. God, yes..."

Slow and steady, he kneels between my legs and thrusts in. This position feels so good, and it only takes me a few seconds to adjust. My thighs wrap around his waist as he buries his face in my neck.

Each time he slams harder, Kane causes a ricochet of emotions to pour through me. His sweet whispers echo in my ear.

"You were made for me."

"So goddamn perfect."

"You make me so fuckin' crazy."

His final words—*"I'm fallin' so hard for you, Ivy"*—have my pussy tightening, and we fall apart together. Kane bites my shoulder as he releases a long, breathless moan.

By the time we come down from our highs, I'm completely spent. Every inch of me is jelly.

Kane leans up on his elbows while still inside me and brushes my wild hair out of my face. "I'm afraid you'll be really sore tomorrow."

I nod with a grin, still trying to slow my racing heart. "It'll be worth it."

He grins, cupping my face and sliding his lips across mine. "You're amazing, baby. I hope you know that."

I kiss him back with as much fire as I can. Our connection was strong before, but now it's forever changed.

In the best way possible.

After Kane helped me clean up, I was surprised to see that I barely bled. I've read about first-time expectations and thought I'd be embarrassed about it, but he was so sweet and tender. He had extra towels in the back seat and made sure I was clean and dry. We lay in the bed for an hour, and when the fire died down, he drove us to his house.

"I know you've told me you're on birth control, but we probably should've talked about using condoms," he confesses while we rinse off in the shower. "If you want me to use them, I will. I kinda got lost in the moment."

Smiling up at him, I shrug. "You weren't the only one."

He lightly grabs my chin, brushing his lips over mine. "Not that I wouldn't love to see you pregnant with my baby, but I want us to be careful until we're ready for that. Hads would kill me if I knocked up her sister before she knew we were dating."

I chuckle because he's right. Hadleigh would lose her shit.

"I never miss a pill. If I do, my cycles get irregular and even more painful than what they are now. I've been taking them consistently since I was fifteen, so my uterus has stronger security than Alcatraz."

He snorts. "Good to know."

Once we've showered and dried off, Kane brings me two pain pills and some water. Then he holds me as I relive the best night of my life.

"Did your stomach just *growl*?" he whispers in my ear.

I giggle, wishing he hadn't heard that. "I guess I worked up an appetite."

"Well, shit. We totally forgot about dessert."

I spin around in his arms. "What was it?"

"Cannoli with extra chocolate chips."

My mouth drools. "That sounds *soooo* good right now."

He flashes me a devious smirk. "Stay here. Be right back."

Before I can say another word, Kane jumps out of bed in only his boxers and returns a few minutes later with a plate.

I sit up and lean against the headboard, salivating at the delicious treats.

"Ready?" He brings one close, and I open wide. As soon as I taste the chocolates and cream, I'm a goner.

"Ohmagah," I say around a mouthful.

Kane takes a bite and moans.

"That is seriously the best I've ever had," I say once I've swallowed. "I swear, Grandma Bishop's secret ingredient is crack. I'm already addicted."

I open my mouth for more, but Kane pulls back. "I have a better idea. Take off your shirt."

He means *his* shirt, really. Even though I packed an overnight bag, he offered me one of his. After the shower, I didn't bother putting on my bra either, so once I remove it, I'm completely bare sans my underwear.

"Beautiful. Now lie back."

I adjust myself on the bed, and once I'm settled, Kane swipes a finger through the cream, then rubs it over my nipple. My breathing grows shallow as I watch him do the same to the other nipple. Then he puts more cream right above my clit.

"Open up," he tells me.

Once I do, he lets me taste his finger.

Kane takes his sweet time licking the dessert off my body. Carefully, he teases and caresses his tongue over my skin, getting me hot and bothered with every slow swipe. He flicks my clit once I'm licked clean, then gives me another earth-shattering orgasm.

"Your turn," I tell him, taking the other cannoli. "Too bad the cannoli shell can't fit around your cock. It'd be a cockoli."

"Uhh...I'm not sure whether to be aroused or hungry."

I burst out laughing, feeling so damn comfortable around him. "Well, clearly both. You just ate off my body while having an erection."

He lies down on the bed, and I remove his boxers, then straddle him. "Impossible not to be when my beautiful girlfriend is naked on top of me. Hell, this sight alone will keep me hard until I'm dead."

Butterflies surface at how he looks at me like I'm his world.

I put a good amount of cream on my finger and place some on his mouth before diving in and tasting him. Then I lower down his body and rub the rest on his cock, then suck and lick it off.

"Fuck," he hisses as our gazes lock. "You do that so good, my sweet girl."

I work him between my hand and mouth until he's shooting his release. Warm and sticky, I don't swallow and wait for his next order.

"Spit it in my mouth, baby. Then kiss me."

I eagerly move toward him, and he hauls me closer until I'm pressed to his chest. He parts his lips, and I slowly let it fall into his mouth. Once he has it all, he kisses me hard.

It shouldn't be as hot as it is, but it turns me the fuck on. Everything about Kane does, even the weird shit, but I like it.

Kane isn't afraid to be himself around me, and it makes me feel like I can be my true self around him too.

"Hands down, *best* dessert."

I chuckle. "Agreed. Remind me to thank your grandmother."

"Ha! Do *not* do that. She already asked who I'm seeing, and when I wouldn't say, she made me promise to tell her first before we go public."

We get back into position, my shirt and his boxers still off. It's late, and we're exhausted, so we agree it's time to call it a night. He lifts the covers over us, then holds me tight to his chest.

Just as I'm drifting off, I hear him whisper, *"I've fallen so hard for you, sweet girl."*

I fall asleep with a full heart and the biggest smile on my face.

CHAPTER TWENTY

KANE

I peel my eyes open and see it's after nine in the morning. It's the latest I've slept in a long time, but I can't find the strength to crawl out of bed. Not when Ivy's wrapped so tightly in my arms.

"Good mornin'..." I whisper in her ear, my cock greeting the small of her back.

"Are you always this excited this early?" she asks in a sleepy haze.

I chuckle against her neck as I press a kiss there. "Only when I've had naughty dreams about you or wake up with your naked body pressed to mine."

"Hmm...lucky me then." She rolls over, but when I lean down to kiss her, she covers her mouth. "Morning breath."

I swat her hand away and slam my lips to hers, then swipe my tongue between them. "I let you snowball my come, and you think I give a shit about bad breath?"

She blushes. "*Jesus*. I guess not. But still, I'll be right back..."

Ivy puts on my T-shirt, then makes her way out of my room. I pull on my boxers, then piss in the other bathroom before walking to the other one.

I knock on the door. "Can I come in, or are you hiding your

naked body from me that I've already seen all of and licked dessert off?"

"Yes, smart-ass," she shouts from the inside.

I smirk as I walk in. "How are you feelin'?"

"I actually don't feel that bad. A little achy, but nothing compared to when I have my period, so I won't complain."

Wrapping my arm around her shoulder, I kiss her forehead. "Last night was really special for me, just so you know."

She smiles up at me, her bedhead a wild mess but looking sexy as hell. "I don't think I've ever felt this happy before, and that scares me a little, but I trust you and this."

My heart hammers as I gaze into her eyes. The words are on the tip of my tongue, but I hold back.

"I'd rather let Knox punch me in the face a hundred times than hurt you." I smile, placing a soft kiss on her lips. "I'm in this for the long haul. No matter what."

"Good to hear that because Hadleigh texted and invited me over to see Hendrix. Then we're supposed to meet everyone for Sunday brunch at the B&B. But after, I was thinking maybe I'd talk to Hadleigh and tell her the truth."

My brows pop up. "Yeah? You're ready?"

She nods happily. "I am. Sneaking around has been pretty hot, but it's getting harder to contain my constant state of happiness. And I *cannot* suffer through another blind date."

"Fuck that. Me neither. Alright, we'll tell her after lunch, together."

She wraps her arms around me, and I pull her closer. "You have time to take a shower before you go?"

Narrowing her eyes, she says, "A regular shower or a sexy shower?"

"Do you even have to ask?" The corner of my lip tilts up.

Contemplating it for all of three seconds, she agrees. "If I'm late, I'll blame traffic."

I snort-laugh. "Yeah, tractor back up on Highway 2129."

She playfully smacks me.

We step into the shower, and I let her soap up and wash her hair first, but once she's done, I pin her to the wall and capture her mouth.

"There's one thing I didn't get to do to you last night," I taunt, pulling her bottom lip between my teeth.

"What's that?"

"Teach you the proper form of edging."

Her eyes widen as water pours down my back. "In the shower? I will fall and bust my ass."

"I would *never* let that happen." My hand slides down between her thighs, and she parts them. "Unless you're too sore."

"No."

"Then tell me to touch you, sweet girl. Tell me you want my fingers inside you."

"Mmm, yes."

My thumb brushes over her clit. "Say it, Ivy. I wanna hear the words."

"Touch me, *please*."

Grinning, I carefully thrust a finger between her folds and feel her tighten around me.

"Fuck, that's super sensitive today."

"If it's too painful, you tell me."

"No, it's okay. Keep goin'," she urges.

I add a second finger as I brush over her sensitive bud. Feeling how wet she is, I know it won't take much to build her up.

"This time, there's one rule."

"What's that?"

"You don't come until I let you. Got it?"

"That might be hard." Her head falls back slightly as she hums. "But okay."

I hold back a chuckle because she's in for a ride.

Twisting my wrist, I slide into her deeper, just barely pushing her to the edge, over and over. I add pressure to her clit, and when her legs shake, I slow down.

"Oh my God, this is torture. I was so close."

"Trust me. It's gonna be fuckin' amazing once you do."

"I can barely stay on my feet," she pouts, breathing hard as the hot steam surrounds us.

"How badly do you wanna come, sweetheart?"

"I *need* it," she pleads.

Sinking deep inside, I finger-fuck her fast and hard. She clasps a hand around my arm, squeezing tight as I relentlessly bring her closer to her release. Just before she starts to fall apart, I pull my fingers out.

"You *asshole!*" she screams. "Move. I'll do it myself."

Laughing at her frustration, I grab her arms and pin them behind her. "Patience."

"I'm all out."

Holding back my amusement, I nudge her feet farther apart. "I wanna taste you when you come, baby. On my face."

She's unsteady as I kneel between her thighs.

"You better not be teasin' me again, or I swear to God, I'll—"

I swipe my tongue up her slit and capture her clit before she can continue scolding me. She uses my shoulders for balance as she moans out in pleasure. Spreading her pussy wider, I sink two fingers deep in her cunt while I lap her sensitive bud. Considering she's so worked up already, it only takes minutes for her legs to tremble before she's releasing on my tongue.

Tapping her hip to get her attention, she looks down at me, and I motion for her to kiss me. She bends over and tastes herself on my lips.

I stand, brushing wet strands of hair off her cheeks. "Fuck, that was hot. Your body was made for me."

"There's no way Hads isn't going to see the words *I had sex* written all over my face."

I snort-laugh. "Just picture Knox naked, and then you'll have a disgusted look instead."

"Ew. Oh my God, you're horrible."

I shrug with a chuckle. "We should get dressed. I'll take you home to get your car, then I'll stop by the barn before I meet y'all there. Gotta find a way to get my own *I had sex* look off my face."

The moment I drop Ivy off at her house, I immediately miss her. I'm anxious as hell that we're going to tell her sister today. Once it's out there, then everyone will know. Literally, *everyone* in Eldorado will know before dawn.

But I couldn't give two shits. Ivy Callaway is mine, and I want the world to know.

Some people might have issues with our age difference, but all that matters is that it works for us. I love listening to her read to me and teaching her things. What we have is special, and I won't let anyone's opinions change that.

I'm sure my parents will have some thoughts about it, but they're supportive, so I'm not worried. Ivy's mom already approves—well, as long as I don't hurt her, which I never plan to. Grandma will be excited that it's another opportunity for her to get more great-grandkids.

That just leaves Hadleigh and the rest of my family.

As soon as I'm done checking on things at the barn, I head over to the B&B and see the parking lot is full. Ivy's car is here, which means Hadleigh and Knox are too.

I remind myself not to make it obvious that Ivy and I are together.

When I enter, I spot Grandma and Grandpa with my parents. The majority of my cousins and aunts and uncles are all here too.

"Hey," I greet my dad. He pulls me in for a side hug.

"Hey, son. Stayin' out of trouble?"

"Yeah, right," Kaitlyn intervenes with a plateful of food. "Trouble's his middle name."

I stick my finger in her mashed potatoes and scoop some into my mouth.

"Ew, you're nasty. Who knows where your fingers have been."

In Ivy's cunt.

Holding back a laugh, I scowl at her. "Payback, little sister."

She rolls her eyes. "Whatever."

I get in line and chat with Payton. As soon as my plate's overfilled, I look around for Ivy and find her sitting next to Hadleigh and Kaitlyn. There's an open seat adjacent to her, so I take it and try my best not to look at her.

"Forgot to ask, has Rhett texted you since your date the other night?" I overhear Hadleigh ask.

Son of a bitch. Of course she wouldn't drop that.

"Umm, no. I think we're better as just friends," Ivy explains.

"Well, there's another guy I can set you up with. He just moved to Eldorado and works at the feed mill."

"Did you say, new guy? How old?" Kaitlyn interrupts, causing a roar of laughter from everyone at the table.

"Calm down. He's like twenty-two."

"Dammit. All these single *boys* and no available men," Kaitlyn groans, then looks at Ivy. "No offense. Perfect age for you, though."

Ivy looks less than thrilled. "Yeah, I'm good. Actually, Hads, I wanted to talk to you later in private about something."

"About—"

"Oh my God! Baby!"

Everyone's heads snap up at the squealing sound of *Raelyn*.

I blink hard, confused as fuck as to what's going on.

She rushes over, weaving between the standing people. "There you are!"

I'm in such shock, I can hardly breathe as she wraps her arms around me and welcomes herself to my lap.

"Did you miss me?" She plants a kiss on my lips before I can avoid it.

Miss her?

I completely forgot she existed.

"Raelyn, what are you doin' here?" I ask, trying to move her off me.

I shift my eyes to Ivy, who's *pissed*.

"Raelyn," Hadleigh sing-songs. "I thought you two broke up?"

Thank God. Bestie to the rescue.

"What? No way! We were just on a short break while I dealt with my busy work schedule and caught up with some old friends. Right, baby?"

Fuck no.

"Umm...I think we should talk in private," I tell her quietly so no one overhears. The last thing I want is to make a scene, and if I tell Raelyn that we aren't together, she'll blow up in the middle of the B&B. My parents and uncle John would kill me if that happened in front of the guests.

"Sure, babe. I brought a bag so we can spend *all* night catching up," she says loud enough for everyone to hear.

I get to my feet so she's forced to get off me. Ivy's jaw is tight as she avoids my gaze. I hope she knows this is a misunderstanding. If she wants to come clean about our relationship right now, I'd do it. But since I can't read her, I keep quiet.

Ivy pushes back to stand and takes her half-full plate with her. "Hads, I gotta run."

"What? But I thought you wanted to talk later?"

"Um, I know. I just remembered I told Mom I'd be home to help with laundry and chores. We can catch up tomorrow."

"I'm gonna grab some food," Raelyn tells me, capturing my hand. "Come with me."

Fuck. How am I gonna get out of this so I can catch Ivy before she leaves? No matter what I do, Raelyn will make a scene, and chasing after Ivy will be too suspicious. Now I'm not sure if Ivy will want to tell everyone, so running after her might be the last thing she wants.

I watch over my shoulder as Ivy hugs Hadleigh goodbye and pleads for her to look at me. She doesn't. Instead, she keeps her face down as if she's trying to hold back tears.

Shit.

As soon as she's out the door, I pull out my phone to text her.

Kane: Please meet me at my house. Raelyn and I are NOT together. I don't know what she's doing here, but I'm going to clear everything up as soon as we're out of the B&B.

I sit with Raelyn as she eats and talks nonstop. I don't know how she's even chewing her food with the amount of talking she's doing. In between, I check for a response from Ivy, but it doesn't come.

"Raelyn, we need to talk," I tell her as soon as her plate's empty.

"Okay, I'll follow you to your house. We have so much catching up to do!" she says giddily. I'm pissed she expects us to start where we left off when she wanted to *take a break* to screw other guys.

As soon as I pull into my driveway, I hoped to see Ivy's car in her hiding spot, but it's not there. She must've really gone home. Just to be sure she got my last message, I text her again.

Kane: Baby, let me know you got this. I promise it's not what it looks like.

Raelyn meets me at my front door, and as soon as I let her in, she notices some of Ivy's things on the coffee table.

"I guess you *enjoyed* our little break too," she says smugly.

The fucking nerve.

"Actually..." I slam the door shut, then decide I'm gonna need a drink for this.

I go to the kitchen and pull down the bottle of vodka.

If I'm gonna deal with my ex, I can't do it sober.

CHAPTER TWENTY-ONE

IVY

I'm a fucking idiot and still so angry about what happened at the B&B yesterday. My mother noticed my mood shift as soon as I got up this morning. She made some light comments about it, but I explained I wasn't feeling the best, and she dropped it.

It's not a lie, though. I slept like total shit and couldn't stop thinking about Raelyn sitting on Kane's lap. As soon as I walked out of the B&B, I blocked his number. I didn't want to hear his "excuses" after Raelyn admitted they never actually broke up. He's been my best-kept secret for weeks—hell years, if you count the time I've crushed on him—and now what we had will have to stay buried. Along with my broken heart. The day after I give myself to him, his girlfriend returns to town to claim her man. Of fucking course.

Seeing her hang all over him made me so sick to my stomach that if I hadn't left, I'd have lost my lunch right then. I've never felt pain like this, but I've also never lost someone I cared this much about. I stupidly believed every word he said like a naïve teenager. As soon as Raelyn was over their "break," she burst back into his life, and he let her.

My life isn't a romance novel, even if it felt like one at times.

Kane had me fooled. Like my mother always said—play stupid games, win stupid prizes. In the end, I lost, and while it's dramatic, I don't know how I'll ever look at another man again.

I saw how Raelyn acted toward him. I heard what she said, and right now, I need time to think before I can face him.

Before I head to work, I make a cup of coffee. I'm running on little to no sleep, but calling in won't help. Today, I need a distraction. After I change clothes, I grab my keys, then leave. I dreadfully drive toward the ranch and take a quick detour on the way to the warehouse. When I pass Kane's house, I spot a car in his driveway, and my stomach drops.

Adrenaline rushes through me when I think about Raelyn staying overnight. Was she in his bed, the same bed I'd kept warm the night before? I grab the steering wheel tighter and press on the gas.

When I arrive at the shop, I grab my earbuds, needing to get lost in a book, one without a romantic subplot. Harper gives me a grin, and I force a smile when she tells me good morning. After she goes over everything that needs to be completed, she searches my face.

"You okay?" she asks.

"Sorry, I'm just in a bad mood," I admit, and she doesn't push me any further.

"If you need anything, let me know," she states, and we go our separate ways, trying to get as many things marked off our task lists as possible. Right now, we're working on the fall scents, a reminder that the seasons will be changing in a few months—just like my life.

The morning passes in a blink, and eventually, Harper speaks up. "I'm gonna leave for lunch. Want me to grab you something?"

I give her a small smile. "Nah, I'm fine. Thanks, though."

"Okay." I can tell she wants to add something more but doesn't. I turn my book back on and continue mixing the vanilla pumpkin cheesecake soap. After ten minutes, it's ready to be poured into the mold. Once they're in the fridge cooling, I pull the ingredients card for the next one. As I'm grabbing the essential oils from a shelf, the door swings open.

Thinking it's Harper, I turn around to ask her why she's back so soon, only to be faced with piercing blue eyes.

"What're you doin' here?" I ask dryly, continuing to line up the items I need.

Kane doesn't deserve an ounce of my attention.

"I've been callin' and textin' you for the past twelve hours. Why aren't you responding?"

I shrug. "I blocked your number. Didn't think it'd be appropriate since you have a girlfriend and all."

He crosses his arms and glares at me. "Stop it, Ivy. We need to talk."

"Kinda like how you and Raelyn *talked* all night long?" I grow more frustrated with every passing second, but I keep my voice steady so he can't see how upset I am.

He blows out a breath filled with annoyance. "Yes, Raelyn and I did talk yesterday, but I needed a drink or two just to get through it. So as we drank, I laid everything out for her so she'd understand where our relationship really stood. Anyway, after our chat, she was too upset and a little tipsy to drive home, so I offered her the couch. *Nothing* happened between us."

I scoff, focusing on my work. "You're single. You can do whatever you want." Even though we've been calling each other boyfriend and girlfriend, I say the words anyway. Single—that's what we both are. It's a low blow, but I want him to understand how I feel.

Instead of addressing what I said, he ignores it and continues. "I did *not* want her to stay, but I wouldn't have been able to live with myself if she drove intoxicated and then something happened to her."

"Pulling out the sympathy card, I see. Good one."

"Why aren't you listenin' to what I'm saying? I'm tellin' you the truth."

I slam the essential oils down on the counter. "I watched her nearly straddle your lap in front of everyone, Kane. *Everyone.* Do you have any idea how humiliated I was? How mad I was when I realized you had lied about your relationship with her? It made me feel used, like everything between us was fake. I'd just given you my virginity!"

"Ivy, I didn't lie, and I'd never hurt you like that. You should know me better than that. I'm not some dickhead who hooks up with random women, and I'm not a cheater. Raelyn and I aren't together, and I don't want anything to do with her. It's been over for *weeks.*"

"And so now I'm just supposed to believe that after what I saw ?"

"Yes, because you should trust me. I had no idea she'd randomly show up like that. We haven't talked since we agreed on a break so she could fuck other people. A break to me meant it was over because I wasn't takin' her back."

"If it was over for you, why didn't you say that in front of your family so it wasn't a secret?"

I watch him carefully as he takes a second to contemplate my question. "Besides not wanting to make a scene, I was in a state of shock. To have her act like nothing had happened was jarring. I explained as much to her as well, so it's crystal clear where we stand."

"And she's okay with y'all not getting back together?"

"She was disappointed, but she had to accept it. I told her there was someone else in my life. I only want you, Ivy. No one else."

My heart flutters with anticipation even though I'm still annoyed about the whole situation. "You mean that?"

"Yes, of course. I'll do whatever I need to do to prove it to you."

"I appreciate that. I was just really blindsided. You might not think it's a big deal, but it is to me. I've never felt this way before about anyone and never been thrown into a situation like that. I've read too many books where the heroine just automatically takes the hero back after a misstep. But I think I need to work through some of these feelings and make sure I'm not rushing into a serious relationship because of a lifelong crush. It was a lot for me to deal with, and it put me in a really dark place. It was a wake-up call in a way. We've moved fast, and maybe it'll be good for me to take a step back and process my emotions."

I meet his eyes, and his expression softens.

"I'll give you as much time as you need, but I'm not giving up on you. And I'm not too big of a man to apologize, Ivy. I'm sorry that I've upset you. I never wanted any of this to happen."

"Thank you," I whisper as a whirlwind of emotions swirls through me. Kane gives me a small smile, then leaves.

The next day at work goes as planned, and when Harper asks me if I want her to bring me back some food, I decline again. Instead, I eat a sandwich and prep through my break. Right now, I need to talk to someone, but no one knows what's going on other than Kane and me.

After my shift, I visit Hadleigh and my nephew. Thankfully, Knox is working late, and we can talk in private.

As soon as I sit on the couch, my sister hands me Hendrix.

"There's my favorite nephew," I tell him, placing kisses on his chubby cheeks. "You're gettin' heavy."

Hadleigh laughs. "He is. I feel like he's growing up so fast."

"Pretty soon, he'll be driving," I joke, and she scowls.

"So what did you want to chat about the other day?" she finally asks.

"Well, there's a guy I've been crushing on, and I thought things were going a certain way, but then something derailed it."

Hadleigh nods as she studies my face. I honestly find it hard to meet her eyes, so I bring all of my focus to Hendrix.

"He ended up hurting my feelings by not telling me the full truth about something, not intentionally, but it still didn't feel good. And I dunno what to do because I still really like him and was looking forward to seeing where things would go. But I'm new to this whole dating thing, and I guess I'm scared of getting my heart broken. And I know that's part of the risk when dating someone—"

"Ivy. I know you're talking about Kane."

Blood rushes from my face, and my heart thumps so hard in my chest that it might actually explode. I'm waiting for my sister to rip me a new asshole, but instead, she smiles.

"Trust me, I'm really freakin' pissed that y'all decided to sneak around behind our backs instead of just being open about it, but I can understand why you might've felt the need to. Regardless, Kane's a good guy. He's sweet, caring, and very compassionate. Plus, I know for a goddamn fact, he'd never do anything to hurt you. It's obvious just by the way he looks at you."

My mouth falls open. "Wait, how'd you…?"

"Raelyn texted me that they were taking a break. Then I saw the signs that something was up between you two. The timing of your period right after he asked for supplies, you wearing the same clothes two days in a row, y'all being stupidly happy all of a sudden while trying to act indifferent around each other, your car being at the B&B after Fourth of July. Mom telling me you stayed on his couch."

I gasp. "She didn't!"

"Then the blind date was the cherry on top. He was acting more like a jealous lover than an overprotective big brother. But that's why I trusted him to take you home."

"Yeah, we didn't exactly go home." My cheeks heat.

Hadleigh lifts a brow. "Figures. Then after Raelyn showed up and you left the B&B upset, it was the nail in the coffin. I was honestly waiting for you two to come clean a few weeks ago, but you were way too persistent and stubborn, thinking y'all were being sneaky. You do realize I'm your sister and his best friend and know you two better than anyone else. It was painfully obvious once I started noticing. Knox and I tried to sneak around for a while, too."

Guilt creeps up my spine, and my neck burns red. "I'm sorry for not telling you, but I didn't know what you would say or if you'd approve. Before everyone chimed in with their opinions, we wanted to make sure what we had was more than a fling. Then another part of me didn't want to hear anyone's concerns over the age difference or be bombarded about getting hitched and knocked up right away. We were actually gonna tell you after brunch, but that got completely derailed once Raelyn showed up."

She snickers. "I know that feelin'. But if the age gap doesn't bother you two, then who cares what anyone else thinks? They can either support you or shut their mouths about it."

I smile, appreciating how she easily makes me feel better. "So who else knows?"

"Harper." She chuckles. "We shared our theories. Y'all aren't as transparent as you might've thought."

"I guess not," I say.

"If Kane is tellin' ya they were broken up, then they were. I would never question him because he's not a liar. Also, if he said he has feelings for you, believe him. When it comes to Raelyn, trust me when I say you have *nothing* to worry about. Kane's the most loyal man you'll ever meet."

I hold Hendrix just a little bit tighter while I take in every word.

"Well, now I feel stupid for overreacting. I blocked him, then told him I needed space."

"Don't. Mom always told us that we needed to protect our hearts, and that's all you were doing. It's okay to be scared, Ivy. I know you're new to this, but don't push him away because you're afraid."

I nod, wishing I could go back and do things differently.

"I never had these problems when I was exclusive to my book boyfriends," I tease, and she laughs.

"You two could be perfect together, but you have to open your heart and take a risk. But don't get me wrong. If he hurts you in any way, I will take great satisfaction in chopping off his balls and serving them to him on a platter covered in his own blood."

This has me laughing and cringing. "Thank you."

"So tell me…did you two, *you know*?" She waggles her brows.

"Hads!" Color returns to my cheeks as I smile. I don't have to tell her because my face gives me away every time.

CHAPTER TWENTY-TWO

IVY

It's been a few days since I talked with Hadleigh and even longer since I talked to Kane. He promised to give me space to think, but truthfully, I miss him like crazy. I know he's who I want, and I trust his intentions weren't to deceive me. Raelyn showing up at the B&B was a total mindfuck, and I let my insecurities win. But I can't lose him over this.

As soon as I'm done with work, I'm going to his house and tell him exactly how much I want him.

"You've been a machine today," Harper says as I clean up at the end of our shift. "You were so focused, I was scared to even speak."

I chuckle. "Sorry, a lot on my mind."

"Yeah, Hadleigh told me. Hope that's okay."

Nodding, I toss any excess trash off the table, then wipe it down. "It's fine. I figured she would."

"Soooo...can I be nosy and ask for an update?"

"We haven't talked yet." I shrug. "But I already decided I was gonna try to see him tonight. Hopefully, he won't slam the door in my face."

She shakes her head with force. "No way. Kane would never. Well, he'd probably make an exception for his brother, but definitely not you."

Laughing, I nod. "Let's hope so."

"Well, listen. We're all caught up, so if things go well tonight, take tomorrow off and enjoy a long weekend."

I give her a puzzled look. "Harper, are you sure?"

"Yes, of course. Plus, it'll give me time to spend with the kids. Ethan's working a half day, and we'll get to have some quality family time together."

I round the table and give her a hug. "Thank you."

"Good luck."

I've never had to grovel for a man before, so I hope showing up and apologizing is enough.

I grab my bag, then we say goodbye. As I walk to my car, the thought of seeing him makes me nervous. I just hope I can repair this strain between us.

Once I open the door and toss my stuff inside, I notice a single rose attached with twine to something wrapped in brown paper. On top, it reads, *To Ivy*.

Already knowing it's from Kane, I collapse into the seat, then grab the rose and smell it. Memories flood in from every time he'd bring me one. Carefully, I undo the paper and tear up at the leather journal he's worked on all summer.

My fingers rub over the cover that's engraved with vines of roses and ivy. In the center, it says, *Ivy Rose Callaway*.

I never told him my middle name, mostly because I grew up hating it. Kids at school teased me for having double floral names and even started calling me Poison Ivy. It was bad enough that I stuttered a lot, but they had a field day once they heard my mom call it out one time.

But seeing it engraved in Kane's handwriting, I've never loved it more.

Flipping it over, I see the same vine design around the edges, but in the center, he wrote my favorite book quote from the book I'd been reading him. Tears surface in the corners of my eyes. I can't believe he did this. After watching him work on some others, I know this took him *hours*.

He did a beautiful job, but it means so much more knowing he took the time to make it perfect just for me. And that he remembered the quote I told him I loved.

When I unravel the leather string and open it, I find a handwritten note on the first page.

To my sweet girl,

I've spent the past four days consumed by thoughts of you. I can hardly remember a time in my life without you even though you came into it not that long ago. That's how much of an impact you've had on me and how much of a hole you left when you told me you needed space. I'm willing to give you anything you ask, so if you need more time, I will wait.
I'll wait because I know without a doubt that I'm in love with you. I'm sorry if that scares you, but when it comes to my feelings, I don't want to hold back. I did that once before, and it bit me in the ass. So I'm giving you my whole heart. It's yours if you want it.
If by chance you don't, please tell me so I don't hold on to hope. And if that's what you decide, I still want you to know I will love you until my last breath.

Forever yours,
Kane

I'm a messy sobbing puddle by the time I finish reading. My cheeks are blotchy and covered in tears. The pounding of my heart is all I can hear over my shallow breaths.

I feel so fucking awful for putting him through this. And even though it was only four days, it was four days of pain I caused.

After I set the journal and rose down on the passenger seat, I drive as fast as the gravel road allows. Hopefully, he's home because I don't want to wait another minute to see him.

When his house comes into view, I'm so relieved to see his truck that I don't even bother parking in my secret spot. I rush out of my car and up the porch, then knock. I wait five seconds before trying the knob and decide to let myself in.

"Kane?" I call out, looking around and noticing how nothing's changed since I was here last weekend. My book is still on the coffee table where I was last reading to him.

Guilt floods in as I walk through his living room.

How could I ever walk away from a man who's been nothing but perfect?

As soon as I round the hallway, I hear the shower running. He must've just gotten home from work.

"Kane?" I repeat, not wanting to startle him. Pushing open the bathroom door, I see his naked body surrounded by hot steam.

Sweet Jesus.

Not only does his shower hold some of the best memories we've shared, but the view in front of me is enough to bring me to my knees and beg him to touch me again.

I tap my knuckles on the door to alert him, and when he finally turns toward me, my gaze falls to his cock. He's not even erect, and it's still thick and long.

"Ivy." His deep baritone vibrates through the air as I take a few steps inside.

Turning off the shower, he opens the door and shows off every hard muscle. Then he grabs a towel off the hook and wraps it around his waist.

"Hi." That's all I can manage.

Kane walks forward, and we meet in the middle. My breath

hitches when he softly strokes my cheek and tucks a piece of my hair back.

"Did you like your gift?" he asks.

I swallow down the lump in my throat. "I loved it, Kane. I can't believe you made that in just a few days."

"Truthfully, I started it a couple of weeks ago. I wanted to surprise you for our one-month anniversary, but since I wasn't sure I'd be able to give it to you then, I wanted you to have it now. So I worked nonstop to finish it."

"What date do you consider our anniversary?" I ask, barely above a whisper. I never thought to keep track.

The corner of his lips tilts up slightly. "July fifth, the first time we kissed."

That's about a week away, and I still managed to screw it up before then.

My eyes water again, but I can't fight it any longer and let the tears fall.

"Baby, don't cry." He cups my face and closes the gap between us, wiping my cheeks. I clear my throat so my words don't get stuck. "I'm so sorry I ran from you and that I ever doubted you. I promise to get a better handle on my emotions so I don't overreact. I let my intrusive thoughts get the best of me when I knew deep down I could trust you."

"It's not all your fault, Ivy. I should've handled it differently. Thinking back, I should've made it crystal clear to Raelyn that we were over for good, so there was no chance of her being near me again. At the B&B, I was more worried about everyone else's reaction and her making a scene, and I hurt you in the process. I should've stood up for us. That will never happen again, I promise you."

I swallow hard as I gaze into his ocean-blue eyes. "I told Hadleigh."

He arches a brow. "And?"

Shrugging, I laugh. "She said she already knew."

He snorts. "Of course. And since she's not bangin' my door down, I take it she didn't threaten my balls?"

"Only if you're a jackass." I snicker. "But no, she's happy for us and wishes we'd told her sooner, but understands why we didn't. It's only a matter of time now before everyone finds out."

"Fuck, I better text Grandma Bishop and tell her before she hears it through the grapevine."

I laugh, wrapping my arms around his waist and pulling him to my chest. "I've missed you."

He captures my chin, pressing a soft kiss to my lips. "I've missed you so goddamn much."

"I think another part of you did too," I tease at the way his erection is poking me in the hip.

"Oh, he did. I also missed hearing you read to me, so I started the book from the beginning."

"Really?"

"Yeah, but it didn't hit the same without your commentary and laughter. You brought it to life, the same way you've brought me to life."

"I can say the same thing about you."

Slowly, he brings his mouth to mine, and I sweep my tongue between his lips.

"Oh! I almost forgot to tell you something." I pull back to meet his eyes. "I'm in love with you too. For probably much longer than I should admit."

His face splits as his smile widens. "I can now die a happy man."

I burst out laughing. "Don't say that!" Then I pull him closer. "You know what else I've always wanted to try?"

"What's that?"

"Makeup sex. I hear it's pretty awesome."

Without warning, Kane lifts me and hauls me over his shoulder. Gasping, I squeal and smack his ass. "What did I say about you actin' like a caveman?"

He locks his arm tighter around my thighs. "That you find it hot."

I snort.

Kane places me on the bed and towers over me as I lean back. "I'm going to fuck all the doubt out of you so you'll think twice about runnin' from me again."

God, yes.

The sound of his promise has every nerve in my body blazing hot.

We scramble to take off my clothes, then with the twist of his towel, he's naked.

"Lift your hips for me, sweet girl."

I do as he says, meeting his cock at my center before he thrusts. We gasp in unison as he slides inside deeper.

"Fuck, your cunt is so tight. I wanna go harder, but…"

"Don't hold back, please. I can take it."

"Flip over and stick your ass out, baby."

Quickly, I get into position and fist the comforter to keep me steady. Kane grips my hips and sheaths himself in me. My eyes roll at how deep and hard he takes me. He smacks my backside over and over, while the sensations of his cock buried inside leave me breathless.

"Who's pussy is this, Ivy?" His deep voice causes tingles to float down my spine.

"*Yours,*" I tell him submissively as he brings a hand between my thighs and rubs my clit. "Only yours."

"That's right, baby. Because you were made for *me*. My sweet Ivy Rose."

Within seconds, I'm screaming through an orgasm and shattering against the bed. Kane slams into me a few more times before groaning out his release, and then we collapse next to each other.

Panting is all that can be heard as we stare at one another.

"I love you," I tell him.

He pulls me into his arms and kisses my lips. "I love you so much. Don't ever leave me again."

"I won't as long as you never give me a reason to."

One side of his mouth tilts up. "Deal." Then he cups my chin and adds, "That's a promise I intend to keep forever."

CHAPTER TWENTY-THREE

KANE

Having Ivy back in my arms is the best feeling in the world, and I never want to live without her again.

I screwed up by allowing Raelyn to think we were still together, but I quickly set her straight. Now, she's free to screw as many guys as she wants. I'd forgotten about her until she waltzed into the B&B—proof that I never really had feelings for her to begin with. Her asking for a break was the best thing that happened to me in a long time.

It brought me Ivy—the woman who's curled up next to me after *thoroughly* making up last night. I'm deeply in love with her and want to spend the rest of our lives together.

Ivy stirs, and I squeeze her a bit tighter. "Good mornin'," I whisper.

"Morning." Her eyes blink open. "What time is it? Aren't you late for work?"

"I told Knox I was takin' a personal day. He replied with eggplant and cherry emojis."

"Oh my God." She buries her face into my chest. "Hadleigh told him."

"Oh yeah." I chuckle. "Also, my grandma texted back. She wants us to come over for lunch."

Her head pops up. "Today?"

"Yep. I figured you'd be okay with it, so we're going over at noon."

Ivy's eyes widen in horror. "I can't go lookin' like the walk of shame."

"You've got an hour."

"*Shit, shit, shit.*" She scrambles out of bed, and I laugh as she runs to the bathroom.

While she showers, I make a pot of coffee, then get dressed. When I texted Grandma last night, she replied with a *"Called it"* GIF. I didn't even know she knew how to do those.

She responded this morning with a lunch invitation, and I figured it was time for us to rip off the Band-Aid.

Now we just need to inform my parents.

"I was thinkin' we'd stop by the barn to visit my parents before we go eat," I tell her as she gets dressed. "Might as well announce us being official to my folks right away too."

Ivy's face pales.

"Baby, it's gonna be fine." I squeeze her shoulders. "I promise."

"I just worry they're going to think I'm too young for you. I know I shouldn't care about others' opinions, but I want your family to like me."

"They already do," I reassure her.

"As Hadleigh's younger sister, not your girlfriend," she counters.

"They're very accepting and will be happy for us."

She nods. "I just hope you're right."

Once Ivy's ready, I drive us to the training facility. When we get out of the truck, I take Ivy's hand, and we walk inside.

"Kane!" my mom greets. "Hi, Ivy." She looks at our

interlocked fingers and smiles, then motions between us. "You two?"

"Two what?" Dad chimes in, walking over. When he realizes what Mom's talking about, he adds, "*Oh.*"

"What in the world? When did this happen?" Kaitlyn blurts out as she rounds the corner and joins us.

"Kaitlyn Rose!" Mom scolds.

"What? I think it's great, but now I'm officially the last single person on this ranch. Might as well carve my name in the old oak tree, Kaitlyn + No One."

I chuckle at her dramatics as Ivy blushes.

"Don't forget the heart with *True love forever* inside," I add.

Kaitlyn glares. "Yeah, thanks."

"Anyway..." I linger. "We're off to have lunch at Grandma's."

"Ivy, you promised you weren't having kids before me. Don't forget that." Kaitlyn shakes her finger at her.

"Don't worry, we aren't rushing." Ivy grins at me. "At least not until we're married."

Kaitlyn folds her arms over her chest. "Okay, fair enough. I'll go to the sperm bank when you get engaged. That way, I'll be nice and pregnant for the wedding and won't have to hear anyone askin' when it's my turn."

"Ignore her," Mom interjects, pushing Kaitlyn toward the stalls. "We're happy to see you two together. Y'all make a cute couple."

"Thanks, Mom."

"Two Bishops with two Callaways. Y'all could run your own country with that bloodline." Dad winks.

"I can't even legally drink, so not quite." Ivy lets out a nervous laugh.

"You let me know if he ain't treatin' ya right, okay?" Dad tells her, then gives me a look.

I roll my eyes. "Remind me to fill you in on the story of how my father waited to kiss my mom until the night before she was gettin' married to another man."

Ivy gasps. "The *night* before?"

"And finally confessed his feelings after fifteen years," I add.

"Don't listen to him. He'll get it all wrong," Dad says.

Mom chimes in, "I'll tell you the whole story over dinner some night."

Ivy smiles wide at the invitation. "That sounds great."

I check the time, and we say our goodbyes. Ivy's relieved that everyone was supportive, but I can sense how nervous she is to face Grandma Bishop.

"Don't worry, baby. We'll eat, chat, and have a good time," I say as we park in front of the big farmhouse.

Ivy nods with a smile, and we get out of the truck. "If I can win her over, I'll call it a successful day."

I grab her hand, kiss her knuckles, then lead her toward the house.

"Y'all are late," Grandma says as soon as she whips open the door.

Ivy's eyes widen, but I give her a reassuring squeeze.

"Not our fault. Mom and Dad kept us."

"Well, we know your dad doesn't care about punctuality. C'mon in, kids. Your grandfather is already at the table." She steps back, and we walk inside. "I told him to hold his horses, but you know how he is. Stubborn as a mule."

I chuckle, leading Ivy through the hallway and into the kitchen.

"There they are," Grandpa announces. "Nearly starved to death waitin' on ya."

"We're seven minutes late," I bemuse. "We quickly stopped at the training facility first."

The three of us take our seats. "How's everythin' going with the stud farm?"

"Great. Stayin' busy as usual."

Grandma turns to Ivy. "And how are things at the warehouse? I hear Harper's soap business is booming."

"Yes, ma'am. Going very well," Ivy responds.

Once Grandma says grace, we dig in. Scalloped potatoes with ham and gravy.

"This is delicious," Ivy says after trying a few bites. "I don't think I've ever had this."

"It's his favorite," Grandma says, pointing at Grandpa. "So I only make it once in a blue moon, or he gets spoiled."

We laugh and continue chatting until we're all full.

"Now y'all save room for some peach cobbler. Would ya like yours à la mode?" Grandma asks both of us, and we nod.

"Ya still engravin' those leather journals?" Grandpa asks while Grandma goes to the kitchen.

"Yes, sir. When I have time. I just made one for Ivy, actually."

"You did?" Grandma squeals as she carries our plates of dessert. "How sweet. You'll need to show me sometime, Ivy."

"Oh yes, of course. It's really pretty. I told him he should open an online store."

I shrug, though I've thought about it. "Right now, I prefer to do them for fun. At least until I get better."

"She has a good point, though, Kane," Grandma says. "They'd make great gifts."

"Is that a hint that you'd like one for Christmas?" I tease.

"Well, as a matter of fact, it was. I could use one to write my thoughts for the day."

"Alright, Grams. Consider it done." I shoot her a wink.

"This is so good," Ivy says around a forkful. "I could eat this every day. Well, if I knew how to make it."

"I'll teach you how," Grandma offers with a wink, and Ivy's eyes widen.

"Really? I'd love that," Ivy says. "Admittedly, I'm not very good in the kitchen."

"Oh honey, we'll fix that." Grandma grins.

I love how Ivy is open to learning new things.

As we continue eating, Ivy chats about her upcoming college classes and how she hopes to partner with Harper after graduation. Grandma offers tons of business advice and shares how much the ladies in her knitting club love their soaps. After we're stuffed full, we help clean up, then head out.

"Well, I think that went well," I say once we're driving back to my house.

"I *love* your grandma!" she gushes.

I snicker at her excited expression. "She has a fan club for a reason."

"I won't lie, she's a little intimidatin', but the sweetest," Ivy continues. "I felt very welcomed and accepted."

"Told ya it'd be fine. And see, she didn't bring up our age difference once."

"I'm sure everybody's thinkin' it, though, but it's fine." She shrugs. "I just hope she doesn't expect me to walk down the aisle next week."

"There's no pressure. We get to move at our own pace without expectations. All of that's on Kaitlyn now." I bellow out a laugh.

"Yeah, I've noticed the past few times I've been around her, she's been worked up about being too old to have kids. I think my mom was in her early thirties when she had me, so I don't know why she's worried."

"She's been that way for years. Even as a teenager, she went on and on about having a big family. I think she's nervous about running out of time."

"If I had any older guy friends, I'd try to set her up."

"I do have guy friends her age, and I still won't," I admit.

Ivy chuckles. "I get the impression that Payton has a thing for her."

"Oh, we all do, everyone except for Kaitlyn. She only sees him as a friend or like another annoying brother."

"Well, that's unfortunate, but I've been where Payton is..." She smirks.

"That so doesn't count. You were barely hitting puberty when your crush started."

"Hey!" She playfully smacks my arm as I park in my driveway. "You can't use that against me."

"Oh, but sweet Ivy, I can and I will. Get your ass in the house. I have plans for you now that we're alone."

As soon as we walk inside, I pin her to the door and capture her mouth. "Do you know how special you are to me?"

"I have a good idea, but how about you show me?" she taunts.

I grab behind her thighs and lift her until her legs instinctively wrap around my waist. She holds on to me tightly while I walk us to my room. Once I set her on the bed, I glance at the large handheld mirror on my nightstand.

"What is that for?" she asks warily.

"You're about to find out." I shoot her a wink, then remove my shirt. "Clothes off, baby."

Once we're both naked, I crawl over her body and settle between her thighs. I suck on her neck, then feather kisses down her chest.

"I got you a present," I murmur, lowering down her stomach.

"Mmm...w-what?" An audible gasp releases from her throat, and I smile in satisfaction as I near her center. "A little toy."

Ivy's eyes pop open when I look up at her.

"You wanna have some fun, baby?"

Her breathing increases as I place pressure over her clit. "As long as you don't stop doin' that."

I give her thigh a playful slap. "Sit tight, be right back."

"You suck," she groans.

Chuckling, I slide open the drawer where the black box is stashed. I turn on the toy and wait for her reaction.

"Is that a...*vibrating* rose?" She leans up on her elbows and examines it while I rub it over her pussy. "Oh my God..." Her eyes roll back.

"It's a clit massager," I confirm. "I want you to use it while I take you from behind, and then we're gonna watch together in the mirror as you come over and over."

She blinks hard. "Wait, *what*? I don't think I'm that flexible."

I chuckle, then grab her hand to pull her up. "Trust me, baby. Bend over."

After she gets into position, I slide the mirror underneath her.

"Do you see your pussy, baby?"

She tilts down and looks. "Mm-hmm."

"Now place the rose on your clit," I order.

"Holy mother of God..." she bursts out, her knees nearly buckling.

"That feel good?"

"This should be illegal," she stammers, struggling with her words.

"Startin' to feel like you don't even need me," I say with a laugh as I position myself behind her and stroke my shaft.

I slide the tip through her wet pussy folds.

"Yes, I do..." she pleads.

"Tell me what you want, sweet girl. You want this cock?"

She moans louder. "*Please*."

"Look down and watch."

Slowly, I sheath myself into her tight body. She draws out a long groan as I fill her full.

"Fuck, you feel so good." I smack one of her ass cheeks. "Look how good we fit together, baby."

We glance in the mirror, our bodies slamming together over and over as the toy vibrates her sensitive bud.

"I'm gonna come," she announces, then breathlessly screams my name and squeezes down on me.

"Holy shit," she pants as I continue to pound into her.

"Keep watchin', baby. I want you to see how we were made for one another."

Her body tenses, and I know she's close again. Witnessing her pussy soak my dick has electricity shooting up my spine.

The buildup comes fast and hard. I pull out, pumping myself over her ass and back. "Fuck...my come all over you is the sexiest thing I've ever seen."

"Clean me up now," she taunts.

"My fuckin' pleasure."

Once I've thoroughly licked every inch of my come off her body, I flip her over and press my mouth to hers.

"You're so goddamn perfect for me."

"That clit massager thing is the devil. I'm numb from the waist down."

I laugh as she sighs and falls back on the bed.

"I can't wait to use it on you while edging you with my fingers."

Her eyes widen. "Only if I get to use Winston on you."

I arch a brow, leaning up on my elbow. "Use it *where* exactly?"

"You'll find out."

"Ivy..." I warn.

"I read a scene in a romance novel, and it was super kinky. Apparently, the area underneath a man's balls is super sensitive because of the prostate. The heroine used a vibrator there, and he came over and over again. I wanna see if it's legit."

I blink hard but then shrug in defeat. "Okay, I'll try anything once."

"I know." She chuckles.

I pin her down, holding her wrists to the mattress. "What's so funny?"

"Nothing." She giggles as I slide my mouth against hers. After we settle in bed, we spend the next hour talking and playing around. I kiss every inch of her soft face. Ivy hums and giggles a little as I find new sensitive areas around her neck.

"Kane Bishop! I know you're home! Open the door!"

The two of us jolt upright in bed. There's no way we can ignore Hadleigh's loud screaming and banging.

"Oh *shit*," Ivy mutters.

"I thought you said she was cool with us being together?" I rush around to find my shorts and slide them on.

"She was!" Ivy screeches, searching for her clothes.

"Should I put on the cup just in case?" I ask with amusement, but deep inside, I'm not kidding. She might actually punch me in the nuts.

"I'm not against bargin' in! So y'all better be dressed!" Hadleigh shouts again.

"Fuck," I murmur. "I'm comin'!" I yell back.

I slip on a pair of jeans while Ivy gets hers on. Then I sprint to the front door before Hadleigh kicks it open.

"What in the world?" I ask breathlessly.

"You slept with my baby sister!" She steps in, pointing her finger at my chest. "You took her *virginity*!"

I hold up my hands in surrender so she doesn't try to kick my ass because I've never seen her so worked up.

"Hads, what're you doin'?" Ivy asks, coming around me. "You said you were happy for us?"

"I am!" She beams, relaxing her shoulders. "Doesn't mean I'm passin' on my right as your big sister to bust his balls."

"Jesus Christ." My arms drop. "I legit thought you were about to try to hurt me," I breathe out in relief.

"*Try*?" she mocks. "If I wanted to, I could."

"Considerin' y'all's history, I think ya should call it even." Ivy gives her a knowing look, and I somewhat hate that she knows about our past, but it's never been a secret. It's not even a big deal anymore, especially since it's been over two years.

"Okay, fair enough," Hadleigh concedes. "You're lucky you're my best friend, or I would've karate chopped your dick in half."

"So you're really okay with this?" I confirm, hugging Ivy

against my side. "Or am I gonna wake up in the middle of the night with a knife to my throat?"

"I think y'all make a cute couple, but you make her cry *one* tear, and I'll come locked and loaded."

I take a step forward, then pull Hadleigh into a hug. "As your best friend, I promise I'd never do anything to harm your sister. I'm in love with her."

"Aw...you didn't tell me that, Ivy." Hadleigh pulls us in for a group hug. "I really am happy for y'all. If there's anyone good enough for my sister, it's my best friend."

CHAPTER TWENTY-FOUR

IVY

THREE MONTHS LATER

I can't believe I only have one semester of college left, and then I'll officially be Harper's business partner.

"Did you grab the extra candy from the back seat?" I ask Kane as I pull a box of supplies from my trunk.

"Yep," he tells me, holding the two large witch cauldrons in his hands. Even though Kane offered me his truck, I loaded everything in my car yesterday. I wanted to prove to Harper how independent and dedicated I am.

Today, Harper has given me an incredible opportunity to run a booth at the fall festival. Over the last few months, she's shared more with me about the business and has been testing my strengths and weaknesses. It's the reason proving myself to her today is so important to me.

Harper knows I'm an introverted bookworm and that public appearances are out of my comfort zone, but I appreciate how much she believes in me.

"Don't be nervous," Kane whispers in my ear as I pull a wagon with our inventory in it.

"I'm just so glad you're here," I admit. "I honestly feel like I can do anything with you by my side."

He waggles his brows. "*Anything*?"

"Okay, not anything, but ya know what I mean. It's gonna take a lot for me to explore voyeurism. That's all I'm sayin'."

"One day," he says just as we arrive at our bright orange tent with a giant inflatable pumpkin on top. Kane had a few of the ranch hands set up our tables, tent, and some minor decorations so all we'd have to do is arrive and put out the products.

"Oh wow." I can't help but gasp because it's amazing. "We're gonna be the talk of the town."

"Considering I'm dressed like a stick of butter and you're Paula Deen, I'd say we already are."

I snicker, fixing my gray wig, and pull my spatula from my back pocket. "Hey, we look cute, and you know it's hilarious!"

"It's pretty fuckin' funny. I woulda never thought of it."

"I'm just happy the ladies at your grandma's quilt club volunteered to sew your costume. They were in stitches over it."

"Somehow, that doesn't surprise me." He pulls out the small shelves and slides them together. After the table is fully set up, I check the time and see we still have twenty minutes before the gates officially open.

"Check out all those people lined up to come in."

I turn to see what looks like the whole town standing out there. Since we're one of the first booths they'll see, I'm expecting to be bombarded. "Okay, now I'm officially nervous."

"Baby, you're gonna do amazin'."

"I hope so," I say, my anxious-excitement nearly getting the best of me. I sit down and pull out the journal Kane gave me and go over my checklist. "We've taken care of everything I wrote down so there's nothing else to do."

"You should take a pic of the setup and text it to Harper so she can see how awesome it looks. Especially before all those people destroy it," he suggests.

"See, this is why I keep you around." I hurry and snap a shot of the table and send it to Harper like he suggested. Then as if someone opened the floodgates, hordes of people rush through, many of who come straight toward us.

A couple of hours pass, and I don't even notice because we're swamped. By the time the initial rush fades, I notice how little we have left in stock.

Kane gently squeezes my shoulder.

"You're doing amazin', baby," he encourages.

"Thank you so much. I would've drowned without you. I didn't expect that," I admit, repositioning my wig. Right now, I'm glad I'm wearing jeans, but then I realize Kane has been busting his ass helping in that costume.

I'll totally make it up to him later.

Once we have a small break, I see my sister and Knox in the distance. I wave, and they return the gesture.

"How did Hadleigh talk him into being a Thing from Dr. Suess?" I ask Kane, and he shrugs. "She has her ways. Hads always gets what she wants from him."

When they're closer, Knox blurts out, "That shit is hilarious."

"Ivy's idea," Kane admits. "But yours. Thing 1, Thing 2, and Hendrix is Thing 4."

"Obviously," Knox states.

"I'm confused," I say to Hadleigh. "You skipped a number."

Then my sister lifts her shirt and reveals another one that says Thing 3 on her belly. I immediately run over to her and squeal. "You're *pregnant*!"

"Yes," she says, and we both start crying.

"I'm so happy for y'all," I say, just as I turn to see Kane hugging his brother. Then he wraps his arms around Hadleigh and smiles at Hendrix.

"Do you have any idea how many people just thought we didn't know how to count?" Hadleigh asks, chuckling. "You're the first one to say anything about the missing number!"

Kane wraps his arm around me as we chat, and I lean into him. "Looks like we're gonna be sharing another niece or nephew."

"It's gonna be twins this time," Knox confirms.

"Do not wish that upon me." Hadleigh playfully smacks him. "Carrying one at a time was enough."

A few more customers walk up, and we say our goodbyes. So many of Kane's aunts and uncles stop by to support the business, and I'm so appreciative of them buying anything. Another hour passes, and that's when I see Grandma Bishop along with Grandpa walking toward us.

"Holy shit," Kane says. "She's dressed like a stripper."

I turn my head and giggle. "No, she's not. She's a sexy devil. Wait. Is your grandpa...*Jesus?*"

As they make their way toward us, the red sequins on her costume glint in the late afternoon sun.

"Grandma!" Kane scolds after we exchange hugs.

Her bright red lips turn into a smirk. "Hi, sweetie."

Kane looks at his grandpa. "Was this your idea?"

"Oh, I can't take credit for this," he states, flipping the long-haired wig he's wearing over his shoulder. "I'm heaven, and she's hell."

All I can do is snort. "I think it's perfect."

"Thank you, dear," she says, then leans in and whispers. "I lost a dare at quilt club so this was my punishment."

I meet her eyes. "Well, we love a spicy devil."

She winks. "A Bishop never passes up a dare."

"Your costume turned out adorable, Kane. Didn't you get Betsy Sue to sew it for you?"

"Yes, ma'am, she did. Needed a lot of material for this big hunk of butter," I explain, squeezing him.

Kane chuckles as some ladies from the church pass by and nod toward us. We both look at Grandma Bishop.

"I'm happy to give everyone somethin' to talk about. At eighty-four, makes life a little more interestin', don't it?"

"It does," I say. Grandma looks over all the soaps we have left and picks up a few. Of course, she gets the family discount, then she puts them in her purse that has flames on it.

"Y'all stay outta trouble, ya hear?" Rose tells us as she and Scott walk away.

"We will because we don't want to go to your eternal hell," Kane shouts back at her. I see his grandma playfully but discreetly shoot him the finger.

His eyes nearly bug out of his head.

"Oh my God," I tell him. "That was the *best* thing I've seen all week."

"She's gonna be the talk of the town," he says as we try to restack and restock the soaps. "You saw the church ladies' expressions."

"It's because your grandma is iconic and gives no fucks. Simple as that. I hope to one day be just like her."

Kane places the rest of the inventory on the table. "She's a queen."

"Yes, she is." I look at what's left, which isn't a whole lot. "This is it?"

"Yep, that's everything."

"Wow. We still have so much time left. I guess I didn't bring enough."

"That means we'll have sold out with time to enjoy the pumpkin patch and maybe bob for apples."

I glance at him with a devilish grin. "Is that code for something?"

"Well, there are some other things you can bob if you want."

A playful growl releases from me. "Don't tempt me, Cowboy."

"You're the temptress here, not me."

"Oh whatever!" I laugh, but before I can say anything else, a customer strolls by, and we greet her.

"You're butter, and you're Paula Deen?" the older woman asks with a snicker. She's well dressed and is wearing several diamond rings on her fingers. Just by the way she presents herself, I know she's rich and probably drives a Cadillac. Most of the wannabe Stepford wives around here do.

"Yes, ma'am," Kane tells her. "All my girlfriend's idea."

"That's cute," she says while smelling the different scents. She starts stacking the ones she's getting on top of one another until it's a leaning tower of goat soap.

"Honey, where'd you get that beautiful journal?" she asks. Her eyes narrowed in on it when I scooted it to the side.

"Oh, this thing?" I'm wearing a cheesy grin. "It was given to me as a gift. Completely handmade."

"Do ya mind?" The woman reaches out, and I willingly give it to her because I'm proud of what Kane made. She studies it with amazement, and I know she's just as impressed as I was the first time I saw it.

"I think I might need one of these for my daily devotionals," she explains, handing it back to me.

I meet Kane's eyes, then bring my attention back to her as she continues to add lotions and everything else to her purchase.

"I know the person who made it. I've been tryin' to get 'em to make a website because others might want something that's so pretty." I give Kane a wink, and the woman quickly catches on.

She turns to him. "Honey, if you start a shop for these, I'll be your first order. Before you tell me how much time it takes to make, I know. My late husband used to do some leatherworkin' for a saddle maker over in El Paso. Reminds me of the good ole days before he passed away."

"It's really just a hobby of mine," he shyly explains.

"Some people have skills, and some people *have skills*. You know what I'm sayin'? That's pure talent. Don't let it go to waste." She pulls out her business card and hands it over to him. He places it in the side pouch of my purse. "I'm serious about gettin' one made. No rush. Money isn't an object."

Kane looks shocked, but all I can do is laugh.

"I've been tellin' him how amazing they are, but he's modest."

The older woman grins wide. "Now, how much do I owe you?"

Kane stands and puts everything in a bag as I ring up each item. I swallow hard when I see her total. "Five hundred and sixty-seven dollars."

"And how much for everything else you've got left?"

My eyes widen in shock. "Seriously?"

"Absolutely. I have a huge family and love to send them gifts. They don't usually get high-quality items like fresh goat milk soaps, so they'll feel special. And smell good too."

We count the rest of the products, and even I'm surprised when I say the new total out loud.

"Fourteen hundred and twenty-three dollars and fifty-five cents."

"Great." She smiles, then hands over her card. Kane swipes it, and I turn the tablet around for her to sign.

"Ma'am, would you like me to help carry these out to your car?" Kane offers because the soaps aren't light.

"That would be fabulous," she tells him.

"Thank you so much." I give her a wave. "We appreciate your business, and you can find us on Instagram!"

"Oh honey, I don't use social media. I'm too old for that."

Kane follows her to her car, and I start cleaning up the booth. After everything is packed and back in the wagon, Kane returns.

He smiles wide. "Do you know who that was?"

"No idea," I confirm. "She seemed nice."

"That was Audrey Adler. The widow of an old rich oil tycoon. I think she's even *seein'* the governor of Texas."

"Seriously? This could be huge for the business and for you!"

"For me? No, for you, sweetheart. She kept going on and on about how much she loved the scents. Even said she'd be making an online order around Christmas."

I gasp. "Harper is going to flip when that happens!"

"The woman has enough money to buy every person in the state a bar of goat soap."

Giddiness fills me. "Wow. I had no idea. But I'm kinda glad I didn't know. I probably wouldn't have been able to talk. Did she say anything else?"

"She's serious about me making her a journal."

"And you're going to do it, right?"

Kane grabs the wagon, and we walk to my car to put everything away so we can enjoy the rest of the evening.

"Yeah, I think so. Her husband was really into leatherworking. The guy was known for his skills in the community, so it's kinda full circle in a way that she likes my work."

"Proud of you, babe."

"Thank you. I'm proud of you too. I know how nervous you were today, but look, you sold out in record time. And you spoke to every single person who walked over. That's progress, sweetheart."

Kane and I load my trunk, and he tells me the ranch hands are coming back later to take down the tent.

"I can't believe it. I just hope Harper is impressed."

He chuckles. "Oh, she will be. She used to get nervous at these things too. Hadleigh would have to walk her off the ledge."

"Really?" I ask.

He nods and wraps his arm around me. We go back into the festival, and several locals ask if they can take pictures with us like our costumes are the main attraction. As we're waiting in line for a caramel apple, I overhear someone talking about the older woman dressed as a devil.

I elbow Kane and nod toward them so he can listen too.

"Was her husband Moses?"

"Dorothy, he was Jesus."

"That's ballsy, considering the whole town is here."

"Yeah, but what a statement."

We grab our sweet treats, and I turn to him. "Rose is gonna be the talk of the town."

"Ma'am, she clearly already is." He snickers.

We walk toward the gigantic wooden spook house built just for this event. As the sun sets, the bright purple and green lights reveal the eyes of an entrance that resembles Frankenstein. Smoke from the machines fills the ground as the kids' and adults' screams echo throughout the structure.

"You wanna do this?" He looks over at me, then chomps into his apple.

"Actually, jump scares really aren't my thing. But can we ride the Ferris wheel?"

"Absolutely," he tells me, but we take a stroll through the pumpkin patch first. There are several different sizes and colors laid all around with hay bales around the perimeter. Teenagers are taking selfies as Kane interlocks his fingers with mine.

I love being with him in public, love letting everyone know he's mine and I'm his. After we buy a few tickets, we wait in line for the only ride I care about. When it's our turn to get on the Ferris wheel, Kane asks the guy if we can be alone in our basket, then slips him a ten.

Somehow, it works. While people are slowly loading, his lips crash into mine. I take the opportunity to devour him as our tongues violently twist together. Moans escape me as his hand moves under my shirt and cups my bare breast.

"Fuck," he whispers. "Your nipples are hard as a rock."

"I need you," I whimper when he pulls away and kisses up my neck to my ear.

"I can't wait to be inside you," he whispers. We stop at the very top, and Kane takes the opportunity to slip his hand inside my pants. When his fingers brush against my clit, my pussy throbs with anticipation. He shoves two digits inside, and the excitement of what we're doing has me ready to combust.

"Kane," I quietly say as he slides his fingers in and out. "Let's get out of here."

When we start moving again, he removes his hands from my panties and places his fingers in his mouth. The eye contact is intense, sexy, and possessive, just the way I like.

"Mmm. Sweet and wet."

I smile as he slides his lips against mine, allowing me to taste myself. "If this damn Ferris wheel doesn't stop and let us off in the next five minutes, I'm gonna fuck you right here."

My eyes shift to where his cock is, and I can see it's raging. The costume isn't doing him any favors of hiding his arousal either.

"Is that a stick of butter in your pocket or…?"

Kane takes my hand and places it on his hardness. "Does it feel *soft* to you?"

He lets out a groan as I trace the outline of his dick with my finger. I need him like the desert needs rain. When the ride finally comes to a halt and we exit, I let out a sigh of relief.

I wrap my arms around his neck and slide my tongue into his mouth.

"Let's get the hell outta here," he states, and we rush to the car.

We contemplate pulling over but go straight home instead.

As soon as we walk inside his house, we remove our clothing. By the time we stumble into the bedroom, we're completely naked. We're ravenous and desperate, and nothing in the world matters right now other than being together. Kane's touch and kisses consume me as he fucks me hard but slow.

Our pants and moans fill the room, and I know I won't be able to last much longer when he flips and bends me over the bed. He slams into me so goddamn hard that my vision blurs. The orgasm takes hold in a blink.

"Shit," he groans out, digging his strong fingers into my hips and skin. "Your pussy's squeezing me so tight."

And within seconds, we're unraveling together, both catapulted to another world. One where only we exist together and forever. When we come down from our high and clean up, Kane pulls me into his arms.

We hold each other completely satiated.

"There's something I wanna talk to you about," he admits, rubbing my arm.

"Mm," I say, so relaxed I nearly fall asleep.

"Move in with me?"

I tilt my head so I can fully meet his gaze. A laugh escapes me. "I already practically live with you."

"I know, but I want you *officially* living here. I want all your shit scattered around my bathroom permanently and your panties on my floor each night. But really, I want to wake up to you every morning."

I grin and slide my lips across his, knowing this means we're really going to the next level. And who knows, maybe an engagement, wedding, and a baby in the near future. Something I've always wanted and dreamed about.

"That sounds amazing," I admit.

"So that's a yes?" he asks.

"It's a *hell yes*."

EPILOGUE
KANE

TWENTY-TWO MONTHS LATER

I'VE BEEN LOOKING FORWARD to celebrating Ivy's birthday in New York City for a long time. I'll be thirty-one in four months, and this will be my first time traveling to the East Coast. I'm not sure who's more excited about this trip, but when she sees what I have planned for her special day, it'll be a moment neither of us will forget.

For the first time in my life, I'll be dropping down to one knee and asking the love of my life if she'll be my wife

IVY

Most people do a bar crawl or go partying on their twenty-first birthday, but I couldn't be less interested in that. Instead, I'm in the Big Apple with the man I've crushed on for half of my life.

"I can't believe I'm inside the infamous New York Public Library!" I whisper-shout as Kane leads us through the Rose Main reading room. "The photos online don't do it justice."

"No, they don't. It's even more beautiful in person," he agrees. "But not more than you." He flashes me a wink, and I shake my head.

Even after two years together, Kane never forgets to tell me how much he loves me and how pretty I am. It's impossible not to fall harder for him each day.

We've been living together for a while, and I never grow tired of spending time with him. Our schedules have been chaotic, so we both need this time away. I'm working full-time with Harper, and recently, Kane started taking custom orders for leather journals on top of the stud farm operation. When he planned this surprise trip, I could hardly contain my excitement. I've always wanted to visit New York City, and touring the public library was a bucket list item.

"Wanna take a picture together?" Kane asks.

"Ahh yes! Of course!" I beam, searching for the perfect background.

Kane finds a nice older lady and quietly gives her a few instructions while I wait. When he returns, he wraps his arm around me, and we smile.

"Let's do one more," Kane mutters, and I agree with a nod.

The lady gives us a thumbs-up.

"Oh shoot, my shoe's untied." Kane kneels, but then I remember he's wearing boots.

When I turn to watch what he's doing, he's down on one knee and holding up a black velvet box with a smirk.

My eyes widen as he opens it and reveals a diamond ring.

"Ivy Rose Callaway, I love you more than words could ever express, and nothing in this world would make me happier than having you as my wife. So would you do me the honor of marrying me?" His words are just above a whisper but loud enough for me to hear. I'm shocked this is happening right here and now.

"Yes, yes, oh my God, yes!" I try to hold back my excitement but fail. I cover my mouth once I realize how loud I am in the library. Kane quickly stands and swoops me in for a hug.

"I love you so much," I tell him, then smack my lips to his. "I can't believe you planned all this."

"I knew how much you'd love it and wanted it to be extra special."

"Like I've said from the very beginning, you were written by a woman."

"And you were made just for me, future Mrs. Kane Bishop."

"Oh my gosh, I love the sound of that."

The woman who had Kane's phone brings it over to us. "Congrats, kids! I got it all on video."

"Thank you, ma'am. And thank you again for helping me capture our special moment."

"It was my pleasure. I wish you two the best."

After she leaves, Kane slides the ring on my finger. As we walk around, I can't stop staring at how it sparkles and reflects the light.

"Does anyone know you planned this?" I ask once we go outside.

"Hadleigh and Harper. They helped me pick out the ring and plan your days off so we could come here. But knowing your sister, she told Knox, and he told someone else and so on. I did tell my parents and Grandma Bishop. Oh, I also asked your mom for permission."

I gasp. "You did?"

"She adores me."

Rolling my eyes, I laugh. "She does."

As we walk hand in hand, Kane asks, "So should we set a date? You know everyone will ask the second we're back."

"Ha! That's true. How about a spring wedding?"

"Hmm...April?"

"That's only seven months away. Think that'll be enough time to plan it?"

"Between your sister and my family, yes. They recruit for wedding planning like the military—all hands on deck."

I smile. "Truthfully, I don't really care when it is because all I want is to be your wife. Nothing else matters."

Kane stops us in the middle of the sidewalk and pulls me closer. "Good because that's all I want too. The first time you tempted me with your sweet smile and brown doe eyes, I knew I wanted forever with you."

BONUS EPILOGUE
KAITLYN

SEVEN MONTHS LATER

"Wasn't the ceremony beautiful?" my mom says as soon as we're done with family photos. "I couldn't stop crying."

"It was. Those vows nearly had me in a puddle of tears on the altar," I admit.

Kane and Ivy got married at the little church on Main Street. The reception will be held at the Event Center just a block away.

Dad follows us while my brother and his new wife finish taking couple photos. "Looks like you're next," he taunts, knowing damn well I hate when people say that to me. "Just FYI, I'm fine with an elopement."

I turn and give him a death glare. "Considering I'm nearly middle age, pretty sure marriage just ain't in my cards."

Dad chuckles. "You know how many times I thought the same thing? I was over thirty when I got married."

"Grandma would track me down and murder me if I eloped."

"*Jackson*." Mom places her hand on his shoulder as we enter the reception hall. "Don't poke the bear."

"Exactly," I say, my mood slightly turning sour as I move to the wine bar. Instead of taking one glass, I grab two and double fist them. I need to drink my way through this reception before I roll into a ball of emotions because I'm the last single kid.

The room looks gorgeous with twinkle lights hanging from the ceiling, creating a warm ambience in the room as the DJ plays love songs. It'd be a million times better if I had someone to dance with.

I'm happy for my brother and excited for them, but I'm definitely jealous. He's loved Ivy for years, and they're perfect for each other. A true match made in heaven. You know, all the things they say about *every* Bishop who's gotten married. But being at weddings is just a reminder that I'll be an old hag before I have the opportunity to even start a family. The pressure that puts on me is intense.

I groan as I look around the room at all the happy couples and begrudgingly drink my chardonnay.

It doesn't bother me as much that I don't have a husband. I only need a man for his sperm and knocking me up. Being a mother is something I've wanted since I was a kid, and if finding true love isn't in my cards, then I'll at least find a way to have a baby.

I've always been independent and taken care of myself. With twin brothers like Knox and Kane, I always had to be able to take and throw punches, but some guys find that intimidating.

"Hey!" Rowan comes my way with two glasses of wine in her hands.

I arch a brow at her. "You're partyin' hard, huh?"

"This weekend is like a staycation, and I'm taking *full* advantage."

I snicker. "You're gonna be sloppy drunk."

"Looks like I'm just followin' your lead." She people-watches with me. Diesel is taking silly pictures at the photo booth with the kids.

"I ain't got nowhere to be tomorrow either. And since

BONUS EPILOGUE

everyone is basically heading back to the ranch, I'll find a designated driver," I explain, then finish off the first glass and start on the second one. "But they need to bring out those hors d'oeuvres because I haven't eaten since breakfast. I'm not tryin' to puke tonight." My stomach growls, and when I take another sip of my second glass, I know I should slow down.

Maize, Harper, and Hadleigh come over and join us. She's holding Hannah who just turned two. After she was born, Hadleigh quit her job indefinitely to stay home since they now had two kids only thirteen months apart.

"The happy couple should be arriving at any moment," Harper says, pulling out her cell phone from her clutch. I do the same. As soon as I unlock it and open the camera app, Kane and Ivy enter.

"Please to welcome Mr. and Mrs. Kane Bishop," the DJ announces as the room hoots and hollers. My brother smiles at me, and we watch them like royalty as they have their first dance.

After it's over, others flood the dance floor, and I make my way to the bar. As I'm grabbing my third or fourth glass, the alcohol hits me like a sack of potatoes.

"Okay, drunky," Knox says from behind me. "You know, maybe you *should* join the convent to clean up your act."

"And maybe you should get your dick chopped off so you'd be less cocky."

He bursts into a roar of laughter. "Whoa, buddy. You're fast with those comebacks tonight. I was kiddin'."

I smirk. "Yeah, well, I wasn't."

"Don't make me tell Mom and Dad on you," he warns with a mischievous grin.

"What are you gonna say? Your adult daughter is drinking wine at a wedding? Fuck off," I whisper.

He sips his wine. "No, I'd explain you're gettin' sloppy drunk, and we know how loose your lips get when you drink."

BONUS EPILOGUE

I roll my eyes and find the table where my grandparents are sitting and join them. A photographer walks around and takes tons of pictures. I think I posed so many times that there's a spot in my vision from the bright-ass flash.

"I'm happy I got to see Kane get married," Grandma says, and I swallow hard as Grandpa agrees. My uncle John and aunt Mila are at the table too, but they're having their own conversation about gardens and vegetables.

"Why wouldn't you?" The words fall from my mouth, and I swallow hard.

"Because I'm not gettin' any younger, sweetheart. So how 'bout you get married and start that family before I kick the bucket?"

I gasp. "Grandma!"

"What? It's true," she says. "Then I can finally die a happy woman."

"Well if me not doing all those things means you'll live forever, then maybe I really will join that convent everyone's been suggesting."

She shoots me a wink. "Honey, I ain't gettin' any younger, so chop-chop. I've had a blessed life, but I'm waitin' for you to give me some more great-grandbabies. And if you don't while I'm still here, I'm gonna haunt you for the rest of *your* life."

I burst out into laughter. "That's a deal I'm willing to make. Just let me find a man to knock me up."

"*Kaitlyn Bishop,*" Grandma gasps.

Uncle John chuckles. "Don't give the poor woman a heart attack with those kinda jokes."

I narrow my eyes at him and smirk. "Who said I was joking?"

Grandma laughs and leans over to pinch me, but I'm too fast for her. Eventually, it's time for dinner to be served, and I find my best friend Payton sitting with a few ranch hands. They're all too young for me. Trust me, I've asked them their ages. "This seat taken?"

BONUS EPILOGUE

"Nope, all yours," Payton says with a smile.

When I plop down, I nearly miss my chair but he helps me.

"Jesus Christ, Kate. How much have you had to drink?"

"Three glasses of wine? Four? Wait. Five? I've lost count. *A lot.*"

"You're slurring," he tells me, shaking his head. "You have to give a speech after dinner."

I laugh and wave my hand. "I've got this. It's fine."

We eat, and I'm thankful pasta and bread were served because Payton is right. For a second there, I thought I was seeing double, but after I devoured a plateful of carbs, I'm fine. Still drunk, but not sloppy.

When it's time for speeches, our parents start, Hadleigh and Knox say a few words, then I make my way to the front and look out at my family and friends.

"Saving the best for last, I see," I say, holding the microphone in one hand and a new glass of wine in the other. "Did y'all know Kane was *always* my favorite brother?" I glance at Knox, and he laughs out loud.

"Caring, compassionate, and not a complete and total...well, you can fill in the blank. Any word would fit. But seriously, Kane, this isn't a roast for your evil twin brother."

Diesel yells out. "It should be!" And everyone laughs. I give him a nod and a grin.

"This is a celebration of love and commitment. Ivy, you're beautiful, and my brother is so lucky to be able to spend the rest of his life with you." Kane grins wide and looks over at her. He places a kiss on her cheek.

"See, he knows," I say. "With that being said, I'd like to make a toast to my brother and his better half. Two of the most wonderful people I've ever had the pleasure to know found love in Eldorado. A miracle, trust me. No ring on this finger."

The room bursts into a roar of laughter at my expense.

"On a serious note, I'm so happy for you and am honored to

be your sister. I've watched your relationship grow into something that people only dream of having, and I'm sure you know how lucky you are to find that. At least I can tell how much you love and adore each other just by how you look at one another. Congrats, you two. Love like this couldn't have happened to anyone better. Now, as Grandma always says, go make some babies. And yes, I'm available to watch your kids whenever you need. Love y'all, wishing you all the happiness, love, and laughter in the world. Congrats."

Everyone begins to clap, and Ivy and Kane both look at me with the sweetest smile. I nod and go back to my seat as the wedding planner announces it's time to cut the cake.

After we stuff ourselves with the best one Maize has ever made, the lights lower, and the real dancing begins.

I think Payton and I are the only ones sitting in a room of at least three hundred people. "Do you wanna dance?" he asks, meeting my eyes.

I'm not much of a dancer, but I am somewhat feeling the FOMOs because everyone does look like they're having fun. Even the little kids are jamming out.

"Sure," I tell him, and he leads me to the dance floor.

I wrap my arms around Payton's neck, and he places his strong hands on my hips. I'd be lying if I said I didn't find him attractive as hell, even if he's quiet sometimes. He's always been there for me because everyone else is too busy being in love. I'm completely lost in my thoughts as he spins me around, and I meet his smoldering gaze.

"Why are you looking at me like that?" he asks, and I wonder if I'm imagining it all. Wine can sometimes be brutal to my perception.

I snort, trying to brush it off, but a blush creeps up my cheeks. Thankfully it's dark. "Wait, was I eye-fucking you?"

A grin touches his plump lips. "Probably the wine."

"*Definitely* the wine," I add, though the thought of being with him has crossed my mind on more than one occasion. Especially when he's working shirtless with sweat running down those washboard abs of his.

Just the thought has me ready to fuck him right here on this dance floor, but then again, it's been a while since I've been with anyone. Payton pulls me closer, and the firmness of his hands resting right above my ass causes my heart to flutter. He leans in, and the warmth of his breath brushes against my ear. The intoxicating smell of his cologne overtakes my senses.

"I'm not lettin' you drive home tonight."

"Mm," I state, smiling. "Are you taking me to *your* house instead?"

"*Woman…*"

"What? Am I not your type or somethin'?"

He bellows out a laugh. We're so close, but I'm happy I can't see his expression.

"Oh, Kate. You've had way too much to drink, and while I find it adorable, it's also dangerous. You already don't have a filter, but this is Kaitlyn with her balls out."

"That was a good non-answer. You know what they say, a drunk man's lies are a sober man's truth," I tell with a chuckle, pushing away to meet his eyes.

There's something behind his expression.

"Honestly, I just need you to pull my hair, fuck me raw, then knock me up," I whisper, and he smiles while he slightly fists the material of my bridesmaid's dress.

We're close, almost too close. The music changes, and it's one of those songs played at the club. A disco ball above casts shards of light around the room as those dancing bump and grind on one another.

"Well?" I ask, moving even closer to Payton. I turn around and rub my ass against him feeling his rock-hard cock. Let me just say he's thick as hell, and I'd be lying if I said I didn't want to take him on a test drive right now.

I *really* should get laid more.

"I don't know how to respond to that, Kate."

"All you need to say is *yes*."

Continue the Circle B Ranch series with Payton & Kaitlyn's story in *Seducing the Cowboy*

If you haven't started the Circle B Ranch series from the beginning, make sure to go back and meet the other couples! They can all be read as stand-alones, but for the best reading experience, start with *Hitching the Cowboy*.

You can also binge-read their parents' stories in the Bishop Brothers series. Each couple's book can be read as a stand-alone and ends in an happily ever after.

WHAT'S NEXT

Next in the Circle B Ranch Series is Payton & Kaitlyn's story in *Seducing the Cowboy*

After leaving his hometown over a decade ago, Payton hasn't returned. One heartbreak was enough to turn him off relationships forever. As soon as he arrived at the Circle B Ranch, they treated him like family—something he's never had—and he met the one woman he shouldn't want.

He's put her in the friend zone, but after agreeing to her proposition, he can't hold back anymore.

Kaitlyn Bishop is the only woman on the ranch without a husband and kids. A family is all she's ever wanted, but it's never been in her cards. Since she's turned thirty, she's decided to go to the sperm bank or ask her best friend to knock her up.

She knows being friends with benefits is a bad idea, but she's willing to take the risk.

Their agreement is purely transactional, but they'll soon find themselves in too deep—something they're too stubborn to admit. However, they only have nine months to figure it out.

ABOUT THE AUTHOR

Brooke Cumberland and Lyra Parish are a duo of romance authors who teamed up under the *USA Today* pseudonym, Kennedy Fox. They share a love of Hallmark movies, overpriced coffee, and making TikToks. When they aren't bonding over romantic comedies, they like to brainstorm new book ideas. One day in 2016, they decided to collaborate under a pseudonym and have some fun creating new characters that'll make you blush and your heart melt. Happily ever afters guaranteed!

CONNECT WITH US

Find us on our website:

kennedyfoxbooks.com

Subscribe to our newsletter:

kennedyfoxbooks.com/newsletter

- facebook.com/kennedyfoxbooks
- twitter.com/kennedyfoxbooks
- instagram.com/kennedyfoxduo
- amazon.com/author/kennedyfoxbooks
- goodreads.com/kennedyfox
- bookbub.com/authors/kennedy-fox

BOOKS BY KENNEDY FOX

DUET SERIES (BEST READ IN ORDER)

CHECKMATE DUET SERIES

ROOMMATE DUET SERIES

LAWTON RIDGE DUET SERIES

MOCKINBIRD DUET

INTERCONNECTED STAND-ALONES

MAKE ME SERIES

BISHOP BROTHERS SERIES

CIRCLE B RANCH SERIES

LOVE IN ISOLATION SERIES

TEXAS HEAT SERIES

Find the entire Kennedy Fox reading order at
Kennedyfoxbooks.com/reading-order

Find all of our current freebies at
Kennedyfoxbooks.com/freeromance

Made in the USA
Las Vegas, NV
28 August 2022